"I wish you'd stop referring to me as a job," Annabelle said.

Conrad paused, then nodded. "Sorry. You're a person, and you have a life of your own. It's a law enforcement trick to help us keep our emotions in check."

"Maybe I feel safer with a bodyguard who actually experiences his emotions," she said.

"You shouldn't." He met her gaze soberly. "I'm faster on my feet when I do things my way. This is for your benefit."

"I take it you've guarded witnesses before?"

"Yup." That was a good thing, wasn't it? He'd done this before. She wasn't a trial run.

"And everything went smoothly?" Annabelle paused next to him. She had to tilt her chin up to look him in the eye.

"You'll be safe," he said. "I'm going to get changed, and then we'll get you saddled up."

It wasn't exactly an answer, was it? For a split second she saw something deeper flicker behind that professional gaze—regret.

Dear Reader,

I have written cowboy romances for years, but more recently I have delved into Amish stories. My readers have said they loved my Amish romances, and some of those books even hit the *Publishers Weekly* bestseller list. What an honor!

This story combines everything I love—rugged, protective cowboys, a light mystery and the down-home charm of Amish neighbors who bring a whole new perspective on simple living. I truly hope you enjoy this story.

If you'd like to connect with me, you can find me on my website at patriciajohns.com, on Twitter and on Facebook, where I hold continual giveaways. Pop by and enter to win some free books—we have a lot of fun!

Patricia Johns

HEARTWARMING

A Deputy in Amish Country

—

Patricia Johns

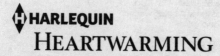

HARLEQUIN®
HEARTWARMING™

Recycling programs
for this product may
not exist in your area.

ISBN-13: 978-1-335-42662-8

A Deputy in Amish Country

Copyright © 2022 by Patricia Johns

This edition published by arrangement with Harlequin Books S.A.

For questions and comments about the quality of this book,
please contact us at CustomerService@Harlequin.com.

Harlequin Enterprises ULC
22 Adelaide St. West, 41st Floor
Toronto, Ontario M5H 4E3, Canada
www.Harlequin.com

Printed in U.S.A.

Patricia Johns is a *Publishers Weekly* bestselling author who writes from Alberta, Canada. She has her Hon. BA in English literature and currently writes for Harlequin's Love Inspired and Heartwarming lines. She also writes Amish romance for Kensington Books. You can find her at patriciajohns.com.

Visit the Author Profile page at Harlequin.com for more titles.

To my husband and son. Without your support, I'd never have been able to follow my dreams this way. I love you both.

CHAPTER ONE

THE OHIO COUNTRYSIDE was a patchwork of green and gold, and Annabelle Richards watched the summer wind bend the crops in the fields, rippling across the heads of wheat and oats like waves on a lake. The hot scent of grain baking in the sun came into the SUV through their air-conditioning vents, and Annabelle found her gaze moving back to that side mirror. No one followed them, the stretch of black asphalt winding out behind them reassuringly empty.

The Amish farms slipped past them, laundry fluttering on clotheslines and flourishing gardens stretching out beside neat white houses. Every once in a while, a buggy would come trundling by, the muscular quarter horses plodding along at an even pace. The drivers didn't look at them as they passed.

Annabelle used to come out to Amish communities to wander through shops and buy some local produce, but she'd never come in this direction before. These roads were far from the tourist attractions, the corn mazes, restaurants, craft shops... Here were just Amish people living their lives, and this gas-powered SUV seemed like an intrusion into their world. It felt almost rude to be coming here to disappear, a stranger in their midst.

Conrad Westhouse, the bulky, muscular sheriff's deputy who was assigned to her protection, wasn't exactly a stranger. They knew each other a little bit from volunteering at the Wooster, Ohio, soup kitchen that provided free hot meals for needy families three times a week.

Annabelle forced a smile. "So...do we keep this professional and I call you Deputy Westhouse? Or are you Conrad, like at the soup kitchen?"

"Conrad is fine." He cast her a smile. "I'm the same guy, you know."

"The uniform does change things," she said.

"It's supposed to, I guess," he agreed. "But I'll try to keep this whole process as painless as possible. I promise."

"I'm curious about the ranch," she said. "You said it's family land? Were you raised there?"

Conrad shot her a look, and for a moment, he was silent.

"The thing is, this is all really intimidating," Annabelle said. "Three days ago, I was just a bank teller doing my job and wondering if I should get a rescue dog. Today, I'm in protective custody so I can be a witness in a murder and robbery trial. This is a lot!"

"You look really scared," he said, his voice softening.

"I am."

"It's going to be okay," he said. "We protect our witnesses, I promise you that." He cleared his throat and said, "I live with my brother."

"Oh?" Annabelle still wasn't comfortable around this big man, although he seemed to be trying to help her to relax.

"His name is Wilder. You'll meet him when we get there. He does a lot of the ranching work while I'm away at my job, so... You'll see him. He's a decent guy."

He tapped his hand on the top of the steering wheel. He didn't look inclined to say more.

"And I'll be living with two men for three weeks?" She'd assumed that she and Conrad would be alone. That was the implication—out there in the country, tucked away from any undue attention. But if she decided to slip out of Conrad's custody, how difficult was that going to be?

Annabelle had agreed to testify, but she had good reason to rethink that now. She'd seen the robber's face, yes. And she'd picked his photo out of a series of mug shots easily. But it had been that easy because she knew him, a fact she hadn't shared with the deputy taking her statement.

Conrad cast her a sympathetic look. "I could see if a female deputy could be assigned to you as well, if that would be more comfortable. We were working pretty fast to figure out a solution until the trial—there wasn't a lot of time to plan, and the sheriff figured you'd be safer right under my nose than anywhere else."

"Is this really necessary?" she asked. "I mean, how bad is Stephen Hope?"

"He's got connections to some gangs, and in the past, witnesses have disappeared."

"How many?"

"Two." He cast her an apologetic look. "And others have simply declined to testify. So we're going to take this very, very seriously, and nothing will happen to you."

She considered that. If the sheriff thought

that Conrad's ranch out in Amish country was the safest place for her, who was Annabelle to quibble? She wanted the same thing—safety. But what was the best way to stay safe? With the police, or on her own as far from Ohio as she could get?

"This is pretty overwhelming," she said.

"Yeah, I get that." His tone softened again.

"And I'm about to spend three weeks with you," she said. "I know that you're a pretty good cook from the soup kitchen, and we've chatted a bit, but I don't know you very well. So if I could get to know you a little bit better, it would go a long way to calming my nerves."

"This is pretty different for me, too," he said. "I've never had a witness in my home before. The thing is, I normally try to keep my professional and personal lives completely separate."

"Why did you change your mind for me?" she asked.

"You're a good person."

"What makes you so sure?" she asked.

He smiled faintly. "I have a good sense of these things. And I've watched you, too. You work hard at the soup kitchen. You treat everyone with respect. You're decent, Anna-belle."

He'd been noticing her? She stole a look at him, but his gaze was locked on the road in front of them.

"Thanks," she said.

"And I can see that this is weird for both of us. So in the spirit of making it less weird…" Conrad slowed for an intersection and came to a stop. He glanced over at her. "The land belonged to my great-grandfather and then my grandfather. My uncle inherited the place when he died. He ran the ranch for the last forty years or so. He and my dad were es-tranged for a lot of my childhood. My dad bought a large acreage, but there were hard feelings about that inheritance. He and my uncle didn't get along real well."

He signaled a turn and stepped on the gas.

"That happens sometimes," she murmured.

"Anyway, Uncle Gray never did have any kids, and when he found out he had lung can-cer, he wrote my brother and me into his will. I guess the rest is history."

"Did he reconcile with your dad before he died?" Annabelle asked.

Conrad shook his head. "Nope. We didn't even know he was sick. That's part of the reason why I'm willing to work the ranch with my brother. We're pretty different, but family has to count for something. So I'm trying to have fewer regrets than the generation before us."

"How…um…different is your brother?" Annabelle surveyed the big man next to her—his clean-shaven face, strong jaw and bulky muscles. He looked relaxed enough, but there was something about him that felt like a coiled spring. He wasn't like this at the soup kitchen. The uniform definitely changed him.

"I'd trust him with my life, if that's what you're asking," Conrad replied. "He's the free spirit, where I'm…" He angled his head to one side. "I guess I'm the stickler for doing things right. You're safe with the two of us—I can guarantee that."

If it came down to a fistfight, she had no doubt that she'd be well protected. Conrad was an intimidating-looking man—the human equivalent of steel and concrete. But even a muscle-bound cop was vulnerable to bullets. An image flashed in her mind of the security guard slumping to the ground and the masked man with his finger still on the trigger. The two masked accomplices had looked surprised and started hollering at each other. It had only taken a second. She hadn't known then who the shooter was. It had only been later, after everyone was on the floor with their hands behind their heads, that she'd seen him lift his mask, just for a moment, and she'd known who he was. Stephen had met her gaze and winked. He'd pulled out her key—one from the set with the Snoopy key fob that had gone missing two days earlier— opened up the door that led into the vault, and her heart had almost stopped. Where had he gotten her keys? She'd been searching everywhere for the set. Had it dropped from her bag? Had he lifted it off her in a store or something? In that moment, she knew that life as she knew it was over.

Could you describe the man you saw?

A little over six feet tall, dark hair, kind of a long nose. He looks friendly—but he's not. You know?

Even after shooting a man, Stephen had that cordial look about him that made her blood run cold. Death meant nothing to him, and apparently money was worth a life.

I wonder if you could look at some mug shots for us...

Annabelle hadn't known that Stephen had a criminal history when she met him two years ago. He'd just been a guy she'd briefly dated who'd had a scary temper. But his picture had been on the fourth page of the mug shots.

There. That's him.

How sure are you?

A hundred percent. That's him. I looked him right in the face. Can I go now?

She'd figured she would head to Texas, where she had an aunt, to hide out, and she'd find a job down there. She'd change her hair and put on some weight…but the sheriff's department hadn't let her leave.

I'm sorry, ma'am. You'll have to stay with us until we have the suspect in custody. And then it was *I'm sorry, ma'am, but you're in a vulnerable position right now, and it's our job to protect you.* And now she was headed out to Amish country with a deputy and a suitcase.

How safe was she while she remained in Ohio? Because Stephen had texted her before Conrad picked her up to hide her in the country. He'd said if she said anything, he was bringing her down, too. And now Conrad had her cell phone, and she was being hustled off to some farm outside of town.

"Annabelle?"

She startled. "Sorry—what was that?"

"I asked if you enjoy visiting Amish country," he said.

"Oh." She nodded. "Yeah, I do. To check out the shops and just relax. It's a slower pace."

"It is," he agreed. "It's like a different world out here."

"Are there many non-Amish farms and ranches in this area?" she asked.

"Not too many," he replied. "In fact, I get the feeling that the Amish are just waiting for us to sell. They run smaller farms than the rest of us do, because they have to do all the work with horses and wagons. So our ranch could probably be split up into two or three Amish farms."

"Do you know your neighbors well?" she asked.

"My brother and I have only had this ranch for two years, so we haven't been around long in the local estimation," he replied. "But we're on friendly terms. They're nice people."

The Westhouse ranch had a big wooden sign over the drive, and wooden rail fences stretched out on either side. Conrad turned into the drive and she noted how he watched his mirrors, his attention fixed on a truck that went rumbling past.

Would anyone outside of law enforcement know where she was for the next three weeks? Well, besides her best friend, Theresa. She'd told her where she was going, but Theresa could be trusted.

Several trees, leafy and heavy with large green apples, hunkered down along the gravel drive. Beyond the trees and past a vast lawn that looked like it needed mowing was a low ranch-style house. Three pickup trucks were parked beside it, two in various states of disrepair, and a man in a grease-streaked white T-shirt stood next to the open hood of one of the more beaten-up vehicles.

The man turned, looking mildly surprised to see her in the front seat of the SUV. He shoved a tool into his back pocket and eyed them as Conrad pulled to a stop.

"I wasn't going to trust this to a phone call," Conrad said. "Give me a minute to fill my brother in, would you?"

She nodded, and Conrad hopped out. He headed over to his brother, and she watched the silent conversation for a moment. Then she looked out her window. There was a small red barn with a corral. On the far side of the farmyard was a squat stable with its own corral, where a glossy chestnut horse stood with

a colt beside her. The colt looked young—
gangly, slender, sticking close to his mother.
And beyond that corral and a few yards of
long grass there was another property that
looked Amish—a two-story white house,
a clothesline with Amish dresses and pants
rippling as the wind strummed across them.
She'd never been quite this close to an Amish
home before, and she was intrigued.

The SUV was getting stuffy, so she opened
her door and got out into the fragrant summer
air. There were some fruit trees in the Amish
front yard, and a black buggy was parked
next to the house. The shafts that would at-
tach to a horse's breeching were resting on
blocks of wood. A window had been raised
and the front door propped open with another piece of wood. She could hear a child's
laughter from inside. The difference between
these two properties was immediately obvious, from the style of house to the mode of
transportation sitting outside. But she had to
admit that she was intrigued to spend some
time here.

The horse in the corral nickered, and Conrad looked up at the sound of her door shutting.

"I want to introduce you to my brother,"
Conrad called.

Annabelle headed over to where the men stood, and the second man eyed her with a curious expression.

"This is Wilder," Conrad said. "I've filled him in on the basics—you witnessed a crime, and we're keeping you under wraps until the trial."

But he wasn't telling his brother which crime, it would seem. Wilder wiped his hand on his jeans, then shook hers.

"I'm Annabelle," she said, and when he released her fingers, she resisted the urge to wipe her hand off.

"Wilder," he replied, then looked down at her hand. "Sorry." He grabbed a rag and gave it to her. "I didn't know we'd have company, so I didn't clean the place up. But you're very welcome to stay as long as you need. Make yourself at home."

"I'll grab your bag," Conrad said, and he headed back over to the SUV. He paused, scanning the road again.

Annabelle glanced over at Wilder, and she found him watching his brother, too, his brow furrowed. Conrad pulled her suitcase out of the back, as well as the shopping bag of toiletries, and as he closed the hatch, he scanned the property one more time.

"He's scared, isn't he?" Annabelle said quietly.

Wilder's gaze snapped over to her, and he smiled faintly.

"Nah, he's just cautious. It's in his nature. It's fine."

"He and I both volunteer at the soup kitchen, so I know he's capable of relaxing more than this," she said. "I've seen him joking around with the guys there."

Wilder chuckled. "Well, you're on the other side of things now. This is Work Conrad. He's a real watchdog. Trust me, you'll be fine so long as he's prowling like that. Come on inside. I was going to open a can of soup for lunch, if you're interested."

"Thanks. That sounds good."

Conrad rejoined them, the suitcase held easily in one hand, the shopping bag in the other, and he nodded for her to go ahead of him. She followed Wilder through the side door that opened into a kitchen that looked like it was last updated in the eighties—brown everything. But it was clean enough, all but a pile of dishes in one sink, and a few boxes of cereal lined up haphazardly on the counter. Wilder headed over to the cupboards and took out some bowls.

Conrad let the screen door bounce shut behind him. "So let's just set up a few ground rules." The gentler man from their ride over seemed to be gone again, and he was back to granite. "No phone calls out to anyone. This is important. I know I have your cell phone, but I still think it's important to say it. We can't let anyone know where you're staying— anyone. A friend could breathe a word, and then your location is blown. You are officially off the map until that trial is over. You already told your family you'd be unavailable for a few weeks, and anyone close enough can hear through them."

His voice was brusque, and she nodded. She'd told Theresa that she'd be at a nearby farm, but not specifically where. It had been one of those moments where she wasn't thinking about the dangers. She wouldn't tell anyone else.

"Okay." She swallowed.

"No answering the door. Stick close to me at all times when you're outside. I'll give you privacy in here, but once you walk outside this house, you need to be with me. No exceptions."

"I thought it was safe out here," Annabelle said, trying to sound like she was joking. "Amish farmland, horses and buggies."

Conrad cast her a flat look, then continued. "You aren't Amish, are you? And they aren't witnesses to a case. If you see anyone on this property besides me or Wilder, let me know. If anything seems odd or suspicious on a gut level, let me know that, too."

The air was warm, but a breeze filtered through the window and worked through the kitchen toward the screen door. She plucked at her tee, holding it away from her collarbone.

"I'm going to need a little bit of personal space," she said. "If no one knows I'm here, we should be fine. If we have three weeks of me being glued to your side, you and I are going to hate each other by the end of it."

His intense gaze caught hers, and she saw something simmer there, a challenge, maybe? Her breath caught.

"I have phenomenal self-control," Conrad said dryly. "I think we'll both survive. We're clear on the rules?"

She felt mildly chastised. "We're clear."

"Good."

So this was going to be her life for the next few weeks. No internet, no phone, no connection to her life…just this big, tough, by-the-book cop who was intent on getting her back to court to do the right thing.

If she decided to forget about the right thing and just save her own hide, what were her chances of getting out of here without Conrad or Wilder noticing?

CONRAD'S BOOTS ECHOED down the hallway as he carried Annabelle's suitcase and toiletries to the spare bedroom. He and his brother had moved in a couple of years ago, and the spare room still had a few boxes stacked in the closet, a twin-size bed in one corner and a couple of shelves filled with their late uncle's fishing trophies. The rest of the contents they'd carried off to the dump, but a man's trophies… Those felt wrong to trash. Uncle Gray might not have been a real friendly sort, but he'd been family, all the same. The room had that slightly musty, old-house smell that he'd always found rather comforting.

He set the suitcase and bag next to the bed.

"I'll grab some sheets and make up your bed," Conrad said. "I'm going to have to ask you to sleep with your window shut for safety. We'll set up a fan in here to cool things off a bit."

The window overlooked the flourishing, albeit rather weedy, back garden. Round green pumpkins were starting to blush with orange, and a row of green beans were already going to seed. There was a patch of kitchen herbs—dill, thyme and oregano—and a row of petunias that had spread and blossomed like a fuchsia carpet. Neither he nor his brother had prioritized keeping the garden this year, and he felt a little bit embarrassed about the state of it now.

"I'm going to be in the way here," Annabelle said, and she tucked her chin-length blond hair behind one ear.

"In the way?" Conrad shot her an incredulous look.

This woman had no idea how seriously he took his work. His job as a deputy filled all his thoughts and waking hours. And she was different, too. He'd noticed her at the soup kitchen, and he'd thought she was an attractive woman. They'd chatted a little bit, and he'd considered asking her out a couple of times, but he'd wanted to be sure she was single first. Besides, she was younger than he was, and less battered by life. After getting an up close and personal view of his brother's divorce, he hadn't been in a rush to punch above his weight.

"It's not like you chose this," he said. "And that shouldn't be your worry. You are officially my full-time job now. I need you underfoot—that's the deal here. Don't feel bad about it."

"I appreciate it." Annabelle's expression was still veiled, though.

Conrad wanted to make her feel better. The thing was, he'd requested to be her bodyguard for the next few weeks. When he'd seen her stricken face after the robbery, he'd known that he wouldn't sleep a wink unless he was 100 percent sure of her safety. He wasn't normally this territorial, but for Annabelle, he felt something different...

"Your stay doesn't have to be all misery." Conrad tucked one thumb into his belt. "We can take you horseback riding, for example. I mean, Wilder and I will be checking the herd, but you can just enjoy a ride in the fields. There are people who pay good money for that experience, you know."

"That would actually be fun." A smile touched her lips. "I haven't been riding in years."

"I know this is hard," he said, lowering his voice. "I know you're giving up your freedom, your home, your routines… I get it. I am, too. But what you're doing is really important here. Your testimony is the one that will put this man behind bars and keep him there. And Wayne County, Wooster and anywhere else he'd decide to target are all safer."

He saw some tears mist her eyes, and his heart sank. Maybe he was taking the wrong tack here. She'd been through an awful lot, and the sheriff's department had made sure that she was safely cut off from everyone else. Conrad was all she had at the moment—and while he had a powerful instinct to keep her safe, he wasn't great with the emotional side of things.

"Did you, um, talk to the victim's services people?" he asked. "They have therapists who specialize in helping people who have witnessed crimes."

She nodded, swallowing hard. "Yep. I talked to a therapist yesterday."

"Do you need to talk some more?" he asked. She'd seen a man shot in front of her. Even for a seasoned cop, that would leave emotional damage that one chat with a therapist wasn't going to smooth over.

"I'm fine." Annabelle's face was pale, and she

had her hands balled up into white-knuckled fists.

Yeah, she wasn't fine. It was that very look on her face that had driven him to ask for this assignment.

"If you do want to talk about it," he said, "I'm here. And I'll understand better than you think. In law enforcement, we see a lot, and we have to go through the steps of dealing with it just like anyone else. So if you want to talk, I will certainly understand what you're feeling."

She nodded. "Thanks."

It was something he could offer—a listening ear, a shoulder to lean on. While he tried to stay in his lane and leave the long talks to the people who were trained for it, there wasn't that luxury here on his land.

Annabelle seemed to notice her clenched fists, and she relaxed her fingers.

"It won't be so bad," he said quietly, and in that moment, he wasn't sure who he was trying to soothe more, her or himself.

"Soup's ready!" Wilder called from the kitchen.

Conrad let out a breath of relief. "Are you hungry?"

"A bit."

Conrad led the way back down the hallway toward the kitchen. He grabbed a pile of flyers from the mail pile on the edge of the table, and as his gaze moved past the screen door, he startled. Standing on the porch, looking inside in solemn silence, was his neighbor's five-year-old daughter. She was dressed in her little pink Amish cape dress—a perfect replica of an adult woman's dress, except she didn't have a white apron. But she did have a child's *kapp* on her head.

"Hello," the child said.

"Jane," Conrad said, "is everything okay?" He went to the screen door and opened it. Jane came inside and she looked around.

"I was looking at the baby horse," the girl said. "And then I came to say hi."

"Hi, Jane," Wilder said, pulling some crackers down from a cupboard.

"How long will the baby be a baby?" Jane asked. "Will you let him stay with his mother forever? Or will you sell him?"

Amish children were farm raised, and the Amish didn't tend to hide the realities of farm life from the little ones. The colt was only a few days old, and this was the first day they'd taken him out of the stable and into the sunlight.

"We'll probably keep him," Conrad said.

"Will you teach him to be ridden?" Jane asked. "Will he like being ridden? Maybe he won't like it. My *mammi* said when she was a little girl that an untrained horse stamped on her like this."

The little girl mimed a rearing horse.

"Oh…" Conrad winced. "That would hurt."

"I think so." Jane nodded, her gaze moving around their kitchen and stopping at the microwave. "Can I touch the buttons?"

"No," Conrad said.

"Oh. Because it's forbidden," she said.

"No, because there's nothing inside. You have to put something inside a microwave, or else you'll break it if you turn it on."

"Why?"

"It's just the way microwaves work." It was always the same. How had he gotten sucked into another lengthy conversation with this chatty little girl?

"Who's that?" Jane asked, pointing at Annabelle, who was watching him with an amused look on her face.

"That's my friend," he said. Not a lie. They did know each other, even if they were very casual acquaintances.

"What's her name?"

How much was he going to tell people around here? Couldn't this child just go back home already?

"I'm—" Annabelle's gaze flickered up toward Conrad. "You can call me Annie. I'm Mr. Westhouse's friend. I'm just visiting for a little while."

Not bad. There were a lot of Annies in Amish communities, too. It just might blend in.

"Do you like baby horses?" Jane asked, bouncing past Conrad and stopping in front of Annabelle. She pulled out a chair at the table and sat down.

"I do like baby horses," Annabelle replied seriously. "That's why I came."

He was impressed by how fluidly she skirted the truth. Maybe Annabelle's presence would be less gossip-worthy if she were just a city dweller who liked horses. Just another tourist.

"That's why I came over here, too!" Jane said. "What are you eating?"

"Vegetable soup," Wilder said.

"My *mammi* makes sausage-and-potato soup," Jane said. "It's the best soup ever."

"Her *mammi* is her grandmother," Conrad said.

Annabelle nodded, but some color had returned to her cheeks and her lips. If nothing else, little Jane was a good distraction.

"Our soup came from a can," Annabelle said. "It's very good, but I'm sure your grandmother's soup is much better."

Conrad looked out the screen door and saw Wollie Schmidt walking briskly across the narrow stretch of grass that separated their two properties. No doubt he was in search of his daughter. Conrad opened the screen door and shot his neighbor a smile.

"Jane dropped by to say hi," Conrad called.

"I always know where to check for her first," Wollie said. "My *mamm* was frantic looking for her. She's got to stop running off like that."

Wollie was tall and solid, and he wore an Amish beard that didn't include a mustache. His white shirt, rolled up to the elbows, was sweat stained. Wollie poked his head into the house and said a few words to his daughter in Pennsylvania Dutch. Jane sat up straight, but didn't move.

"I told her to wait for me," Wollie said, and he angled his head away from the house. "I was going to come by and talk to you anyway. Are you missing any cattle?"

"No, I was out there this morning. We're

fine," Wilder said. "Don't tell me you're missing another calf."

Wollie sighed. "That's the second one this week. They cut my fence and snatch them right out of the pasture," Wollie said. "And they don't take yours?"

"They aren't touching ours." Conrad crossed his arms over his chest. "Is anyone else missing calves?"

The screen door clattered shut, and they both moved a couple of paces away from the door.

"Morty Esh lost one last week," Wollie said. "And his cousin Elijah lost four the week before. Mose Schrock on the other side of me has lost three so far. They don't hit the same farm every time, but they don't seem to touch yours at all. I wonder why that might be."

Wollie's sharp gaze caught Conrad's, then dropped to the ground, where he kicked a tuft of grass with his boot. Was it suspicion? Or just irritability at being picked on?

"Maybe they know that my brother would shoot a man for cattle rustling on his property," Conrad said. "And an Amish man wouldn't do that."

Because the Amish were peaceful people. They worked hard, and they lived by their ideals, even when it hurt. Even when it cost them a great deal.

Wollie let out a huff of breath. "Maybe so."

There was someone out there stealing cattle and profiting from a peaceful people's refusal to cause hurt, and that didn't sit right with Conrad. It was the behavior of not just a criminal, but a bully.

"We'll help you fix your fence," Conrad said. "How about after we have lunch? We'll be done in about fifteen minutes."

"I appreciate it, Conrad," Wollie said. "You're a good neighbor."

"We try." Conrad nodded. "And we'll try and keep an eye out for mischief."

"I'd appreciate that, too," Wollie replied. "I can't afford much more of this."

If Conrad ever spotted someone rustling the Amish cattle, he'd do what an Amish man wouldn't. Conrad wasn't made of the same stuff. His ideals included dealing with bullies head-on. There was a certain type of person who didn't understand the grace and forgiveness the Amish offered, but they did understand a pair of handcuffs.

CHAPTER TWO

"...AND WE HAVE a rooster named Methuse-lah," Jane said, twisting the hem of her pink dress in one hand. "He's mean. He'll peck your bare feet. And he flies at you if he gets mad."

Jane's nose was freckled, and her honey-blond hair fell in loose tangles around her shoulders. Her sun-browned bare feet pad-ded across the kitchen floor as she paced. She hadn't stopped talking or moving since she arrived. Outside the door, Annabelle could see Conrad and the little girl's father talk-ing. The Amish man was rubbing at his wiry beard, and Conrad's arms were crossed over his chest and his gaze was flinty. Something was up, and she was curious if it was related to her situation.

She knew Conrad only a little, but she had seen his no-nonsense glare before. A guy had come into the dining area of the soup kitchen and started making trouble for someone else who had come there to eat. Something about owing him money. So she knew Conrad was capable of getting tough when he needed to. The single women who volunteered there had all swooned that day.

Conrad's gaze snapped in her direction, but he wouldn't be able to see her inside from where he stood in the sun. There was a directness in his dark gaze that made her breath catch anyway. He looked bigger out there where she could see him at full height. His shoulders were broad and thick. His uniform fit him well, and she could see the latent strength in the man. He stood with his legs akimbo, and when he uncrossed his arms, he rested one large hand on his belt. He turned back to the Amish farmer.

"Oh, wow," Annabelle said, pulling her attention back to the girl. "Will you get a nicer rooster to replace Meth... What's his name again?"

"His name is Methuselah," Jane repeated. "But mean roosters are doing their job. That's what my *daet* says. Mean roosters are taking care of their hens, and they'll peck at a dog or a coyote or anything that wants to eat the chickens."

Conrad was older than she was, and definitely more experienced in life. He seemed to be all testosterone, hardened and slightly jaded, but she still felt sparks when she saw him. It was a purely chemical reaction, and he was probably used to causing women to feel this way. He seemed to sidestep the blatant flirting from the women they volunteered with, and Annabelle had no intention of embarrassing herself.

"And Methuselah is as mean as they come," Jane chattered on. "So that's not a bad thing when it comes to coyotes."

"Oh." Annabelle nodded. "That's a good point."

"I saw Methuselah chase off a cat, and when he came back, he had fur in his beak, and that cat was yowling."

"He's a good guard rooster, then," Annabelle said.

"He's the best, but he doesn't know who's going to eat the chickens and who's just taking care of them." Jane spun in a circle, looking around the kitchen. "So my *daet* has to be the one to gather the eggs, because he can make Methuselah behave."

"How does he do that?" Annabelle asked.

"*Daet* says he shows him his boot."

Annabelle chuckled. "Maybe Methuselah knows your father won't eat the hens."

"Oh, we'll eat them, but only when they stop laying." Jane cocked her head to one side. "How many chickens have you got?"

Annabelle couldn't help but smile at this little girl's matter-of-fact view of her world.

"I don't have any. I live in a city," she replied. "We buy our eggs and meat at a grocery store."

"Huh." Jane seemed to consider this for a moment. "We sometimes butcher a cow, and then my *daet* will do a trade with a turkey farmer for some turkeys. Then we can eat turkey and beef both."

"That's smart."

"Do you like to play with baby chicks? I do. They're so cute when they peep."

From outside, Wollie called Jane's name, and the girl perked up and went to the door. She shaded her eyes, then hollered something in Pennsylvania Dutch. Her father answered her in the same language.

"I have to go now," Jane said. "'Bye."

Then she disappeared outside. Annabelle looked over at Wilder, who just shrugged.

"She comes by pretty often," Wilder said.

"And she chatters the entire time. She's a cute kid."

"Is it just her and her father and grandmother over there?" Annabelle asked.

"Yeah. Wollie's wife died when Jane was a baby, and his mother came to help him with her. But he hasn't remarried yet."

"Is that strange that he'd stay single?" Annabelle glanced out the screen door. Conrad stood there in the sunlight, a thoughtful look on his face. Then he started toward the house.

"For the Amish, it's a bit weird, yeah," Wilder replied. "They have some pretty practical marriages. A man has to do the farmwork, and a woman needs to do the work inside the house. With no electricity, there's a lot of hard work between them. Besides, someone has to take care of the kids."

"But Wollie's held out." Annabelle wasn't sure why she liked that, but she did. Practicality made sense, but what about love? She couldn't imagine marrying someone for their ability to run a farm and nothing else.

"He definitely held out," Wilder confirmed. "He told me that they keep throwing single women in his path, but he's not ready to remarry. He's not over the death of his wife. She was the love of his life."

Conrad came into the kitchen. He stooped over the sink and washed his hands, then came back to the table.

"Wollie's concerned about that lost calf," Conrad said, pulling out a chair, and she felt a wash of relief that this had nothing to do with her. His gaze moved over her, including her in the moment, but he was obviously speaking with his brother.

"Yeah, I would be, too." Wilder crossed his arms.

"How was our herd this morning?"

"Like I said before, we're fine and accounted for. We've got the eight new calves, and they're all doing well."

"I said we'd help him fix his fence. They just cut the wire and were in and out in minutes, I imagine."

Wilder muttered a curse. "I've got half a mind to sit out by his fence with a shotgun to make a point."

"Are you going to do that for every single Amish farm?" Conrad asked. "They've been hitting even more Amish farms, according to Wollie. We need to do more than scare them—it doesn't last. We need some evidence and a few arrests."

"Right—the legal way." Wilder shot his brother a grin, and Annabelle couldn't help but smile, too, at the brotherly teasing.

"Let's eat," Conrad said. He glanced at Annabelle. "How do you feel about a horseback ride this afternoon?"

"Sounds good to me," she replied. "Is cattle rustling still a thing? It sounds like something from an old Western movie."

"Cattle are worth money. Thieves will take whatever they can, including livestock."

"Do you think you can catch them?" she asked.

"I'm more focused on getting you to a trial," he replied, then sighed. "But maybe. I don't like people who take advantage of the Amish."

Conrad nudged the dish of microwaved vegetable soup toward Annabelle, and she filled her bowl. Then the two men took theirs. Conrad pushed bread in a plastic bag in her direction.

"The Amish have shotguns, too, don't they?" She took a piece of bread and slathered it with butter.

"They hunt, so yes," Conrad said. "But

they'd never use those weapons to threaten people, no matter what."

"And everyone knows it," Wilder added. "Some people respect that—they appreciate the ideals. Other people just see an easy target."

"You think they wouldn't fight back?" Annabelle asked.

"They won't." Conrad sipped a spoonful of soup. "It's a fact."

Annabelle was a peace-loving woman, too, but if she was backed into a corner, she'd fight. Self-preservation was a strong instinct, and people dropped their ideals all the time in order to protect themselves. There was a lot of gray area in life, she was realizing, and maybe that Amish farmer next door would come to some similar conclusions.

"Jane was telling us about their vicious rooster," Annabelle said. "She says that a mean rooster is doing his job, protecting his hens. I don't see a difference."

"They see one," Conrad replied. "People aren't supposed to act like animals."

Like Stephen Hope—who could shoot a man in the chest and just keep walking. She felt a shiver go up her spine.

"They make a good point about that," she murmured.

Conrad shot her a sympathetic look. "Look, I respect their beliefs. I even admire them, but while the Amish feel called to forgive and turn the other cheek, I feel obligated to make criminals face justice. It takes all kinds to make the world turn."

"The world needs sheepdogs," Wilder said, then took a jaw-cracking bite of bread.

Annabelle understood the army reference. There were sheep, there were wolves that would eat those sheep, and then there were sheepdogs, who protected the sheep and fought back against threats just as viciously as they had to. The tranquil life of sheep wasn't possible without the sheepdogs to protect them.

So what did that make Annabelle—one of the sheep in Conrad's care? She had to admit that she was counting on him to keep a wolf at bay for her.

They finished eating. It was a simple meal, but satisfying, and after the stress of her hurried packing and the long drive, her stomach needed something simple. In fact, she felt like she needed something simple right now on a soul level, too. After all she'd seen the last few days, after the fear, the adrenaline… right now this ranch with its Amish neighbors was oddly comforting, even with the threat of cattle rustlers along the fence line. Because here, with Conrad and his brother, nothing was going to touch her. Maybe this wasn't so crazy after all—a few weeks with horses and a wild sky might be exactly what she needed to get her equilibrium back before she decided if she was going to testify or not.

Wilder headed out to start saddling the horses, leaving his brother and Annabelle alone in the kitchen. Conrad drained a glass of water, then looked over at her.

"If it's ever too much for you, my brother can take care of the ranch on his own for a while. It won't kill him. You're my full-time job. Just so you know how this will work."

That was the second time he'd called her his job. Not quite the way she wanted to be seen, and that wasn't her pining for a romantic connection, either. It just felt…sterile.

"I'm fine," Annabelle said. "I wish you'd stop referring to me as a job, though."

Conrad paused, then nodded. "Sorry. You're a person, and you have a life of your own. It's a law enforcement trick to help us keep our emotions in check."

"Maybe I'd feel safer with a bodyguard who actually experiences his emotions," she said.

"You shouldn't." He met her gaze soberly. "I'm faster on my feet when I do things my way. This is for your benefit."

"I take it you've guarded witnesses before?"

"Yep." That was a good thing, wasn't it? He'd done this before. She wasn't a trial run.

"And everything went smoothly?" Annabelle paused next to him. She had to tilt her chin up to look him in the face.

"You'll be safe," he said. "I'm going to get changed, and then we'll get you saddled up."

It wasn't exactly an answer, was it? For a split second, she saw something deeper flicker behind that professional gaze—regret.

CONRAD'S BEDROOM WAS across the hall from Annabelle's—which would work well for keeping an eye on her. He glanced over his shoulder toward the guest room where Annabelle stood with her back to him. Then he shut his bedroom door to change.

Annabelle didn't like being his job, but it was better if he kept her relegated to that part of his brain. The truth was, he'd felt something powerful when he saw her tearstained face after that robbery, like every atom in his being was being magnetically drawn to protect her. And in all his years of policing, he'd only felt that way once before...

His partner, Terri. She'd ended up badly injured, and it was all because Conrad had developed feelings for her. He'd been thinking of her as his girlfriend when he should have been seeing her as the competent cop she was. He'd gone in too soon during a drug bust, and she got beaten up badly when the buyer realized she was a cop. If Conrad had just waited until her signal instead of reacting like an overprotective boyfriend, she would have been fine.

Terri quit the force, got married to someone else, had some kids and was now working in computer sales, the last he'd heard. They didn't keep in touch. Law enforcement ties were supposed to be closer than family, but he'd messed that up. He hadn't made that mistake again—work was work. He kept those lines firm.

No, Annabelle was better off as his assignment, although he could see that he'd have to soften up with her somewhat.

Conrad pulled off his uniform shirt and

replaced it with a T-shirt. He grabbed a pair of jeans, and once he was dressed, he put his badge and gun into place on his belt where he could feel the familiar bulk and weight of them.

When he headed out of his bedroom, he saw Annabelle standing in the doorway of the guest room where he'd left her. She was still wearing the same jeans and T-shirt, form-fitting in a way he was determined not to notice. Her hair was down, and her shoulders were tensed as if she was curling in on herself protectively. He sighed.

That softening up was going to have to start now. His feelings around the robbery, around her, around his own history, were not her problem. She had one problem right now—she'd seen someone shot. The hallway floorboards creaked beneath his feet.

"I don't have riding boots," Annabelle said, turning to him.

As if that was what was occupying her thoughts. But he could also understand a woman's desire to keep some things private.

"My uncle had a few different pairs for guests," Conrad said. "You can try on a pair and see what fits."

She nodded slowly, then pulled a hand

through her hair, tugging a blond tendril away from her face. Her eyes were filled with a mixture of emotions, and she quickly blinked it back.

"Are you okay?" Conrad asked.

"That's dangerously close to caring," she said, her voice low.

Conrad smiled faintly. "I didn't say that I didn't care. I just said that I try to keep my head in the job. That's really important right now. I want you to look back on this in ten or fifteen years and remember that robot of a cop who kept you alive."

Annabelle looked up at him, searching his face, which only made him turn his expression to granite. She didn't need to know what was under his practiced reserve. It wouldn't instill confidence.

"You say you're better at your job when you're all—" she moved her hand in front of him "—this."

He looked down at himself. "Professional?"

"Unfeeling."

"I never said I didn't feel," he said. "I just don't inflict it on you."

She winced, and he sighed. "I don't mean that I can't handle your feelings. I just—" He'd never had a witness push back like this before. But then, he'd never had one living with him, either. "You've gone through enough, okay? You get to feel it all—anger, fear, sadness, anxiety…all of it! You have a right to it. But what you don't need right now is to concern yourself with what I'm feeling."

"What *are* you feeling?" she asked.

He chuckled. "It doesn't matter. See? This is about you. Sensitive people want to gauge everyone else's feelings around them, but I'm not your burden. I'm okay. That's all you have to know—I'm strong enough to handle all of this."

Annabelle didn't answer that. Her gaze moved back to the window. Was she thinking about freedom—getting out of here? What did she need right now? There were no state psychologists here or trauma therapists to take over—just him.

"What's freaking you out the most?" he asked at last.

"I saw him—" Annabelle lifted her hand, one finger held out like a gun. "I saw him point the gun at that security guard, and I thought to myself, he's just acting tough. This robber is putting up this big act. And the security guard was already putting his hands up. I mean, he wasn't going to risk his life for what he gets paid, you know? Everyone knows that. None of us were going to risk our lives for that money!"

Conrad was silent.

"And then—" She made a soft sound with her mouth and dropped her hand. "He just shot him. And he kept walking. It was like that guard wasn't even a person to him. It was like—" Her gaze moved around the room as if searching for the words. "It was like he didn't recognize anyone else's right to breathe. What kind of person does that?"

"He's a con man," Conrad said. "Stephen Hope has done one stint in prison for defrauding an elderly woman. That was what we could nail him with. He's pretty slippery, and he's got those gang connections where he calls in favors. He's got a rap sheet a mile long for disorderly conduct, domestic violence, driving under the influence... He's been in the system since he was a teenager."

"Domestic violence?"

"About three different assault charges, yeah."

Goose bumps rose on her arms. "Maybe I'm not quite so dedicated to the right thing as your Amish neighbors seem to be. I'm not willing to die to bring that man to justice."

"Good. That's two of us. I'm not willing to let you die, either," he said. "Or get hurt, for that matter. I think you underestimate just what a pain in the butt I am for detail and security."

She smiled at his rueful tone, and he felt a wave of relief to see it. Was she getting an idea of how dedicated he was to her safety?

"A real stickler, are you?" she said.

"I drive my brother crazy with it," he said. "But all of my instinctive, obstinate focus on detail—that's yours for the next few weeks. A hundred percent."

She licked her lips, and for a split second, he caught himself thinking how pretty she looked, even when she was completely off balance. But he'd seen her when she was more relaxed at the soup kitchen, and she was absolutely gorgeous. He wanted to bring that level of confidence back for her. He *needed* to bring it back—not for him, but for her. If he could see her safe and volunteering her time for the less fortunate again, then he'd feel like he set something right.

"You're safer with me than anywhere else, you know," Conrad added, and he'd stop there. That was all she needed to know. What he was feeling needn't concern her. His motivation, his satisfaction with a job well done—none of that was her business. But with him, he'd use every last ounce of strength in his body to protect her. He'd be vigilant, watching for any sign that the wrong people had discovered where she was. His training, his experience, his dedication would be for her.

"Maybe some distraction would be good for me today," Annabelle said, and she straightened.

"Yes. Let's go fix a fence," he said.

It wouldn't solve all of this, but it would give them something to do, hopefully give her some temporary purpose here, and completing a task had a way of tricking a brain into feeling like it was in control of uncontrollable things. Everyone needed that deception once in a while. Worries could eat a person from the inside out. But a job—even a job in the form of this pretty blonde woman who'd seen more than she wanted to—helped to give life some shape.

WILDER HAD THE horses saddled by the time Conrad and Annabelle got to the stable. Conrad paused at the corral and held a hand out to the colt. The little guy clambered over to him, all legs and enthusiasm, looking for the sugar cube he knew that Conrad would have. The mare, Sophie, waited patiently, watching him with a liquid stare.

"You want some sugar, too, Sophie?" he asked her.

The horse strode regally over to him, and he fed her the promised sugar cube and stroked her velvet nose. Then he headed over to his brother and the waiting horses. Wilder had saddled up Mona for Annabelle—a good choice. She was quiet and hard to spook.

Something bright flickered in the periphery of his vision, and he spotted a small pink-frocked figure who appeared at the other side of the corral.

"Jane, you've got to go back home," Conrad said firmly. "What did your father say about staying in the house?"

"Can I feed the baby horse?" Jane asked softly, ignoring his question.

"We're going to meet up with your father, so we won't be here to keep an eye on you," Conrad said. "You need to go back to your *mammi*. I'm serious. You can't be here by yourself."

Jane hesitated, her eyes moving back to the horses. He could see the hope shining in her round face. She wanted to feed the colt, but he couldn't let her get used to that. Besides, his mind was spinning with other potential risks and how to defend against them. He couldn't take on the responsibility of a little girl, too. She had a family.

"Jane!" he barked. "Go back home, now!"

The little girl startled, her eyes widening. Her lower lip trembled, and she turned and ran back the way she'd come, the strings from her *kapp* trailing out behind her. When he turned, he saw Annabelle's surprised gaze locked on him. He hated this—having his weaknesses on full display. He was very good at his job, but he wasn't good at everything, and that included kids.

"It's not safe," Conrad said curtly. "That's how accidents happen, and she needs to go back home, where her family can keep an eye on her."

This was the price of being the sheepdog. Everyone else saw the teeth and heard the snarl. He was the one who could visualize all the potential dangers—like the damage an overprotective mare could do. All the best intentions in the world didn't matter a bit next to the consequences of one monumental mistake.

CHAPTER THREE

ANNABELLE'S HORSE FOLLOWED after Conrad and Wilder without any encouragement. She settled into the horse's rolling gait, letting her hips absorb the bumps as they rode toward the vandalized fence. Conrad reined his horse in to bring him to Annabelle's side. He seemed ill at ease.

"She's just a little girl," Annabelle said.

Conrad sighed. "She's safer at home."

"Agreed," she replied. "I'm not arguing that. But little girls remember things like that—being barked at by some beefy rancher next door, being scared of him. That sort of thing sinks into a girl's heart and stays there."

It sank in when it was her father who had done it, too. Annabelle's father had been of the belief that his daughter should be resilient and never need a man to take care of her. Not a bad goal, except that his way of getting her there was more of a tough-love approach.

Ahead of them, Wilder started off in the direction of the house next door.

"I'm not great with kids," Conrad said.

"I can see that," she replied ruefully. "What's the story there?"

"What do you mean?"

"Don't you have nieces and nephews?" she asked.

"Nope."

"Do your cousins have kids?"

"A few," he replied.

"And?"

Conrad shook his head. "Kids are phenomenally bad at rules, in my experience. They do things their own way. That's all fine and good, but if I'm responsible for their safety, chaos doesn't work for me."

"Not all kids are little hellions," she replied. "Jane, for example, isn't some brat just waiting to annoy you. She likes you."

"I know…"

"They say that children that are drawn to horses are deeper feeling and more compassionate," she added. "I'd see it as a good sign."

"Look, I'm good at a lot of things," Conrad said. "I'm a very good shot, I've got a great instinct for security and I can smell a rat a mile away. But I'm not good with kids."

And yet Jane kept coming over anyway. Maybe the little girl saw something in Conrad that appealed to her—a deeper kindness, perhaps. Annabelle had seen that gentler side of him.

"You seem okay with kids at the soup kitchen," she said.

"There aren't any horses there to trample them," he replied. "It's a relatively safe environment. And they have parents watching them, for the most part. Send a passel of kids into the kitchen with the stoves on and see me bark then."

She chuckled. "Okay, okay. That's a valid point."

They rode onto the Schmidt property, and Wollie met them on horseback. Jane stood on the front porch watching them with a dismal look on her face. Annabelle waved at her, but the girl didn't respond. Wollie said something to her in Pennsylvania Dutch, and she heaved a sigh.

"She wants to come along," Wollie said as he fell in beside them. "I told her she has to stay home."

"She's lonely," Annabelle said.

Wollie glanced over at her, looking mildly surprised.

"Yah," he said. "I think she is."

Wollie and Wilder pulled ahead, their horses moving at a quicker pace. Conrad seemed happy to let some space spread between them, but he stayed close to Annabelle.

"So you like predictability," Annabelle said, casting him a smile.

"How come you're trying to figure me out?" Conrad asked. "I don't think I'm that interesting."

"I don't know about that." Annabelle flicked a fly off her arm. "At the soup kitchen, the single women are wildly curious about you."

"Including you?" He caught her eye, and she felt her cheeks heat.

"I find people interesting, not just you. But you're a hard one to figure out."

Conrad looked behind them, that flinty gaze of his sweeping left and right. Then he settled in his saddle again.

"So what do you do for fun?" she asked. "Humor me here. I'll be a whole lot easier to deal with if I feel like I know you a little bit."

Conrad rolled his eyes. "You don't give up."

"I've got nothing better to do," she said, but she smiled to show she didn't mean any harm.

"I like to ride." He shrugged. "See? Nothing interesting there. Before my brother and I inherited this place, I used to go trail riding with some buddies. I also like to hunt."

She nodded. "Man versus nature?"

"Sometimes just man in nature," he replied. "Something might want to eat me, but you don't come across the same ugliness that you get with people."

Did anyone ever get used to dealing with the darkest corners of humanity? She let her gaze move out over the fields. A barbed-wire fence stretched like stitches between the Westhouse and Schmidt land, and the horses plodded along at a comfortable pace.

"I'm taking a yoga class," she said. "I didn't think I'd be any good at it, but it's soothing. Or I used to think so. I'm not sure it'll be enough to combat my newfound anxiety." She caught a smile tickling the corners of Conrad's lips. "I'm also part of a book club. Theresa, Alana and I joined together. They work at the bank."

She and Theresa had had plans to see a movie this weekend. And Theresa was the one person Annabelle wanted to hash all of this out with, because the robbery didn't make complete sense. How did Stephen know the right time to hit the bank? She knew now that he had her keys—although how he'd lifted them, she had no idea. But he knew the exact moment to rob the place, when there was a very large cash order on the premises. The crooks got a massive amount of money, and the bank worked hard to make sure those big cash orders weren't under their roof for long for this very reason.

"The three of you are good friends?" Conrad pushed his hat back with one hand, the reins held expertly in the other.

"Yeah, we are."

"You didn't mention that in our interview with you."

She hadn't mentioned her missing bank keys, either. She wanted to be completely open, but she didn't dare.

Annabelle shook her head. "A lot of us are friends. In a place the size of Wooster, you know people. Why? Is that important?"

"Just good to know," he replied.

That was right—she was trying to get to know the man who'd be responsible for her safety, and he was accumulating information for a case. There was a difference here in what they were trying to accomplish. He'd called her his job, and that was what she was. They weren't going to be friends. This wasn't personal.

And Annabelle wasn't going to tell him every last detail that he might find incredibly interesting, either. Like the text message that she'd immediately deleted, though the words were still seared in her mind:

You were part of it. You helped us plan it. You had a cut of the cash. If you say a word, you go down with me. That's a promise, Princess.

It was from a number she didn't recognize, but she knew who'd sent it. There was only one person who could have. While she hadn't been a part of anything with that robbery, and while she hadn't done more than bump into him a few times in the last two years, she could see with nauseating clarity exactly how guilty he could make her look.

The police could probably dig that text message back up again, but what would it do but make her look guilty? Stephen worded it the way he had for a reason. Those few weeks she'd dated him, she'd gotten to know a very intelligent but emotionally shallow man. He'd taken the breakup rather well, to her relief. He'd said he understood—they wanted different things. He'd had a terrible temper when a situation didn't go his way. But she hadn't seen this particular darkness inside him. She'd never even suspected…

But would the police believe that?

A breeze lifted her hair away from her face, and despite the August heat, Annabelle shivered.

They crested a hill, and over the top, she saw a herd of cattle dotting the landscape. Golden August sunshine warmed the scene, the scent of grass and cattle coming to her on the breeze. A cow with a calf looked at them warily and then bawled out a low moo. The grass was lush and long, and the cattle roamed lazily, their backs shining like burnished bronze in the afternoon sun.

"There's the hole in the fence." Wilder pointed, and Annabelle shielded her eyes to get a better view. There was a spot near a dirt road with some muddy wheel tracks, and she could see wooden rails that had been broken off to open up part of the fence. A couple of cows had wandered through the hole in the fence, crossed the road and grazed next to some trees.

"I guess we can fix that with wire for now," Wollie said, over his shoulder.

"Let's go get the cows back into your pasture," Wilder said, and he kicked his horse into motion.

When Annabelle looked up at Conrad, she saw him eyeing the scene thoughtfully, but he didn't follow Wilder down the slope.

"Conrad, can I ask you something?"

He turned toward her. "Sure."

"What happens if I don't testify?"

His eyebrows went up, and he pulled off his hat. He pressed his lips together for a moment, then said, "Why?"

"I'm just wondering. You all asked if I'd testify. What if...I wasn't so certain about who I saw?"

He frowned slightly. "You aren't sure?"

"What if I wasn't?" she pressed. "What if I didn't testify against Stephen Hope? Would you still have enough to put him away?"

"It would be a whole lot harder." He looked down into his hat, then replaced it on his head. "You seemed pretty certain back at the station. Really certain. You knew who you saw. What changed?"

Annabelle looked around, and her heartbeat started to speed up again. She blinked back unexpected tears. Crying wouldn't help—it wasn't going to change facts, and it certainly wouldn't protect her from the man out there who wanted to keep her quiet.

"What changed?" Conrad repeated quietly.

She knew who she saw. She knew what Stephen had done. There was no doubt in her mind about his guilt, but he'd promised to bring her down with him, and heaven help her, but she believed him.

"I'm scared." Annabelle met his gaze, then shrugged feebly. "I looked a killer in the eye, and he knows who I am. What happens if I change my mind about testifying?"

Conrad licked his lips. "I guess I'd just ask you to tell me straight. Because if you disappear on me, I'm going to assume something bad happened and I'll use every weapon in my arsenal to get to you and make sure you're okay. I will go through any walls I have to. It'll probably cost a lot of taxpayers' money and waste a good amount of time." He caught her gaze and held it. "So if you do change your mind about what you saw, I'm asking you to tell me. It'll save us both a lot of trouble."

Annabelle's heart hammered hard in her throat. Somehow, she believed Conrad as much as she believed Stephen. There were two very powerful men who wanted something from her, and all she wanted was to go back to her quiet little life.

"It's nothing," she said. "I was just asking... You know, seeing how it all works."

THE NEXT COUPLE of hours slid by on the grass-scented breeze. Wollie and Wilder herded the escaped cows back onto Wollie's land, and they worked on the fence. For a little while, Conrad rode back and forth along the road that edged their property. She could almost see his gears turning.

The cattle grazed on, all but the mama cow whose baby had been stolen. She kept bawling out her call. She'd walk a few paces in one direction and moo loudly, then take a few more steps and repeat the call.

"Cows are very sensitive creatures," Conrad said as he reined in next to Annabelle. "I can't figure out how they got that calf away from the mother, unless she was sleeping and they were incredibly quiet. Even so, that's a dangerous undertaking."

"What will Wollie do about the mother?" Annabelle asked.

"That's a cow with milk and a longing to care for a calf. There might be a solution there. I've got a bottle baby calf in our barn,"

Conrad replied. "The cow just wouldn't feed him, so we had to take him away. Maybe if we put them together, nature will take its course and the cow will adopt the calf."

"Really?" she asked.

"It's worth a try. I'll have a word with Wollie about it and see what he thinks. We might be able to help each other out."

Wollie and Wilder had finished with the fence, meanwhile, and when they loaded up their tools and came back in their direction, Conrad and Wollie spoke for a few minutes out of Annabelle's earshot.

"So what do you think about ranch life so far?" Wilder asked, shooting her a grin.

"I doubt it gets boring," she replied.

"It never seems to," Wilder agreed. "I've been trying to get my brother to ranch full-time with me for the last two years, but he can't be budged."

"I should be glad of that," Annabelle said.

"He's dedicated," Wilder agreed.

Conrad rode back over and fell into place on the other side of Annabelle, leaving her securely sandwiched between the two men on horseback.

"It's a go," Conrad said.

"What's a go?" Wilder asked.

"We're going to bring that heartbroken mama cow together with our bottle baby up in the barn corral and see if we can make a match between them," Conrad replied. "It'll solve both of our problems at once if they take to each other."

Annabelle looked over her shoulder toward the forlorn cow. Her milk was dripping, and while she'd stopped her frantic mooing for the moment, she still seemed on edge.

"Can we do it now?" Annabelle asked, turning straight in her saddle again.

"You want to give it a try?" Conrad asked his brother.

"Let's do it," Wilder said. "You two get the calf into the corral, and Wollie and I can drive the cow up. What do you say, Wollie? Do you have the time?"

"*Yah,*" Wollie replied. "I'll feel better knowing she's not pining down there. The saddest sounds in the world are crying babies and crying cows."

Wollie and Wilder peeled off and headed back down the slope, and Annabelle followed Conrad up toward the barn.

"I'm surprised that you guys care so much about that cow," Annabelle said. "I thought ranchers and farmers were a little tougher about this stuff."

"We still care," Conrad replied. "We aren't dead inside. Besides, this is what neighbors are for—a little bit of creative problem-solving. That mama might not get her own baby back, but she needs a baby to take care of."

Conrad swung down to the ground in one smooth movement, and she hesitated, looking down at the rocky ground beneath her.

"Need a hand?" Conrad asked.

"I think so." She laughed nervously. "It's been a while since I've dismounted."

The last time she went riding, there was a dismounting station for the participants, and she was only appreciating now just how much of a city slicker she was.

Conrad put a gentle hand on the horse's neck, and the mare stilled under his touch. Then he tapped the top of her boot.

"Keep this foot in the stirrup. Then you're going to put all your weight on this foot, and swing your other leg over, and I'll catch you."

"I do know that much," she said ruefully, but then she hesitated. "You'll catch me?"

"Yeah." He squinted up at her. "You think I can't?"

"How much can you bench-press?" she joked.

"More than you." He grinned. "Come on."

It wasn't often that Annabelle trusted anyone to catch her and support her weight—not in her adult years, at least. She doubted this would be graceful, but if she wanted to get off this horse's back, she'd need a hand.

Annabelle did as he instructed, and as she started coming down toward the ground, she felt his strong hands clamp down on her waist, suspending her momentarily in the air. Then he lowered her to the ground. His strength shouldn't have surprised her, but as her boots came gently down, her knees were a little weak.

Conrad took a step back, and she rubbed her hands on the front of her jeans.

"Thanks," she said, her voice sounding breathy in her own ears.

"No problem." He caught the mare's reins, then his own horse's, and led them toward the stable corral a few yards away. He sent them both inside with the mare and her colt, and then gave the gate a shake to check it before he rejoined her.

Conrad walked with a cowboy's rolling gait, and she couldn't help but notice that the boots and hat suited him. He was a cop, but he was also a cowboy to the bone.

"Let's bring the calf out to the other corral. If you bring a bottle of milk, he'll follow you."

Conrad led the way into the barn. It was dim and smelled of hay.

"When we're done with this calf, I'm going to set up some perimeter alarms the department is letting me use," Conrad said.

"Fancy alarms?" she said, trying to sound more joking than she felt. The seriousness of her visit was coming back.

"They're fairly easy to set up," he said. "They'll give us a heads-up if anyone crosses them."

Anyone coming in, or anyone going out, presumably. How much of this was meant to keep her on the property?

"Do they set off sirens or something?" she asked.

"Nope, just a ping to my phone telling me which alarms were triggered," he replied. "If someone is coming onto the property, I don't necessarily want them to know that I know. They're easier to catch if they're surprised."

"Right..."

Conrad caught her eye, then paused. "It's just a precaution."

"Better safe than sorry," she quipped, forcing a smile.

"You are safe," he said. "My nerdy tech side is as strong as my by-the-book rule side. It all comes together nicely in your favor." A smile tickled the corners of his lips. Then he nodded toward a stall. "Come on. We'll lure this little guy out and see if we can give him a new mama."

Conrad continued on past her toward a stall where a leggy red-and-white calf stood. He gave the calf a scratch on the head and then moved past him to grab a white plastic bottle.

"We won't give him much milk." He picked up a paper package and scooped some powder into the bottle, then turned on a tap to add water. "Hopefully the cow will let him feed from her. We'll see."

He started to shake the half-filled bottle and the calf's gaze locked on to the frothing milk. Then he handed the bottle to Annabelle and put a hand on the stall door.

"You might want a head start," Conrad said. "This guy is coming straight for that bottle. Out the door there."

Annabelle opened the door into a corral. The ground was dusty, but the air was sweet with the scent of grass and wheat from a nearby field. She held the door open and Conrad released the calf, who galloped joyfully in her direction. When he got to her, he started immediately nosing for the bottle.

Annabelle stepped outside and lowered the bottle so he could latch on. The calf drank hungrily, foam collecting on his chin and dripping to the ground. Conrad came outside then, and she noticed how his gaze swung in a full 360-degree turn around the corral before he shot her a smile.

"This little guy will be a lot less work if he can have a cow to feed him," he said.

"I bet." The bottle was draining quickly, and she heard the whoops and hyas of Wilder and Wollie as they drove the cow up in their direction. The cow appeared over the crest of the hill, Wollie and Wilder right behind her. She galloped forward a few paces and then slowed once more.

The calf finished the bottle, and Annabelle dropped it to the side. The calf kept nosing at her hand, but the rest of his meal would hopefully come from the cow.

"Wait here," Conrad said, and he went over to open the corral's wide gate. With some extra prodding from the cowboys behind her, the cow came thundering into the corral and Conrad pulled the gate shut with a clang.

It took a couple of minutes for the cow to relax, and Conrad brought over some hay for her to eat. Once the cow was munching her meal, Conrad led the calf toward her.

"Hey, girl," Conrad said softly. "I've got a baby here who needs you..."

The cow took a step back.

"Come on, now..." Conrad picked up a handful of hay and held it out toward her. The cow took a step forward again for the hay and gave the calf another look. Watching Conrad squatting there with this cow, Annabelle thought the man had softened somehow. He seemed different from the concrete block of a cop she'd been seeing so far. This was closer to the man she knew from the charity kitchen.

The calf had spotted the milk dripping from the cow's udder, and he slipped past Conrad and went straight for it. The cow startled and stepped to the side, but it was too late—the calf had latched on and was drinking hungrily. After all that time not being suckled, the pressure release must have been a relief, because she settled down and let the calf continue to drink.

Conrad leaned against the rail next to Annabelle, but his gaze stayed locked on the cow.

"This might work," he said.

"It might," she replied.

The cow was sniffing the calf now as he drank, and when she licked his back hip—all she could really reach—it looked to Annabelle like she'd accepted him.

Wollie and Wilder watched from outside the corral, and they were smiling and talking together, their voices too low to make out from where she stood. The sun shone warm, and a fly buzzed lazily past Annabelle's head.

She looked up at Conrad and he nodded toward the house.

"I've got motion detectors to set," he said. "We'd better get the horses unsaddled, and then I'll have to ask you to stay inside until I come back."

Annabelle knew the odds were stacked against her, and she wasn't foolish enough to be able to ignore that. But somehow, as she watched calf and cow together, she was starting to feel like she might have some hope.

CHAPTER FOUR

THROUGH THE BACK window of the kitchen, Annabelle could see the corral. Wollie and Wilder were both gone now, but the cow remained. The calf had finished drinking and was standing close to the cow, who was still sniffing it. Annabelle watched them for a moment. There seemed to be a sense of relief in both creatures, the mama cow and the newly adopted baby. They needed each other. Needing someone to care for was a sentiment that Annabelle could appreciate. It wasn't that she was longing for motherhood, particularly, but her need to care might explain her desire to understand this cop a bit better. Somewhere, deep down inside of that muscular, tough exterior, she sensed a man who could use a little nurturing himself.

At the same time, her own world had tipped sideways, and what she wouldn't give for some reassurance that everything would be okay. The problem was, no one could guarantee anything for her—not with the current state of things. Conrad could protect her, but could he stop the slow grind of justice if she got caught in the machinery? She doubted it.

Annabelle leaned forward to see past the corral and farther up the drive. She could just make out Conrad, who was looking up into a tree thoughtfully, before he took a few steps and disappeared from her line of sight. She let out a slow breath.

She missed her apartment—her own little kitchen, the way the sunlight came in through her balcony doors, the smell of the neighbor's phenomenal baking that always made her snackish late at night. She missed her cat, Herman, most of all. He was an absolute brat, but she couldn't help but love that furry face of his. She'd asked her mother to pick Herman up and take him home. Her father didn't like cats—add that to the list of things he didn't like. Here was hoping Herman was getting enough attention.

And here she was in someone else's home, running from people who'd silence her using intimidation, or worse. Funny—she hadn't appreciated the blessing of a boring existence until now.

Annabelle looked around the kitchen, her gaze sliding over Formica countertops and a big sink. This was going to be the next few weeks of her life, apparently. She touched her pocket, instinctively reaching for her phone, and let her hand drop. It was hard to get used to not having access to the world at her fingertips. Ordinarily, she'd text Theresa to see how she was doing, or flick through some social media on her phone. What would her friends think had happened to her when she went social media silent? Was Theresa keeping her secret? Her stomach flipped at that thought, but of course she would. Theresa knew how dangerous this was.

She headed through the kitchen into a sitting room. A woodstove dominated one corner, and a flat-screen TV hung on the opposite wall. There were some mismatched easy chairs and a couch with a cowhide rug on the worn hardwood floor in the center of the room. She could see Conrad out the picture window, walking up and down the drive, watching his cell phone screen, then pausing, his weight on one foot. He looked back over his shoulder and strode in that direction again, reached into a leafy little nook in a bush and stepped back a few paces, his attention on his cell phone screen. He was an incredibly large man, but he was in proportion. Other than on TV, she'd never seen a man who looked quite that well muscled.

Conrad looked up from his phone, and his steely gaze swung over the house, his brow furrowed. Then he seemed to see her in the window, because his gaze snapped back to meet hers. There was something in his expression—protective, competent, determined—that made her cheeks heat. And maybe it was just a little bit of embarrassment at being caught staring. She fluttered her fingers in a wave, and while he didn't wave back, he did cast her a lopsided smile.

"Dang," she murmured. Did he have any idea the effect he had on women?

Annabelle tore her attention away from the window and glanced around the living room. She'd have to while away the hours somehow, and she might as well watch some mindless television. She just needed the remote.

She scanned the surfaces—an antique record player combo unit against one wall, a sideboard with a collection of magazines and newspapers piled on one side, and a bookshelf, which was where she spotted the remote.

She paused when she saw a photo album lying on the shelf with a picture of Conrad on the front in full deputy uniform. She smiled, picked it up and flipped it open. The first pictures were of a much younger, less muscled Conrad at his sheriff's department graduation. He looked proud—standing tall next to an older couple who beamed into the camera. Probably his parents.

There were various snapshots from that day, and then a few other pictures of Conrad leaning against a sheriff's department cruiser, and another one of him looking annoyed while sitting at a desk, again in full uniform.

The side door banged shut, and Annabelle startled. She held her breath as footsteps came across the linoleum in the kitchen before Wilder appeared in the doorway.

"Hi," Wilder said. "Oh, you found our mom's brag book about Conrad, did you?"

"Your mom put this together?" That made sense—the focus on his career, the sorts of pictures that had been chosen.

"Yep. She has one for me, too, but mine is less impressive." Wilder grinned. "She gave those to us last Christmas—she's been putting them together for years."

"That's rather sweet," Annabelle said. "Do you think Conrad minds if I take a look?"

"Who cares if he does?" Wilder quipped. "Feel free. There's just a lot of pictures of Conrad in uniform."

She turned the page, and this time she saw some pictures of Conrad with a woman in uniform. She was tall, lithe, with dark hair and a pretty smile. The uniform looked good on her.

"His partner?" she asked.

"Yeah, that was his first partner on the force. Terri."

"He doesn't have a partner now?" she asked.

"They hop around. The newest sheriff wants them to work with lots of different officers. It's about inclusivity and breadth of training…something like that. He's complained about it often enough," Wilder replied.

She flipped forward and found another couple of pictures—an awards ceremony of some sort, and there was another photo of Conrad with the same older couple, their hair a little whiter. The old man stood on one side of Conrad, and the woman on the other side. They both had wide smiles, and the older man had a hand on Conrad's shoulder in a sweetly protective gesture. Her own father hadn't been that supportive. He'd booted her out of the house at eighteen and told her to make her own way.

She flipped the page to see a shot with Conrad and Wilder together, Conrad's arm flung around Wilder's shoulders. There on the next page was a picture of Conrad and Terri together, his arm around her waist and her hand on top of his.

She looked closer at that one, and she felt a tiny twinge of jealousy that she knew she had no right to. But she had to wonder what it would feel like to be the woman in Conrad's embrace...

"A little more than a partner?" Annabelle said, quirking a smile in Wilder's direction.

He came over and looked down at the photo. "Yeah, they dated for about six months. Then there was an accident on the job, Terri got hurt and she quit the force."

That must have been quite the accident. And it appeared that Conrad and Terri's relationship hadn't lasted.

"What happened?" she asked.

Wilder looked like he was about to answer. Then he pressed his lips together.

"That's a story Conrad should tell."

"Okay. Sorry, I didn't mean to pry."

"Don't worry about it."

"If I asked Conrad, do you think he'd answer?" she asked.

Wilder chuckled. "That would depend on his mood."

She'd expected Wilder to say no. But maybe Conrad would open up a little bit and give her some insight into how he ticked. She had quite a stretch in front of her with not much to do. She might as well dissect this beefy cop and see how he worked.

"We're not that interesting, unfortunately," Wilder said with a laugh. "We run a ranch, and my brother nitpicks the rules. We're pretty boring."

"Boring is a good thing," she said with a chuckle. "I've had enough drama this week to last me a lifetime."

"I'll bet."

Annabelle flipped the page again, and it looked like a few years might have passed, because Conrad suddenly looked bulkier, more muscled, and there were a few more lines around his eyes. These must be more recent photos, because this was the man she recognized.

There was another award ceremony, and this time there was a picture of just Conrad and his mother. She looked even grayer, and Conrad had also changed. There was that look of concrete and steel about him now, bulky muscles and a professional stare. He was older, tougher and somehow changed.

"Did something happen to your dad?" Annabelle asked. "I don't see him in this last picture."

"Dad passed away about three years ago," Wilder said.

"Oh, I'm sorry." She cast Wilder a sympathetic look. "That's tough."

"Thanks. It took us all by surprise," Wilder replied.

That was the end of the album—nothing more in the empty, waiting pages. Somehow, it struck her as sad, that one last picture without his father's proud smile. She might not have enjoyed that kind of relationship with her own father, but she could appreciate it for other people. His mother was more like her own—proud, supportive, and the love in these pages was evident. Annabelle closed the album and placed it back on the shelf.

"Are you okay here in the house?" Wilder asked. "I mean…is there anything you need?"

"No, I'm okay," she said.

"I'm going to grab some water and then

head back out for more chores," Wilder said. "There's always work around here."

"I've been told to stay put until Conrad comes back in," she replied.

"Ah." Wilder grinned. "I'd do that, then. He's a stickler, but there's always a reason. If you need anything, feel free to poke around."

"Thanks."

She heard the thunk of Wilder's cowboy boots against linoleum and then the sound of the tap turning on in the kitchen. Annabelle's gaze lingered on the closed album.

What had happened in that accident that made Conrad's partner leave the force? That would be a very big step if she'd loved her job. And what had changed Conrad like that? Was it just the work of policing, or was it that same accident?

CONRAD HAD FINISHED setting up his motion detector sensors and was satisfied with the results. At least he'd get a heads-up if someone snuck past them.

The problem was, Annabelle's safety wasn't his only concern. She'd just been through an incredibly traumatic event, and now she'd landed in his home. She needed more than physical protection for the next little while—

she needed to be able to relax a bit, process her feelings, talk if she needed to. Goodness knew he wasn't a therapist, and he didn't pretend to be, but he did have a strong enough shoulder for her to lean on.

Dinner that evening was sausages on the barbecue, and it hit the spot. Wilder had discussed the cow-and-calf situation with Wollie next door, and they'd decided to leave the pair together in the Westhouse barn for a few more days to let them bond more effectively before sending them together back to the field. They didn't need to bottle-feed the calf anymore, which would be one less chore to do.

After Conrad and Wilder did the dishes, Conrad looked out the kitchen window thoughtfully.

"Are we on a fire ban right now?" Conrad asked.

"Not right now. We've had enough rain," Wilder replied.

"We have that brush and the wood from those old fences that need to be burned," Conrad said. "I figured I might do that this evening."

"Add a couple of marshmallows to the mix, and you might end up having fun," his brother said.

Conrad chuckled. "That's the plan, at least."

He lowered his voice. "How does she seem to you...stressed out?"

"A bit," Wilder said.

Conrad nodded. Yeah, a bonfire wasn't a bad idea. His perimeter alarms were set, so he wouldn't be taken by surprise, and he had a feeling Annabelle could use something to reduce her stress the first night under his roof.

"My job is supposed to be her safety," Conrad said. And that was the easier job, to be sure. He could keep her in one piece for a few weeks. But people were never as simple as that. She needed more than safety, and he wasn't sure how to provide the rest, or if he should even be trying.

"You want my humble opinion?" Wilder asked.

"Sure."

"She's a flight risk," Wilder said.

"What makes you think that?" Conrad asked. Because he hadn't breathed a word of Annabelle's worries about testifying.

"She's jumpy, she watches the road and she knows where every single one of your motion detectors are set up." Wilder shrugged. "I don't know details, obviously, but just watching her, I'd say she's keeping an eye out for a way out of here—with or without you."

"She saw a man killed," Conrad said, his voice low.

Wilder didn't answer, but his expression turned grim.

"That'll be tough to deal with," Conrad went on. "For anyone, but especially someone like her—a regular civilian who's probably never seen anyone die before. She needs more than physical safety—and I don't know how to even start with the other stuff."

"Talking does wonders sometimes," Wilder said.

"It does." Conrad sighed. But talking involved opening up on both sides. "I'm going to have to relax my rule about no personal connections on work time."

Wilder barked out a laugh. "Yeah, you might. This is no regular day on the job, is it?"

So that evening, Conrad stacked wood next to the firepit out behind the house, and he kindled up a nice blaze. He put a couple of citronella candles around to chase off the nighttime mosquitoes and dropped two lawn chairs around the newly crackling flames. Next door at the Schmidt farm, three buggies arrived. The doors were propped open, and he could hear laughter and talking from the visitors surf the breeze in their direction.

"Where's your brother?" Annabelle asked as she came out of the house, the bag of marshmallows Conrad had dug out of a cupboard in one hand.

"He's got a date," Conrad replied.

"Does he?" Annabelle shot him a smile. "Well, good for him."

Wilder was the kind of cowboy who lived up to his name, and he'd never had a shortage of female attention. Conrad glanced across at the Schmidt farm next door. The warm yellow light of kerosene lamps illuminated the little farmhouse, and a sudden eruption of male laughter made him smile in unconscious response.

"They're having a party," Annabelle said, sinking into a chair by the fire.

"I doubt they'd call it that, but they've got some visitors," he said.

"What do they do?" she asked.

"They visit and chat," Conrad said. "They also enjoy board games a lot. They're super-competitive Pictionary players."

"Really?"

"Yeah. They've had my brother and me over before for dinner. They had a few other people over, too, and they had this cracking Pictionary game going. They made their own cards with Pennsylvania Dutch words and phrases on them, but they played in English for my sake."

"Huh." She smiled. "The Amish life is a whole different world, isn't it?"

"In a lot of ways," he agreed, and he pulled up the other lawn chair next to her and eased into it. "But they're really decent people. You can trust their handshake."

Conrad grabbed the two roasting sticks he'd brought out with him and handed one to Annabelle.

"I saw the news earlier," she said.

"Yeah?" He shot her a cautious look.

"The robbery and the shooting were the lead story for every channel you get," she said.

"I'm sorry," he said. "It might be a good idea to avoid the news for the next few weeks."

"Journalists are suggesting that Stephen Hope had an accomplice working in the bank," she said. "And they said the police are looking into the possibility."

"Well, he did know an awful lot about the right time to hit the bank, how to get in, how to get out…" Conrad shrugged. "He had to get that information from someone."

"So you're telling me that I have a co-worker who willingly gave information to a criminal to rob us?" she asked.

So much for relaxing out here and letting her unwind a bit.

"It's the only thing that makes sense," Conrad said.

She was silent, and Conrad reached for the bag of marshmallows and tore it open. He leaned over and pressed a plump marshmallow onto the end of her stick.

"Roast that," he said.

She smiled faintly. "You're trying to distract me."

"Yep." He put another one onto the end of his own stick and held it toward the heat. Then he cast her a smile. "You've got to trust us to do our job. We're good at it."

She nodded, but didn't return his smile.

"Do you have any suspicions—anyone you work with who seems…I don't know… disgruntled, or off in some way?" he asked.

"No." She shook her head. "It's a really great place to work. We all get along really well. Alana, Theresa and I hang out after work hours, and I know a few others do, too.

We have the best Christmas parties for the branch. I know that some people complain about toxic work environments, but ours is fantastic. The thought that someone would betray us like that—" She sucked in a breath.

"You're going to be too close to it," he said. "And I know that doesn't stop you from thinking about it constantly, but it's the truth. It'll be hard for you to see who was willing to aid a bank robber. If you'd recognized it before, you probably would have told us. But it's okay to realize that you're not in a position to see what was happening, and let us look into it."

She nodded. "I know. I'm trying."

It was enough if she'd be willing to testify, but he didn't want to push that this evening. He turned his marshmallow, the browned bubbling side now upward. Annabelle leaned forward to put her stick over the fire, and the marshmallow went up in a burst of blue flame. She turned it a couple of times, then blew it out.

"You like yours burned," he said with a chuckle.

"Yep." She pulled off the blackened shell and popped it into her mouth. "I see you have more patience."

He adjusted his marshmallow over the heat. It was swelling, and turning a nice shade of tan on the underside.

"I take my time," he said with a slow smile.

Was that a blush he saw on her cheeks? She dropped her gaze and pulled the rest of the gooey marshmallow off her stick.

"Can I ask you something?" she asked.

Conrad pulled his marshmallow away from the heat to inspect it, then let his gaze swing over the darkened yard.

"Sure."

"I was looking at a photo album in your living room," she said. "I hope you don't mind. But you had a partner—Terri. Your brother said there was an accident. What happened?"

So Wilder had gotten chatty, had he? Conrad couldn't help the surge of annoyance toward his brother. Annabelle was here for protection, not to get into the quagmire of Conrad's personal issues.

He put his marshmallow back over the heat again, pressing his lips together.

"It's a long story," he said.

And it wasn't the kind of tale that would make her feel safer in his care.

"Apparently, we have time."

Conrad sighed. "It was an undercover operation, and something went wrong. She ended up getting hurt."

"That sounds like there's a story there to me," she said.

She wasn't going to leave this alone, was she? Conrad slowly turned his roasting stick.

"She was wearing a wire," Conrad said. "She was close to getting a confession from a drug dealer, but then her wire went dead. There was a choice to make—go in and get her, or wait for her to break out a window, the signal for us to move in. I went with my gut."

"You waited?"

"No, I went in," he replied.

"That sounds like the right choice, though," she countered.

"It ended up being the wrong one," he replied. "It tipped off the drug dealers that she was a cop, and it put her between me and three armed criminals. They roughed her up and shot her. Thankfully, she recovered, but…"

"She quit," Annabelle said. "That's what your brother said."

"Yeah." He pulled his marshmallow back—perfectly roasted. "It scared her really badly. But she's okay now. She married a nice guy, she's got a couple of kids and she lives out of state."

Annabelle nodded. "Do you miss her?"

Did he miss Terri? She'd been his first real partner and his first big love. She'd meant a lot to him, and when she quit the force, she'd broken up with him at the same time. He'd been heartbroken for a very long time after that.

"Nah," he said. "I'm fine. I deeply regret that she got hurt, though."

"Is that what changed you?" she asked.

"Me?" He lifted his eyebrows.

"In the photo album, there's a change that happens. You get tougher all of a sudden, harder, and definitely bigger."

He remembered those first weeks after Terri left both him and the force, and he'd learned several hard lessons at once. Dealing with it hadn't been easy, but he'd found his way.

"I used the gym as therapy after that," he admitted. "Maybe that's what you noticed."

"It wasn't just that," she said. "You looked… so much harder."

"Some things change you," he said quietly. "My dad died shortly after, and I think his passing was even harder on me. Dad was al-

ways so proud of me—he'd brag about his
son the deputy to anyone who'd listen. Losing him… I don't know. It was tough."

"I noticed that you seemed pretty close
with your parents in those pictures," she said
quietly.

"Yeah…" He glanced over at her. "Are you
close to yours?"

"My mom, yeah," she said. "My dad…not
so much. It's nice you had a father who was
proud of you. If mine was proud, he never
told me."

"Are your parents still together?" he asked.

She nodded. "Yep. Mom makes excuses for
him, and he just carries on being stubbornly
angry with the world."

"That's tough, too," he said.

"They're taking care of my cat," she said.
"Dad hates cats, but Mom loves them. I never
got any pets until I was an adult, out on my
own. Dad was like that—it was his way or
nothing."

"Was he abusive?" Conrad asked.

"No," she replied. "My dad wanted a son
and got me instead. And he raised me so that
I'd never need a man to do anything for me.
He taught me how to change a tire, change the
oil in my car, to drive defensively and to al-

ways have enough money tucked away that I didn't need to take any garbage from anyone. And then when I turned eighteen and graduated high school, he showed me the door."

"Just like that?" Conrad frowned.

"It was my turn to take care of myself," she said. "Mom was so upset. She cried and demanded that Dad let me come back. I told her not to worry about it. I had a part-time job, got a roommate, and I've been on my own ever since." She fell silent. "So, yeah… be grateful you had something better."

He was grateful. He knew his parents were really fantastic people, but hearing of others who'd had less support always stabbed a little bit. Especially for Annabelle. She gave off an air of confidence that covered some deeper pain, it seemed. He couldn't fix it, obviously, but wanted to give her something.

Conrad held his marshmallow, still on the stick, toward Annabelle.

"For me?" she said.

"Yep." It wasn't any wisdom, or even moral support.

She pulled it off the stick and smiled. "Thanks."

"I think you turned out great," he said. "With or without your dad's support."

Look at her—she was smart, gorgeous, compassionate and mildly intimidating. She was the kind of woman he didn't want to sully with his own ragged edges.

"That's a perfect marshmallow, by the way," he said, when she hadn't answered.

Annabelle pushed it into her mouth, then nodded. "Mmm. It is."

"It takes patience. You have to resist the urge to torch it," he said, and he chuckled when her cheeks turned pink.

He grabbed another one from the bag and speared it onto the end of his stick. Annabelle did the same.

He looked around the property, as far as he could see in the darkness, but apart from the stamp of a horse's hoof in the corral, there was no movement. The problem with Terri was that he hadn't trusted her. Before she went in, she'd told him that if her wire went dead, he was to wait.

He hadn't been reacting like a partner. He'd been reacting like a boyfriend. That had almost gotten Terri killed. He had a lot more regrets than he was willing to talk about, but he'd learned the hard way that keeping his emotions separate from his job was absolutely imperative to not only get the job done, but to keep the women he cared about safe. His heart did nothing but get in the way.

Annabelle leaned toward the fire, and the warm glow lit up her face and the sweep of her golden hair. Her knees were angled toward him, a couple of inches from touching his own. She fiddled with the stick, and he could read the worry in those deep blue eyes.

He reached out and squeezed her forearm.

"It will be okay," he said.

She turned to look at him, and his heart nearly stopped in his chest. The open, worried, complicated look in those eyes got through all his defenses. She was more than beautiful— she was intoxicating—and his first instinct was to put an arm around her and pull her close. He pushed back the thought.

"It'll only be okay when it's over," she said. She pushed her marshmallow into the flames and let it catch fire.

He watched her as she spun the marshmallow, the line of fire moving over the white surface and leaving crispy char behind. Then she blew it out.

"No patience," he said with a small smile.

She didn't answer, but she did smile, and this time she looked more relaxed. She leaned back in her chair, and her gaze moved upward toward the darkened sky and the first few stars that pricked through. He leaned back, too, but he didn't look up at the stars. He pulled out his phone and looked at the proximity alarms.

Someone had to keep an eye out—be the sheepdog. Tonight, at least, she'd be able to look up at the stars, listen to her own thoughts and let her stress melt away.

He'd make that possible.

From across the narrow field, he saw a family with four young children come out the front door, followed by Wollie and his mother. The group paused, and two men headed out— to get the buggy harnessed up, no doubt. The women stayed on the porch in the golden circle of kerosene lamplight. They laughed at something that was said. A toddler started to cry, and one of the women bent down to pick him up.

For the Amish neighbors, it was just an evening with friends, and he felt the edge of his responsibilities stretch. There were crooks who were taking advantage of these peaceful people, stealing their cattle. How long before they tightened their web and started robbing houses, too?

A peaceful life was only ever possible because of the sheepdogs who kept watch. He looked over at Annabelle, and she was looking up at the sky, where one by one more stars winked into view as the night darkened around them. She had a tiny piece of melted marshmallow stuck to her chin, and he was tempted to reach over and remove it, but he didn't want to disturb her.

He turned back to his silent guard duty. At least for tonight, nothing was going to get past Conrad.

CHAPTER FIVE

THERE WAS SOMETHING about looking up at the stars that made Annabelle's own problems, overwhelming as they were, feel a little bit smaller.

She'd been thinking about her father. The ironic part was, if she'd followed her dad's advice, she never would have gone out with Stephen Hope. Stephen was smooth. He'd simply walked up to her and said, "You're beautiful. I want to take you to dinner." She'd told her mother about it, and apparently the phone had been on speaker, because her father had overheard.

"He sounds like a loser to me," her father had grumped. "Who does that? Something's wrong with him."

She'd been so offended by her father's dismissal of this big romantic gesture in downtown Wooster. Why shouldn't she inspire some passion in a man? Why shouldn't he find her beautiful?

But Dad had been right. There had been a whole lot wrong with Stephen, and now it seemed he'd targeted her because of her place of employment.

How stupid was she?

But when Annabelle turned her attention to the night sky, her own regrets felt smaller. She could see the three stars that made up Orion's Belt, and she followed them up to the top star in the constellation and then down to the bottom one... Far away in the cold depths of space, these stars were burning their hearts out, so far away that all she could make out was a pinprick of light. There were dramas bigger than her own.

That was what she was thinking about as she picked out constellations in the night sky until the fire burned low, and Conrad held his hand out to her.

"We should turn in. It's late."

She put her hand in his strong palm, and he hoisted her up.

"It's been a long time since I've sat by a fire," she said.

"Me, too." His voice was low. "You have some—"

He touched her chin, then held up his finger. She felt the heat hit her cheeks. She'd had marshmallow on her face. He smiled faintly, then grabbed the chairs, folded them and tucked them under his arm. Her gaze lingered on his muscled arms for a moment. What would her father say about Conrad? That he was only being professional and she was naive if she read anything else into his thoughtfulness? But Conrad's gaze was warm and enveloping, and whatever her father might say about him drained away.

"Thank you for making this easier on me," she said. "I know this part isn't really your job, but I appreciate it."

"It's no problem." He met her gaze. "You'd be amazed at how much I can squeeze into one job description."

She chuckled. "You're an overachiever, then."

"Maybe so," he said. "I just hope that you're feeling a bit better tonight."

"I am."

He smiled, then put a warm hand on her back as he nudged her ahead of him toward the side door. His touch was sure, and she felt a shiver slide down her arms.

She went into the dark kitchen, and Conrad flicked on a light behind her.

"You go ahead and turn in," Conrad said.

"I'm going to douse the fire and do one more perimeter check."

"Okay. Good night." She did feel a whole lot safer knowing that this man was on duty.

Annabelle glanced over her shoulder on her way to her bedroom, and she found Conrad's gaze locked on her, his expression softened.

She liked him better this way—gentler, more human. She felt safer with a man who felt *something*.

True to his word, Conrad had left her in privacy once she came indoors, and she'd slept more soundly than she had in months. Maybe it was the exhaustion of everything catching up to her, but when she woke the next morning to the sound of birdsong outside and a honky-tonk tune playing on the radio from the kitchen, she felt like she'd slept for a year.

Wilder had made some breakfast and put it in the oven to keep warm—oatmeal, store-bought cinnamon buns and a plate of scrambled eggs. Conrad fried up some bacon to go on the side, and they ate breakfast together in companionable silence.

Then Conrad got a call on his cell—police business—and he stepped outside to take it.

Annabelle washed the last dish and put it

onto the dish rack. Outside the kitchen window, she could see Conrad standing with his arms crossed over his chest, the bass sound of his voice filtering back into the house. With his earbuds in, it looked like he was talking to some invisible entity in front of him.

There was a tap on the screen door, and Annabelle turned to see Jane standing on the step. She went to open it, giving the little girl a welcoming smile. Jane held a foil-covered plate in her hands, and she wore a yellow dress as bright as the August sunshine outside. She hopped from foot to foot in anticipation, holding up the plate.

"Hi, there," Annabelle said.

"Hi," Jane said. "I made cookies."

"All by yourself?" Annabelle asked, accepting the plate from the girl. "Come inside, Jane."

"Almost all by myself," the little girl declared. "*Mammi* helped me a little bit, because I'm not allowed to stoke up the stove by myself, but I did all the mixing and measuring, and *Mammi* just handed me the measuring cups."

Annabelle lifted the foil and discovered oatmeal cookies with raisins in them, still warm from the oven.

"These look wonderful," Annabelle said with a smile. "Thank you so much, Jane."

"What are you doing today?" Jane asked.

"I'm—" It was a good question. "I'm just relaxing a little bit."

"My *mammi* said you could come over for a visit if you wanted to," Jane said. "She says that when women are stuck with men for too long, we get all wound up, and it's good for us girls to get together and unwind ourselves again. We're nicer to everybody when we get our girl time."

Annabelle chuckled. "Your grandmother is a very wise woman."

She looked out the window toward Conrad, who was heading back toward the house.

"And *Mammi* says that if she was stuck in a house with these *Englisher* men for hours on end, she'd tear out her hair." Jane announced this with a bright smile on her face just as Conrad pushed open the screen door.

Annabelle laughed out loud—kids were honest to a fault, but Jane's grandmother wasn't entirely wrong. Conrad and Wilder were nice men, but spending this much time with the stern, complicated cop wasn't exactly easy, and perhaps not in the way the older woman was anticipating. He was just a little too handsome to make this effortless.

"Hi, Jane," Conrad said, and his gaze flickered toward Annabelle for a moment. "How are you doing?"

If he'd heard what Jane had said, he didn't let on. He seemed to be trying to be nicer.

Jane eyed him uncertainly.

"Did you bake something?" he prompted.

"I made cookies," Jane said. "They're oatmeal and raisin and very, very good. I already ate four, so I know."

"Did you?" Conrad picked up a cookie from the plate. "Are these for us?"

"*Yah.* You should try them." She seemed to be relaxing again, and she fixed her gaze on Conrad expectantly until he took a bite.

"Mmm," he said. "These are really good."

Jane blushed. "*Yah*, I know."

"Are you helping your *mammi* with housework today?" he asked.

"I always help *Mammi*," she replied. "But I came over to invite Annie over for a visit. *Mammi* sent me."

"Oh?" Conrad looked out the kitchen window, his expression firming. "I'm not sure that's a good idea."

Jane looked up at him, her eyes round, and

Annabelle could almost see the wheels in her head turning.

"I think it's a nice offer," Annabelle said. "I'd love to have a visit with her grandmother."

Conrad's gaze dropped to the little girl who was still watching him attentively, and he glanced over at Annabelle. He couldn't say much in front of Jane, and Annabelle could feel the irritation coming off him in waves.

"It'll be fine," Annabelle said, lowering her voice. "It's right next door."

"It's not part of my plan," he said.

"And yet I'll very likely still survive." She smiled to soften the words. "You know where I'll be. It'll be fine."

Conrad sighed and shrugged. "Fine. Forty-five minutes, and then I come get you."

"Deal." Annabelle nodded toward the door. "Let's go, kiddo."

"What's a kiddo?" Jane asked.

"You. A small child. A little girl who makes very good cookies."

"That's me!" Jane skipped toward the door. "*Mammi* is making pie! It's lemon meringue. And there's some apple pie, too, and some cherry from yesterday…"

Annabelle looked over her shoulder at Conrad and mouthed the word *Pie!*

A smile tickled the corners of his lips. It was the only sign he gave of softening at all, but she felt a little surge of victory at having gotten that much out of him.

She'd eat pie and chat with a nice older woman. It was just the dose of normal she needed.

JANE LED THE way around the back of the house, past a neatly weeded garden—a vast garden, big enough to feed more than the three people who lived here. The chicken coop was beyond, surrounded by wire netting. Inside, Annabelle could see the ornery rooster, pacing in front of the wire fence, and he stopped when he saw Annabelle, fixing a beady eye on her.

"Is that Methuselah?" Annabelle asked.

"That's him," Jane replied. "You can talk to him if you want, but he's not friendly."

"That's okay," Annabelle said, and she looked over her shoulder to see Conrad still standing on the porch. At least she knew Conrad to be significantly friendlier than the rooster. "We'd better go say hello to your grandmother."

They went down the hill to Jane's house, and the little girl opened a side door that looked lower than the main floor of the house. Annabelle noticed a flight of stairs going down into a dark basement, and another eight steps heading up. Jane went up, tramping up the stairs where she cheerfully announced, "She's here!"

Annabelle followed the little girl and peered over her head into a spacious, fragrant kitchen. Sunlight spilled through a generous kitchen window and over a countertop that had three pies already cooling on racks. Jane's grandmother was pulling a lemon meringue pie out of a black wood-burning oven. Her face was pink from the heat and dewy with sweat. She blew out a breath and carefully placed the perfectly browned lemon meringue pie onto the last wire rack on the counter.

"Come in, come in." She looked up with a smile. "I'm glad you decided to come. My granddaughter took such a liking to you." She crossed the kitchen. "I'm Linda Schmidt, Wollie's *mamm*, and Jane's *mammi*."

"I'm Annie." She smiled and held out a hand.

Linda shook it.

"And how are you related to the Westhouse brothers?" Linda asked.

"I'm—" Annabelle shrugged. "I'm a friend. I'm just visiting for a little while. It's an adventure for me to see ranching life."

Did that sound reasonable—a friend who just dropped in for a visit? She looked out the side window, and she could make out Conrad standing on the porch, his muscular physique easily recognizable, even from here. He was still standing guard, and she was oddly relieved to know that he was.

"A friend?" Linda nodded. "We Amish do those things differently. We wouldn't have a young woman staying with two men. We'd have another woman there to keep up appearances."

"Oh, I see." Annabelle glanced around at the kitchen. "They're both perfect gentlemen. I have a bedroom to myself, and they're very respectful of my privacy."

"They would be," Linda said. "We've gotten to know them pretty well...mostly because our little Jane keeps running over there to visit and we have to go fetch her."

Annabelle chuckled. "I noticed that."

"I like them," Jane said. "They have the baby horse, and *Daet* says that they have our cow for a little while. The calf needs a *mamm* to take care of him, and our cow needs a baby."

"That's exactly what happened," Annabelle agreed.

"Can I get you a piece of pie?" Linda asked.

"I'd love some. That cherry pie looks wonderful." It was already cut into and it would be polite to request a piece of that one.

Linda cut her a slice and handed it over with a fork and a smile. Jane chattered on about the situation with the cow and the calf, not seeming to mind if anyone was listening.

"So, what's happening with the cattle?" Linda asked, gesturing to a spot at a big kitchen table. "My son doesn't want to worry me so won't say anything. All he says is that it's under control."

Was this the reason for the invitation— a little bit of information gathering? If so, Annabelle didn't hold it against the other woman.

"There seem to be cattle rustlers targeting Amish farms," Annabelle replied.

"Is it just the Amish farms?" Linda asked. "There aren't too many *Englisher* farms around here, but you'd think there wouldn't be any difference between the two."

"From what I understand, the Westhouse ranch hasn't lost any," Annabelle said. "I can't speak for any other...*Englisher* farms around here."

"We call them *Englisher* because they're

English speakers," she said. "It's just what we Amish call them."

Outsiders. Yes, she understood.

"I don't know too much more about it myself, but Conrad wants to catch them."

"I hope he's able to," Linda said seriously. "We Amish have small farms. We might only get three or four calves, and if they're stolen, we've lost all our growth."

"Forgive me if this is an ignorant question, but Conrad said you won't use guns to protect your cattle. Why is that? You don't have to shoot to kill."

Linda was thoughtful for a moment. "It's our way. It goes back hundreds of years. There was a man named Dirk Willems who inspires our people."

"Tell her that story, *Mammi*," Jane said, her mouth full of pie.

"Swallow before you speak, dear," Linda said, giving her granddaughter a fond look. Then she turned to Annabelle. "Back in the fifteen hundreds, Anabaptists were being persecuted in the Netherlands. Dirk Willems was arrested for his faith and imprisoned. Now, we don't believe in dying for nothing—we value life, including our own. But there are times when a man can't back down, when it comes down to right and wrong. Anyway, Dirk managed to escape from the jail—a miracle in itself—but it was very cold weather, and he was running away, across a frozen lake. A soldier spotted him and started off in pursuit. As Dirk ran, he heard the ice crack and looked back in time to see the soldier go down into the icy lake."

"Wow," Annabelle murmured.

"What would you do?" Linda asked. "If you were in his shoes?"

"Keep running," Annabelle said. "That was a near miss."

"Even if the soldier died?" Linda asked.

Annabelle felt the disapproval in that question. "I'd want to survive, Linda."

"And I understand that," Linda replied. "Ideals are very nice, but survival and the instincts deep in the human heart are something else altogether, aren't they? Well, Dirk believed in the value of human life—all human life—and he went back to help the soldier. He dragged him out of the icy water and saved his life."

Doing the right thing, no matter the risk to himself… That did sound noble, but Annabelle was currently in a situation where her own desire to do the right thing—testifying in court or just telling Conrad absolutely everything—could ruin the rest of her life. That kind of transparency seemed like a luxury right now.

"Did the soldier let him go?" Annabelle asked. "Out of gratefulness, perhaps?"

"No. The others caught up, Dirk was taken into custody, brought back to prison and eventually executed." Linda leaned back in her chair.

Annabelle blinked at her.

"And that's the story of Dirk Willems," Jane said cheerily. "He was a very *gut* man."

Annabelle looked over at Jane, who seemed entirely unruffled by this story. Likely she'd heard it a hundred times already.

"He could have survived if he'd just kept running," Annabelle said, turning back to Linda.

"He chose his beliefs over his own life," Linda replied. "And we remember him for that. So we look at things a little bit differently. Those cattle rustlers are people, too. They have families, and hopes and dreams. Obviously, they've gone off course, but that doesn't take away their value as human beings."

"I know that your people are pacifists,"

Annabelle said. "And I respect that, but surely you could at least look a little more threatening. You could have big dogs, for example. You'd know that you wouldn't act on it, but sometimes a tough appearance can be helpful."

Look at Conrad—he was turning out to be gentle, but his look was about as soft as concrete.

"Looking a certain way and acting a certain way go hand in hand," Linda replied. "If you look like you're ready to fight, a fight often comes to you. If you have your finger on a trigger, all it takes is one flex of a finger muscle... No, we don't play with the line. We stand very firmly on our side of it. We don't intimidate and threaten. We say what we mean and we mean what we say."

Honesty to a fault.

"But if Conrad were to catch them..." Annabelle said.

"That is the solution," Linda said with a smile. "In that, we're no different than you are. We pay taxes, we vote in elections and we enjoy the American protection that you enjoy, too. We just don't encourage our *kinner* to follow that line of work, but that doesn't mean we don't appreciate it. We know that the law enforcement officers protect us as well as they protect you. And we're grateful for them."

Conrad had been right. But Linda didn't seem naive to what made their peaceful, ideal-driven life possible. Someone bigger and tougher needed to be there to keep their peace in place, to work outside the ideals they held most dear.

Which was what Annabelle needed, too, but she wasn't standing on ideals. When she'd called her parents to say she'd be under the sheriff's department protection, her father had one blunt piece of advice. "Don't do it, Annabelle. There will always be dangerous men, and you don't need to attract his attention. Don't testify." Her mother had been in teary agreement.

Should she be listening to her parents' advice right now?

"Jane, would you go out and pick me some carrots?" Linda asked.

Jane scraped her last bit of cherry pie filling from her plate and brought it to the sink. It dropped in with a clatter and Linda winced.

"Okay!" Jane said, and she headed to the stairs, her footsteps bouncing down.

"Would *you* have done what Dirk Willems

did?" Annabelle asked as the screen door slammed shut. "You asked what I would have done… What would you, personally, have done in that position?"

Linda's cheeks turned slightly pink. "First of all, Dirk had no way of knowing he'd die, even if we give him the credit for it. But I'll be honest. I like to think I'd do the right thing and go back to help a floundering man. I'm not sure if I'm that strong, though. I'd be terrified, and my ideals might slip. I'm not proud to say it."

Annabelle smiled. "You're just as human as I am, then."

"Human, yes," Linda said. "But I'm aiming at something a little better. I haven't given up my ideals."

"I appreciate your honesty, all the same." Annabelle put her fork down.

"It's the only way to be," Linda said. "I might not be as spiritually strong as I'd like, but I can be honest."

And that was exactly what she'd thought when she'd agreed to testify. She let out a slow breath.

"I'm sorry to bring you down," Linda said. "That's all a little too depressing for a bright afternoon like this one."

"It's okay," Annabelle said. "That's life sometimes, right?"

"I do hope that Conrad can catch whoever is doing this," Linda said. "I'll just feel safer when we can get back to normal again."

Annabelle would, too.

"Let's talk about happier things," Linda said. "Are you married? Do you have anyone special?"

With everything Annabelle was facing recently, it was the hope for a happy, simple future of her own that kept her going. Looking around this fragrant Amish kitchen, she had a sudden longing to go back home again. She wanted to snuggle her cat, make herself some hot buttered toast and enjoy an afternoon in her own apartment.

When she had gotten past this danger, she'd never take her simple life for granted again.

THIS WAS AWKWARD. Conrad wasn't normally the kind of man who went stomping after a woman to drag her home, but he couldn't very well protect Annabelle if she was over at the Schmidt house. If anything happened to her between now and that trial, it was his badge on the line. He felt a shiver at the thought—not of a demotion, but of Annabelle getting hurt.

Awkward or not, this was his job, and while she'd been over at the Schmidt house, he'd seen three pickup trucks pass their properties. Two of the three had slowed down on their way past. It wasn't proof of anything, but it did put his hackles up. He normally saw no more than three vehicles pass in a day, not in one hour. He had half a mind to set up a camera to read license plates, but nothing announced "There's something to see here" like police traffic cameras on a rural gravel road.

Conrad pulled the door closed and trotted down the steps. If this were a regular vacation, he wouldn't care what she did with her time. Heck, he'd be out with the herd and keeping an eye out for whoever was targeting Amish cattle. But she wasn't here on vacation. And his number one priority wasn't the cattle rustlers...even if they were a close second.

He headed across the short scrub grass, and as he approached the Schmidt land, he spotted Wollie coming in his direction from the barn.

"Hello!" Wollie called, waving.

Conrad slowed his pace and waved back at his neighbor. He didn't have time for this, but he had to act normal to avoid the local rumor mill.

"How are things?" Wollie said as he sauntered up. His dark pants were streaked with dust, and he pulled off his straw hat to wipe the sweat from his forehead.

"Not too bad," Conrad said.

"You came to collect her, did you?" Wollie asked with a faint smile. "Afraid she'd lay eyes on me and you'd have competition?"

This was the first time Conrad had ever heard Wollie joke about anything romantic, and he shot the Amish man a look of surprise as Wollie laughed good-naturedly.

"Never fear," Wollie said. "I'll only marry Amish. Your *Englisher* girl is safe from me."

"What a relief," Conrad joked back. "But she's not my girlfriend, so that isn't a worry."

"Ah." Wollie eyed him for a moment. "Then what is she to you?"

"A friend," he said quickly. "She's just visiting the ranch."

"Ah." Wollie nodded a couple of times. His gaze moved toward his daughter, who was picking carrots from the garden and piling them onto the grass beside her. He said something in Pennsylvania Dutch, and she scampered off toward the house. "It's been a long time since I was married, or courting, or denying that I was courting—" he smiled teasingly "—but I do have one piece of advice, if you want to hear it."

Conrad shrugged. "Sure."

"Don't try to control a woman," Wollie said. "This coming to bring her home—it can give a woman the wrong impression. She might think you're trying to control her actions, lock her down, keep her with you only."

Conrad felt his face grow warm. Ironic as it was, he was trying to do just that, but it wasn't for romantic reasons. Eventually, in a month or so, he'd be able to explain himself, but for the next little while, he was going to look like a real jerk, wasn't he?

"This isn't what it looks like," Conrad said. "She's…she's a friend. Nothing more."

"Ah." Wollie's expression turned amused. "I said that for nearly a year when I first met my wife."

"Well, with me it's the truth," Conrad said. "There is no romantic connection between us."

There couldn't be. She might not like the description, and she might be beautiful and oddly enticing to him, but she was *his job*.

"I'm not a man with a lot of experience with women, as you might count it," Wollie said. "But I was married. I never worried that she'd look at another man the way she looked at me. She was a woman of character. I know with you *Englishers* there is the idea that your woman might leave you for another man if he were more appealing in some way. But marriage is long, and if she's going to have her head turned, it's better that it happen earlier than later. Because there are women who don't do that—women with character you can count on."

"The Amish way," Conrad said quietly.

"*Yah*. That's our way. Not every woman lives up to that standard, so the choice of wife needs to be a careful one, but a lot of Amish women do. And it's worth finding."

Conrad swallowed. "That's...that's very sound advice, Wollie. I appreciate it."

"I won't bring it up again," Wollie said. "And for what it's worth, she seems like a nice woman."

The side door to the house opened and Jane came out with a woven basket, skipping toward the carrots she'd left on the grass. Then Annabelle emerged, letting the screen door bang shut.

She looked fresh, and certainly more relaxed. Maybe a visit with the neighbors had been just what she needed.

"How was your visit?" Conrad asked.

"That was the best pie I've ever tasted." Annabelle shot him a brilliant smile.

Conrad gave Wollie a nod that he hoped looked casual, and he and Annabelle started back toward the house. He could feel Wollie's eyes on his back, and he tried to pull his brain back into work mode. He scanned the road to their left, and it was empty. But somehow, he was incredibly aware of exactly how close to him Annabelle was walking. If he stretched out his hand, he could easily catch hers...

No, he wasn't going to be that suggestible.

"Linda's really nice, isn't she?" Conrad said. There, they could chat like normal people.

"She is, and she's a great baker, too," Annabelle replied. "How's Wollie doing? Linda seems pretty stressed out about the missing calves. Apparently, he doesn't tell her much."

"The Amish are like that," he said. "The men are very protective of the women. They don't like to worry them."

"I don't think it works. She's just as worried about the calves as he is—maybe more so because she has no information to go on."

"So you filled her in?" he asked.

"Just that you were looking into it," she replied. "It made her feel better."

It was nice to know that Linda felt better, but he'd have to find whoever was stealing these calves if he was going to make good on it.

"Actually, Wollie didn't mention the calves this time," Conrad said. "He was giving me relationship advice about you."

Annabelle chuckled. "Oh no. Does he think we're involved?"

There was a playful glitter in her blue eyes, and he suddenly felt bashful. He wasn't exactly an exciting option for someone like her.

"He thinks we're not ready to make it public," Conrad replied, "and that I'm following you around out of some deep-seated insecurity."

"Ouch." She grinned. "How does that feel, to be considered a creep by your kindly Amish neighbor?"

"Not great." Conrad smiled ruefully. "For the record, when I'm in a relationship, I'm not a controlling boyfriend. I need *someone* to believe that."

Annabelle cast him an amused look. "What kind of boyfriend are you? Because I'm still trying to figure you out."

"I'm...proper," he said. "I do things right.

I open doors, I pay for dinner and I don't demand to know where she is every second."

"So you aren't the jealous type?" she asked.

"Nope."

"Not even a little bit?"

She was teasing now. He shook his head. "I'm a believer in what's meant to be. Wollie's advice was spot-on—if I'm not going to be enough for a woman, I'd rather know that sooner than later."

"And has any woman ever told you that you weren't enough for her?" Annabelle asked, but the laughter was gone from her voice. She looked up, blue eyes meeting his.

"Yeah," he said. "Of course."

"That is shocking, quite frankly." She stopped in her tracks. "You aren't joking?"

"No. Terri was pretty clear when she broke it off with me," he replied. "And for various reasons, other girlfriends haven't worked out."

"What various reasons?" she asked.

"We wanted different things at different times," he said.

"They wanted more than you did?" she asked.

"You're making me sound like a cad," he said with a low laugh. "They wanted less than I did."

He had some pretty high expectations from a relationship these days, and maybe it wasn't fair to the women who'd expressed interest in him, but no one had really turned his head until now.

"I just think that a sweet guy with both ethics and biceps of steel is a pretty good catch," she said.

Conrad felt his face heat. He felt suddenly aware of how much younger she was. She was twenty-five, and hadn't been through the wringer like he had. "Thanks."

"Now, if we walk off with this distance between us," Annabelle said, nodding to the six inches between them, "Wollie is going to think that you're all controlling and that I'm generally uninterested. It casts you in an even worse light. I doubt that's the rumor you want to spread."

"What's your suggestion?" he asked.

"This." She slid her arm through his. "Now you aren't some needy cowboy trying to control his woman."

"That's a relief. What am I?"

"A cowboy who already won her over," she replied with a brilliant smile. "Trust me. This is a better rumor, if they're going to spread one anyway. Juicy rumors fly faster than reasonable explanations."

"They do," he agreed, and he slid a hand over hers, tugging her in close against his side. If he was going to walk with her, let it look believable, at least. Her hand was soft under his, and having her this close made it so that he could smell something faintly sweet around her—perfume? Shampoo? He wasn't sure, but he liked it.

"So what do you want for dinner tonight?" he asked.

"What are my choices?" she asked.

"I've got some steaks in the fridge," he said. "And I make a pretty mean lasagna."

"You cook, too?" Was she flirting with him?

"I'm a grown man. I'd better be able to cook. Heaven knows Wilder is terrible in the kitchen."

She laughed. "You're telling me that you're the domesticated one?"

"I'm the one who cares about a good meal at my own table," he replied. "And I'm not some kind of Neanderthal who expects a woman to feed him. Even if I look like one."

"So steak or lasagna?" she asked.

"Yep."

"I'd love steak."

"Then steak it is."

He liked this—walking with her, feeling the slight weight of her hand on his arm. But even after the robbery, she was much less scuffed and damaged than he was. She was too young, optimistic, pretty.

He glanced over his shoulder, and Wollie and his little girl had disappeared from sight.

"He's not watching anymore," Conrad said.

Annabelle looked back the way they'd come, and it took an extra beat for her to pull her hand off his arm. And in that moment of hesitation, his heart skipped.

Dang. He was feeling more than a responsibility to protect her. This was a hesitant, fledgling tenderness that he knew he had no right to.

"Let's get the food on," Conrad said, and he let his fingers brush against the small of her back.

But he had to stop this. It wasn't a game or just a more appealing rumor to cover up Annabelle's real reason for being here. He was more vulnerable than people might think. All his bulk shielded a heart that longed for the kind of love that Wollie had described— the kind he could count on. And it wasn't something a man could demand, either. The connection and dedication to each other was either there or it wasn't. That was what he'd discovered in girlfriends past—the lack of something deeper that he knew he needed to be fully satisfied. Whatever his Amish neighbors thought, he wasn't the kind of man to demand anything. Not when it came to romance.

But it didn't stop his heart from longing for it, all the same.

CHAPTER SIX

CONRAD RUMMAGED THROUGH the fridge, pulling out the package of steaks, some onions and some mushrooms. His mind was already running ahead to the meal he planned to cook. He deposited the ingredients on the counter, then grabbed the plastic shopping bag of potatoes from under the sink.

"Farm-fresh potatoes?" Annabelle smiled. "Do you grow your own?"

"These are a gift from next door," he replied. "Linda always keeps us in fresh produce. I've started to feel bad about it, quite honestly. I want to do something in return, but I don't have a lot to offer that they appreciate."

"Besides protection," she replied.

Of course, he'd look out for his neighbors, but they didn't need just a reassuring cop presence. They needed actual arrests.

"I'll do what I can." Conrad pulled out a potato peeler and held it toward Annabelle. "Care to peel potatoes?"

Annabelle came up beside him and accepted the peeler. She turned on the tap and started to rinse potatoes while Conrad fetched a pot. As he passed her, she was just turning from the sink, and he put a hand out to catch her waist as he slid by. It was an instinctive gesture to avoid collision, but he found his hands resting on her back.

"Careful," he murmured, and he put the pot down next to her.

"Sorry." She cast him a quick smile and didn't seem to notice the familiarity of his touch. Maybe this was easier for her—Annabelle being younger and obviously not dazzled by his grim, world-weary allure. He smiled ruefully to himself at that thought.

"You know, if you want to check into these cattle rustlers, I could come along," she said.

"It would involve some night patrols," he said. "I'm following strict orders from the sheriff. I'm supposed to let you relax a bit, but I'm not sure staking out country roads late at night is going to help you unwind."

"It's something else to think about," she replied. "I'm just putting it out there."

He was tempted. He glanced out the kitchen window, his eyes taking in the familiar scene of the backyard, the fence and the farm beyond, but his mind was already clicking forward to surveillance possibilities. If Annabelle was by his side, she'd be just as safe as she'd be in the house, right?

"You're thinking about it, aren't you?" she said.

Conrad chuckled. "Yeah."

But the tempting part wasn't just the chance to lock handcuffs on the lowlifes who'd been robbing the Amish. He was also thinking about sitting in his SUV in the velvet darkness, with some snack food to share with Annabelle. That was dangerously appealing. She'd be scandalized if she knew, no doubt, he thought facetiously.

Conrad pulled off his cowboy hat and rubbed a handkerchief over his glistening forehead. Then he spotted his brother coming in their direction across the yard.

"Wilder's back," Conrad said. "Tell you what. Let's have dinner, rest up a bit, and then when it's good and dark, we'll take a drive around some of these back roads and see who's out and about."

Annabelle smiled. "Thought you'd never ask."

And in that moment, he pictured Terri. Or maybe it was himself he was seeing all those years ago, when he was younger, more ide-alistic, and convinced that his own emotions were under control. That was back when he lifted weights for strength and flexibility, and not in a desperate bid to shred the muscles and forget his deepest regrets.

But this was a different situation. He unex-pectedly had a beautiful woman living with him, cooking with him, sliding her hand into the crook of his arm as they walked through scrub grass together. Annabelle said she needed some distraction from her worries, and maybe he needed a bit of distraction, too. Because this job *couldn't* get personal, no matter how easy it would be to tumble into that territory. Her safety depended on his professionalism, and fo-cusing on work had always been an easy way to get his balance back.

He'd made this mistake already, and he wasn't a man who liked to make the same mistake twice.

IT WAS ELEVEN O'CLOCK before Conrad pulled out of the drive. He glanced at his phone on the dash as it pinged on his way past the mo-tion detectors. The headlights carved out a path in the darkness as he turned onto the gravel road. Outside, the evening had cooled off a little bit, a hint of fall already touching the air. He put his window down. Letting a wave of grain-scented air flood into the vehicle, he felt his nerves start to settle.

There was something about night driving that soothed him. It always had.

"It's a pretty night," Annabelle said.

"Sure is," he agreed. "Are you sure you don't mind this?"

"I'm the one who suggested it," she replied. "I've been looking forward to it. There is only so much relaxing I can take. My thoughts aren't going to settle down until this trial is over." She paused. "Anyway, my brain is like a puppy. I can give it something to chew on, but I might not like what it chooses."

He smiled. "I get it. I normally give in to work."

"I enjoy my job, but it isn't like yours," she said. "I can see how police work could take over your entire existence. Being a bank teller? Not so much. So I like to take community classes, attend a book club, go out with friends. There are ways to keep myself occupied. Or there used to be."

"Sorry about that," he said.

"Not your fault." The leather seat creaked as she leaned back into it. He noticed that she angled her knees in his direction. Not a detail that should matter.

"Can't you ask your boss for more patrol vehicles out here?" Annabelle asked.

"I've already requested it, but we only have so many deputies, and it's a big county to cover."

And cattle rustlers, while they were definitely breaking the law, weren't as high on the sheriff's list of priorities as three bank robbers who shot someone. If the cattle rustlers got violent, that might change, but as it stood, their best bet was preventative.

"It might reassure you to know that our resources are currently focused on the bank robbery case," he added.

"It should, shouldn't it?" she said softly.

What did that mean? He shot her a curious look. "You don't think we'll find the evidence we need?"

"I don't know," she replied seriously. "If this were someone else's life, I'd tell them not to worry because the police are very good at what they do. But when it's my own life…"

"We'll get them," he said. "Every criminal leaves a trail, no matter how hard he tries to hide it. We know who pulled the trigger, and it's just a matter of working backward."

She sucked in a slow breath, and when he glanced over at her again, he could see her pulse fluttering in her neck. She had her hands gripped together in her lap, her fingertips white from the pressure. She was stressed and trying to keep it under control.

"Is there something you aren't telling me?" he asked.

"Nope." She released the tight grip in her lap and rubbed her palms down her jeans.

"Your body language says otherwise," he said. "What is it?"

For a moment, Annabelle was silent, and he watched the slice of wheat fields in his headlight beams.

"Look, I believe in your abilities to find the clues you need to put those men behind bars," she said.

"You don't seem so sure about that," he countered.

"I'm really hoping you can do it, okay?" Annabelle pressed her lips together and looked away. Her body language was clearly evasive, as was her tone of voice, and somehow, that stung.

"You're lying," he said simply.

"That's rude," she replied.

"I'm trained to recognize deceit," he said quietly. "And you're exhibiting all the signs."

Annabelle looked over at him, and he met her gaze for a moment, slowing his vehicle to the speed of a buggy as he approached a four-way stop. They didn't say anything for a moment, and he stepped on the brakes at the stop sign.

"I lost my keys," she said at last.

"What?" He looked over at her.

"I lost them two days before the robbery. It's a big deal if you lose your keys. You get written up, and if you do it more than once, it's a fireable offense. I'd misplaced my keys once very early in my time working at the branch. I left them in the employee bathroom on the counter, and the head manager wrote me up. It's been a few years since, and they likely wouldn't fire me for it, but if they wrote me up again for lost keys, it wouldn't be good, you know?"

Conrad's heartbeat sped up. "Keys for what, exactly?"

He turned the corner and pulled over. On the opposite side of the road, some cattle were sleeping, and one cow looked up at the head-lights, blinking.

"The vault," she said. "When it isn't closed

and locked for the night, it has a locking door made of bulletproof glass that allows people in and out of the first section," she continued. "We have boxes of coin in there, for example, or large money orders for people who have ordered in cash or foreign currency. I had keys to that first section of the vault, to the employee lounge and to the night deposit box where our business customers drop their deposits."

"Okay…" He nodded slowly, his mind clicking ahead. "And you didn't report it?"

"I did," she said. "I told Theresa, and she was going to write me up again. I mean, it wasn't personal. It was her job to do it. But I begged her to give me one more evening to look over my apartment and the parking lot… anywhere I might have dropped them."

"So she didn't report the missing keys," he said. "She's the branch assistant manager, right?"

"Yes, she is," she replied. "She was going to write up the report the next day if I didn't find them."

"Why didn't you tell us this before?" Conrad asked.

"Because when I was answering questions, I didn't remember. I was pretty overwhelmed with having seen someone shot," she replied.

"And when I did remember, the questioning was over, and I thought I'd look guilty. I'm in no way connected to that robbery, but the timing was damning. I answered the questions I was asked, and I was scared."

A police questioning could be intense, especially for someone already traumatized. He could appreciate that.

"Look, lost keys end up in gutters most of the time," Conrad said. "I'll pass this along, and we can start looking."

"You won't find them." Her voice shook, and she licked her lips.

"What do you mean?" he demanded, locking her down with a look.

"I saw my key ring in his hand..." Her chest rose and fell with shaky breaths. "I saw it when he lifted the mask."

"And you're sure they're yours?" he asked.

"I had a Snoopy key fob," she said. "And one ear was rubbed clean of paint. I'd know my keys anywhere."

Conrad blew out a breath. Stephen Hope had her keys. Yes, this looked very bad, but there were still a hundred different ways to explain it. It didn't make her guilty.

"Do you have any idea how he might have gotten them?" he asked.

"None. It makes no sense!"

Conrad let out a slow breath. Her worried gaze was locked on his face as if she could get some kind of reassurance from him. A guilty person would be looking down, looking away, looking at his forehead—anything but eye contact. She was scared, and she was looking him straight in the face.

"I don't know what to tell you," he said. "Obviously, Stephen Hope got ahold of your keys. The question is how."

"Do you believe me?" she asked, and he saw her chest stop moving—she was holding her breath.

Did he believe that she wasn't connected to the robbery?

He'd believed she was innocent from the first moment he saw her frantic face in the aftermath. He'd believed in her strongly enough to request to be her protection until the trial. And he knew her from her volunteer work...

"I don't see how you turning in Stephen Hope makes any sense if you were involved," he said. "If you were, you would never have come forward and said you saw his face. Yes, I believe you."

She deflated against the seat again, then nodded. "Thank you."

Conrad had seen a lot of people who'd lied before—good liars, bad liars, phenomenally skilled liars—and she didn't match with any of them. She was a freaked-out civilian who'd watched a man die, and she'd forgotten to mention an important detail in the heat of the moment. She was a good person. Yes, he believed her.

"We'll just have to find out how he did it," Conrad said. "There's nothing wrong with something we can explain. I'll contact my boss, and we'll add it to the list of things we're investigating."

She didn't look reassured, but she nodded. "Okay."

He could still remember the way she'd looked when she'd told them with a blanket over her shoulders, and shaking despite the August heat.

I saw his face. Oh, God, I saw his face! He looked right at me!

Annabelle was a victim here. Conrad didn't need convincing of that. But he'd better keep an even closer eye on her, because if she took off, she'd definitely look guilty.

ANNABELLE PRESSED HER shaking hands against her jean-clad thighs to still them. She hadn't been planning on telling Conrad anything, but he'd read her better than she'd anticipated... and he'd believed her. She stole a look over at him. He put the SUV back into gear and pulled onto the long, straight gravel road. His hand was relaxed on the top of the steering wheel.

"So you *do* believe me?" Annabelle watched his face.

"Yep." He cast her a gentler look. "You aren't much of a liar, Annabelle."

"That's probably a good thing." She looked away, though. She was still hiding her relationship with Stephen, and the text he'd sent her.

"I think there's more to you than you let on, but I also know what a sincerely freaked-out person looks like, and when you saw his face, you were freaked out," he said. "You couldn't have faked that if you were part of the robbery. I know you're innocent there."

"Do the other cops know it?" she asked.

"We're protecting you for a reason," he said.

After a few minutes, he asked, "Why don't you tell me more about you?"

"Like what?"

"Oh, I don't know. I know that you like book clubs and keeping busy," he said. "I know you enjoy good food and that you have very little debt."

"How do you know about the debt?" she asked. All she had was one credit card, and she was a stickler about paying that off. Then she laughed uncomfortably. "You guys looked into my finances?"

"It's all part of the investigation," he replied. "We looked into all the employees' finances. It gives us an idea of who might feel desperate enough to earn some extra money by giving a crook information."

Or keys. That thought sat like lead in her chest.

"Did you find anything...enlightening?" she asked.

"In your finances?" he asked. "No. In other people's? I'm not at liberty to say."

"Right, of course." She leaned her head back against the seat. It was an investigation, after all. But were there people she worked with who'd be desperate enough to do this? "I like this radio guy named Dave Ramsey. He's all about living debt free, and I guess I find it inspiring."

She hadn't grown up rich, but she'd never lacked anything, and Annabelle had always gotten a certain sense of security from knowing that she could make a comfortable life out of less.

"That's not a bad thing," he said. "I like to stay in the black, too."

"It just makes sense, right?" She looked over at him.

"Can I ask what drew you to volunteering at the soup kitchen?" Conrad looked over at her.

"Well, I told you before that at eighteen my dad kicked me out. He figured it was good for my character, or something like that. Well, I wasn't quite as prepared to take on life on my own as he figured I should be. I paid my bills the best I could, and sometimes I ran out of money between paychecks. So I ate at my parents' house whenever I could be sure my dad wasn't home. And I used the food bank sometimes. I always said I'd pay it back. I know what it's like to be a good person who just can't quite make ends meet."

"Wow..." he said quietly.

"What about you?" she asked.

He was silent for a moment.

"Fair is fair, Conrad," she said quietly.

"I guess I just need to see people doing okay," he said. "Or getting the help they need. I see people in their traumatic situations. I'm there for emergencies. Seeing people getting a warm meal into them—it helps me."

"This job *is* hard on you," she said.

"You shouldn't worry about that," he said.

"I'm not worrying—I'm noticing." She turned toward him so she could see his face in profile. "It's not easy."

"It's harder for the people I'm helping," he said. "It's harder on you than it is on me. And I know it. At least I have a chance to make a difference."

They were both silent, and Conrad's eyes stayed on the road as he navigated another turn.

"I think you do make a difference," she said. "You help a lot of people."

"Thanks," he said. "I really do try to improve things. But so do you. You're different than the other volunteers at the soup kitchen. They do good work, but you treat people with a level of respect that doesn't come around too often."

"You noticed me?"

"Of course." His voice was low, and he didn't look over at her. "How could I not?"

She felt her cheeks warm. He'd noticed her... The other single women who volunteered would have given a limb for that. "I learned a great strawberry cake recipe at that soup kitchen. It's the best you've ever tasted. Guaranteed."

"Those are strong words." A smile touched his lips.

"I stand by them." She met his smile. "I'll make that recipe one of these days. All I need is a bucket of fresh strawberries, some flour and unlimited power in your kitchen."

"It's a deal."

He slowed and signaled a turn. Everything looked the same out here, just a variation of pasture and maturing crops. The farmhouses were all dark, except for one that had the faint glow of a kerosene lamp from an upstairs window. It made her wonder what was keeping that person up tonight.

"Do you know many of the families around here?" she asked.

Conrad shook his head. "Not a lot. The Amish tend to keep to themselves, for the most part. I know the Schmidts because our houses are shouting distance apart, and we help each other out. The other farms around here have closer neighbors. They all socialize together in their community."

"If only they knew you were trying to help them," she said.

"If I catch these guys, I might find myself getting some good Amish baking dropped off," he said.

"Be nice to me, and you'll get that strawberry cake," she replied with a chuckle.

"I'm going to turn off the headlights now," he said, and he flicked them off. The only light now was from the three-quarter moon high in the sky. "Headlights are a dead giveaway, if someone is out here."

"And now we wait?" she asked.

"Now we wait."

Conrad slowed, and she looked out the window at the fields. Cows were sleeping or chewing their cud, spread out over the silvery pasture on the driver's side of the road. On her side was a field, she thought of oats. Annabelle lowered her window a couple of inches, and the smell of cattle and pasture wafted through the vehicle. It brought back memories from her childhood, visiting her grandparents out in the country—the smell of the house, the feel of the cold kitchen floor against her bare feet in the summer.

"I grew up in town," Annabelle said, "but my grandparents lived on an acreage out the other direction. They had trouble with some people robbing places, too. Thieves would scope out the properties during the day and put a bag over the mile markers so they'd know where to come back to at night."

"This is the same idea," Conrad said. "It's a crime of opportunity. Were your grandparents ever robbed?"

"No," Annabelle said. "But some neighbors were. My grandfather had a motion detector floodlight in front of the garage, and I remember sleeping on the floor of the living room and seeing the floodlight come on in the middle of the night. Mostly it was rabbits, but it did seem to deter the robbers."

"Unfortunately, these cattle rustlers are hitting the edges of pastures. They aren't coming up to houses, barns or stables. Makes them more difficult to nail down."

Conrad slowed further as they crept up a hill, and when they got to the top, he cut the engine. Down the incline of the hill, rolling fields swept out before them. Moonlight shone on the patchwork of properties, glowing off the metal tops of silos and sparkling off of irrigation canals. Copses of trees erupted from the land here and there, and she could see cattle dotting hills where they slept in the warm summer night.

There was a truck parked by a barbed-wire

fence farther along the road, lights on. Faint male voices drifted up toward them on the breeze. Annabelle could make out a figure moving over the field in the direction of a cow sleeping next to her calf.

"They're going to steal that calf," she said.

"Shh. Keep your voice down. Sound travels out here." He pulled out a pair of binoculars and peered through them, then heaved a frustrated sigh. "I can't see any license plate numbers, and that's what we need."

"What do we do?" she whispered.

"This." He started the engine, flicked on the lights and revved it hard. The men down the road started to scuttle back toward the truck. The one in the field bolted toward the fence and jumped it in one clean leap. The truck's tires spun as it managed a turn that looked far too tight to pull off with a trailer behind, and it roared off in the opposite direction.

"Are you going to follow them?" she asked.

"Nope." His gaze was fixed on the receding trailer, though, his jaw tensed. "They know they're being watched now, and that might slow them down a bit. Besides, if I'm going to make an arrest, I need to be just about on top of them before they know I'm there."

"How will you do that?" she asked.

"By putting some calves right by the fence," he said. "You have to make it too easy to pass up. Then I arrest them."

Conrad pulled a three-point turn, and they headed back the way they'd come. He tapped a tuneless rhythm on his knee, and she noticed that he checked the rearview mirror and the side mirrors a few times.

"You think they'll follow us?" she asked.

"Nah."

"You're checking, though."

"I told you I was a stickler." He reached over and gave her hand a squeeze. She felt her cheeks warm—that had been an unexpectedly tender gesture. He released her fingers as quickly as he'd squeezed them. She swallowed.

A few minutes passed in silence. Her eyes started feeling heavy. A glance at the clock told her it was after one. Conrad flicked on the radio, keeping it low. There was a cowboy ballad playing, something emotional and twangy, and somehow it reminded her of Conrad. He had more depth to him than he liked to show without some digging.

"So tell me, are you more cop or cowboy?" she asked after a stretch of silence.

Conrad's laugh was low and comforting. "I'm a corn-fed, Ohio-raised, pickup-driving male. Put me on horseback or in a sheriff's department cruiser, I'm still the same. I'm competitive and stubbornly attached to my personal ethics. Right is right, and wrong is wrong. Regardless of the hat I'm wearing." He glanced over at her, his gaze warm and tender. "You're tired."

"Hmm…"

"We're almost home…"

They slowed, and the tick-tick of the turn signal made her blink her eyes open once more. They turned into the drive, passing under the sign that said Westhouse Ranch. *Home.* Funny—when he'd called it that, she'd felt her own little tug toward this house and the land, and the safety they provided. The way he'd said it sounded domestic. He hadn't meant it that way, she was sure, but it was enticing, all the same.

CHAPTER SEVEN

CONRAD TURNED THE key in the lock quietly, and he noticed the faint squeak as he pushed the door open. He nudged Annabelle into the house ahead of him, and he locked the door firmly as he came into the kitchen.

The house was hot—keeping everything locked up tight meant no night breezes to cool things off. He and Wilder would have to make up for it when they got up for chores in three short hours. Moonlight spilled through the kitchen window, and he looked down at Annabelle. Her cheeks were flushed, and she brushed her hair away from her face.

"Thank you for bringing me along," she said softly. "I enjoyed that."

"Really?" He smiled ruefully. "You like skulking around on back roads, do you?"

"For a cause," she said and laughed softly. "I hope you catch those rustlers while I'm still here."

"We'll see," he said. "I'm not sure how long it'll take, but they're in my sights."

She didn't answer, but looking down into those clear eyes, he couldn't help wanting to close that case while she was here to see it. Maybe it was showing off a little, but she sparked that male, competitive part of him. He wouldn't mind being her hero.

He couldn't think like this. He shut his eyes for a moment, trying to reset his brain, and when he opened them, she'd dropped her gaze.

"We should turn in," he whispered. "I don't know about you, but I'm an early riser, no matter how late I get to bed."

"Same."

"Just a reminder to keep your window closed and locked," he said. "I've left a fan for you in your room in case it gets stuffy."

"Thanks."

Annabelle turned toward the door of the kitchen, and he felt a longing to catch her hand so strong that he had to ball his hand into a fist to stop himself.

"Annabelle," he whispered.

She turned back, and Conrad suddenly felt foolish. Because he had nothing to say. He just hadn't wanted her to leave quite yet.

There was something about the moonlight and the way it made her eyes shine. His heart sped up, and it was like there was more in this dark moment in the kitchen than there was in the rest of the day.

"If you need anything, don't hesitate to knock on my door," he said. And what kind of an idiot was he that he was hoping she'd need something, anything—a towel, a washcloth...

Annabelle smiled, then stifled a yawn. "Okay. Good night."

WHEN CONRAD SLIPPED between his cool, clean sheets that night, all he could hear was Wilder's snores coming from the other room. He picked up his cell phone from his bedside table and looked at the perimeter alarms. They were all set, and he put the volume up on his phone. Then he let out a slow breath and shut his eyes. Morning would be here before he knew it.

His sleep was fitful, and he dreamed strange dreams that blended together. Then a beep roused him, followed by another beep, shriller than the last. He blinked himself awake and reached for his phone. His brain was still sleep fogged as he focused on the screen. The first perimeter alarm had been set off in two places—one at ankle level, which could be any animal, and the other simultaneously at about chest level. That was something significantly bigger. Then another alarm was tripped farther down the drive. His pulse sped up and the sleep swept from his brain.

He slipped out of bed, stepped into a pair of jeans and tucked his gun into the waistband at the small of his back. He didn't bother with a shirt, didn't want to waste the time or blind himself putting it on, even for a few seconds. Then he went to his bedroom window. He couldn't see any movement outside, but the window didn't look in the right direction. He opened his bedroom door and crept down the hallway toward the living room, which gave him a full view of the front drive.

Nothing. He opened the front door and stepped softly outside. He pulled the door almost all the way shut behind him and crept down the three steps to ground level. He pulled his gun from the back of his pants and scanned the yard.

The moonlight from earlier had dimmed, some clouds moving over the night sky, blocking out the moon and blanketing over half the stars. A cooler breeze blew against his chest, brisk and smelling of far-off rain, but it was welcome cool after the heat of the house.

His phone blipped again, and he pulled it out to see another perimeter alarm had been set off, this one around the other side of the house, and he headed quickly in that direction, the grass cool and prickly against his bare feet.

But as he got around the house, it was the same—no one was there. Was this a false alarm, maybe something in the wind setting it off? But then he saw the footprint—just one, and it wasn't made by a cowboy boot or an Amish boot. It had the sharp, recognizable shape of a tactical boot.

He held his gun out with two hands, sweeping the area.

Nothing. Farther down the road he heard an engine start up, and a vehicle roared away into the night.

Someone had been here—testing his reaction time? Just snooping around? Was this cattle rustlers getting bolder, or had Annabelle's presence here gotten out to the wrong people?

"Conrad?"

He spun around to see Annabelle standing behind him. She wore a knee-length cotton nightgown, and her face was almost as white as the garment. He exhaled a slow breath.

"Go back inside," he whispered.

"What's wrong?"

"I said go back in!" He didn't mean to bark, but she startled and turned back toward the door. He scanned the yard once more to be sure he couldn't see any movement, checked his phone for those proximity alarms and then jogged to catch up with her.

He opened the front door and gestured her in first, then shut it and locked the dead bolt behind him.

A shadow and the creak of a floorboard snapped Conrad's training into gear, and he slid forward, grabbed a shirtfront and pointed his gun. Wilder put his hands up, a look of surprise on his face.

"Whoa, whoa," Wilder said. "It's me… What's going on?"

He let go of his brother's shirt and lowered his gun. Annabelle stood against the wall, her bright eyes locked on him questioningly. He cast her an apologetic smile.

"Sorry, I think we're fine." He glanced back at his brother. "What woke you up?"

"Chores. It's four."

"Right…" He realized then that he wasn't

wearing a shirt, and his brother eyed his bare chest and raised an eyebrow. "Shut up."

Wilder chuckled, then sobered. "Did you hear someone?"

"The alarms went off," Conrad replied. "And I saw a fresh footprint out in the garden. I also heard a vehicle start up and take off. So I'm assuming they're gone."

"Is this to do with—" Wilder's gaze flickered in Annabelle's direction. Her eyes were fixed on his face, the question in her gaze clear.

"I don't know," Conrad said. "But I'm not taking any chances."

Annabelle still hadn't spoken, and Conrad nodded toward the kitchen. "Go ahead and get started, Wilder."

His brother disappeared from the room, and Conrad reached out and put a hand on Annabelle's shoulder.

"You okay?" he asked, softening his tone.

She nodded. "I heard you moving around. I wasn't sure what was going on, but I wasn't about to be stuck in that bedroom on my own."

"Yeah, I get that," he said. "But if that was someone after you outside, what exactly were you going to do?"

"Stand behind you?" She smiled faintly, without humor.

"Better than nothing," he muttered. "Look, I'm sorry I snapped, but you've got to do what I say the second I say it. There's no time for explanations, okay?"

She nodded. "Sorry."

"It's okay." He swallowed. "You can go back to bed if you want. Get some rest. I'm up and I'll take care of things."

"I don't think I could sleep if I tried," she said.

"Well, you're going to have to stick to my side today," he said. "No pie with the neighbors—I need you close."

"Got it," she said with a nod.

Whoever had been skulking around outside was up to no good—there was no doubt about that. But who was it? Someone after the cows, or after some revenge after Conrad had scared them last night? It was no secret that he was law enforcement. Or someone after Annabelle?

He sincerely hoped they were after him, because they'd get what they came for and then some if they tried confronting him. All he needed was an opportunity for an arrest with those cowards.

But if this was someone a little nastier who was after Annabelle...

"Should we help my brother with chores?" he asked, trying to sound relaxed. He didn't need to freak her out, but he was going to be keeping her in sight at all times going forward. And it might be a good thing to get out in the fields and the barns, away from the house.

"We might as well be useful," she said, and she rubbed her hands over her bare arms.

"It's a plan," he said. "Go get dressed, and I'll get a shirt on."

Annabelle's gaze flickered down to his chest. "That's a good idea."

Conrad would get a picture of that boot print before it got muddied, just in case. Whoever had triggered those alarms had come onto private property, and whatever they were after, it was officially personal.

ANNABELLE SHUT HER bedroom door and leaned against it. She let out a shaky breath. Who'd been creeping around outside? Theresa wouldn't have told anyone, would she? Annabelle had felt the need to tell someone. Just slipping off with a cop into the country and not telling a soul felt pretty dangerous, too.

But her jangled nerves weren't only about the trespasser. So far, Conrad must have been trying to appear somewhat gentler for her benefit, because seeing the massive man with a gun in his hand and his jaw clenched like that had given her a start. Anyone who saw Conrad targeting them would be quaking.

And then there was seeing him without a shirt. Her cheeks warmed with embarrassment at the memory. He was even more muscular than she'd thought, and she would bet that he spent a lot of time in a gym to get that kind of physique. He looked like an action hero under that uniform, not that she should have been surprised.

Still… She rubbed her hands over her face. She was tied at the hip with a ridiculously good-looking man who was dedicated to her safety, and there was nothing easy about it. It would be better if he was a portly man closer to her father's age instead of the gym-hardened Conrad Westhouse.

She went to the bathroom to wash up and brush her teeth, and she could hear cupboards closing in the kitchen, the rumble of the brothers' voices. Whoever had come onto this property had been chased off, but tell her pulse that. She went to the chest of drawers that had been emptied for her use and pulled out a fresh pair of jeans and a tank top. The day would be another hot one, judging by how stuffy the room was already.

When she finished in the bathroom, she quickly made the bed, pulled on her clothes and ran a comb through her hair. She was already feeling a twinge of embarrassment at having been seen in her nightgown. She looked rumpled in the morning, while Conrad managed to look like…that.

From the other end of the house, she heard the door close solidly. She pulled back the curtain and looked outside at the tangled garden. Wilder walked past the house, and she watched as he stopped, looking around with the same apprehension that she felt.

She wasn't overreacting if Wilder was scared, too.

The sun was just cresting the horizon, the sky alight with orange and pink. A man's dark form appeared from the Schmidt house beyond, tramping slowly toward the chicken coop. He paused and raised a hand, and Wilder waved back. Then the Amish man disappeared from view.

The day was starting for everyone, it seemed. A songbird began to sing just outside the window, and then another, and another, their twitters and chirps filling the morning air.

This quiet country scene was soothing, and the danger from a few minutes ago seemed to be evaporating like morning dew.

Another form came out from the Schmidt house—it would be Linda. She was plump, wearing an Amish dress, and she was carrying some buckets. She went to the garden, bent down and began to work.

The first rays of sunlight slipped over the horizon and dazzled Annabelle's eyes. The people next door had such quiet confidence as they began their day of work. There were outsiders targeting their livestock, dangers untold out there, but they took the next step forward with a determined kind of faith. There was reassurance in eggs collected and a garden tended to. Maybe there'd be some reassurance for Annabelle in some ranch chores done this morning, too.

"Annabelle?" It was Conrad's voice at her door.

She rallied herself and went to open it. Conrad was fully dressed, and he held his black cowboy hat in one hand.

"I'm ready," she said.

"Good." He paused. "There's something

about getting out there and slinging some hay that makes me feel better. You don't have to work at all—but you've got to be with me."

What was she going to do, stand back and watch him lift things? That seemed a little creepy.

"I'll work," she said.

He gave her a look that seemed to say, *That's cute*. And she chuckled.

"I will!" she said.

"We'll see." He smiled teasingly. "All right. Let's head out."

CHAPTER EIGHT

CONRAD LED THE way across the grass to the far gate, which opened into the farmyard. He scanned the area, looking for anything amiss. He didn't know what he was looking for. This was more of a gut-level search—his instincts were normally dead right—but he didn't see anything. The sky was brushed with gold and coral pink, which illuminated Annabelle's features and made her even more beautiful, if that were possible. Though she kept up with his pace, he slowed down when he noticed her breathing hard.

"Thanks," she said.

"Let's check in on the Schmidt cow and the calf," Conrad said.

"How have they been doing?" she asked.

"My brother says they're great," he replied. "I'll feel better to see it myself, though."

It wasn't that he didn't believe his brother so much as it would do his heart good to see that calf being cared for and the cow's grief soothed.

"You're spooked," Annabelle said.

"No, I'm not." He glanced down at her.

"Yes, you are," she countered. "I'm looking at you, and you're wound up so tight, you could snap."

He considered reassuring her—but her gaze was so direct that he almost squirmed. Could she see through him so easily?

"Okay, I'm still coming down from the intruder alert," he said.

"Was it scary?"

He barked out a laugh. "No—I mean, it got my adrenaline up. Honestly, when you came out in your nightgown, that upped the stakes a bit. If you were inside, I had a plan to protect you."

"Oh…" They went through the gate and in the direction of the cow barn beyond. "So I messed with the system, did I?"

"A little bit."

"You do realize that, standing outside shirtless, you had nothing to protect you, right?" she said. "No bulletproof vest."

"I wasn't thinking about that in the moment," he replied.

"Maybe you should have been," she replied.

Conrad stopped and turned to face her. "Are you worried about me?"

Annabelle opened her mouth to answer, paused a moment and then said, "I think I am."

"It's my job to worry about you," he said, softening his tone. "If we stick to our roles, this whole thing works very smoothly."

"As long as you don't get shot," she replied, and there was no joking in her voice this time. A tangle of hair blew in front of her eyes, and before he could think better of it, he reached out and brushed it away. Her skin was silky soft under his touch, and he froze, his fingers still lingering on her temple.

She was concerned for his safety when she should be more concerned about her own. The sincerity in her face softened him, and that adrenaline started to drain away.

"I'll be okay," he said. "I promise."

"Well, if you promise," she said, and a smile tickled her lips, breaking the moment. He dropped his hand.

He glanced over his shoulder and spotted Linda Schmidt standing in her garden, hands on her ample hips, looking at them. If looking like a couple made her real reason for being here less obvious, this moment would help the illusion. Linda bent down again to her work.

Conrad started toward the barn again, and Annabelle caught up. Birdsong surfed the morning breeze from the trees by the house. He could see his brother on horseback already, growing smaller as he headed out west to check on the herd.

"Doing chores, working with my hands," Conrad said. "This stuff relaxes me."

"So this ranch is your place to get away from it all," she said. "It's your line between work and rest."

"Yeah…" He shrugged. "Normally."

"With me here, you don't get that rest," she concluded.

Exactly true, but it wasn't how he felt about having her here. "Let's put it this way. I'd rather have you here with me on the ranch than have us holed up together in a hotel while we wait this out. At least out here we have some distraction besides daytime television."

"Is that a silver lining?"

Oddly, *she* was the silver lining. If he'd been stuck with anyone else, this would be a whole lot more of a chore, but he enjoyed being around her. Her safety soothed a place very deep inside him, but she was also interesting, and dare he say it—fun.

"Let's just say I'm not suffering," he said.

They arrived at the barn and he pulled open the door, letting her go inside first. The lighting was dim, and dust motes danced in the air. Annabelle sneezed.

"Bless you," he said, and he let his hand linger on her back as he slipped past her. He was finding himself touching her in passing more often these days.

The cow and calf were standing close together, and when he approached the oversize stall where they were staying, the cow mooed protectively and shuffled her feet. It was a good sign—she'd accepted the calf as her own.

He leaned against the railing and regarded the pair thoughtfully.

"Success?" Annabelle asked, leaning against the rail next to him.

"Looks that way to me," he replied. "We'll put them out with the rest of our herd pretty soon. I hate to say it, but I think this calf is safer with our cattle for the time being."

"You knew this would work, didn't you?" she asked.

"It was worth a try," he replied.

"You're too humble," she replied.

Conrad chuckled. "With police work and ranching, it's best not to get too cocky. The minute you figure you're a pro, it's going to kick you in the teeth. You stay humble and work your tail off. That's the way to succeed at it."

"So you won't admit that you're good at it?" she asked.

He shot her a grin. "Nope. Bad luck." He turned his attention to the empty corner that used to hold a few bales of hay. All that was left was a dirty floor. Then he looked up at the ladder that led to the hayloft.

"What's up there?" she asked.

"More hay," he said. "And a great view. I need to toss down a bale or two. You want to come up, or wait here?"

"I'll come up."

Conrad went up the ladder first, and when she got to the top, he grabbed her hand so she could step safely to the solid loft floor. She didn't pull away, and for a moment, he resisted the urge to twine his fingers through hers.

He released her hand and walked over to the large sliding door, grabbed the metal handle and heaved it to the side. The door slid open with a rumble of worn metal wheels moving over the track, and the expanse of the landscape spilled out in front of him.

"I used to climb up into the hayloft when I visited my grandfather as a kid," he said.

"This one?" she asked.

"This very one."

Annabelle came to his side and looked out the open door. Early-morning sunlight splashed over the rolling hills, and from where they stood, they could see the house, the garden and even the Schmidt place next door, all bathed in golden light. Linda Schmidt bent over a garden row, working steadily, and Conrad saw little Jane appear on the grass, her feet bare and her golden hair shining in the sunlight.

Annabelle's arm brushed against his, and he heard her sigh.

"Wow..."

"Told you it was a great view," he said.

Her hand moved into the crook of his arm as she leaned forward, looking out as far as she could.

"My head swims a bit being up this high," she said.

He stood there, letting her use him for

balance as she looked out. Funny—standing here looking at the early-morning scene with a beautiful woman hanging off his arm, he was reminded of being a kid up here. Not that he'd had any beautiful girls hanging off him in those days, but he used to like to sit up here and think, and the girls he had crushes on but no bravery to speak to had factored into his thoughts a fair bit back then.

But from where he stood, he could see the skid marks on the side of the road where the truck had spun off earlier this morning. He wished he knew who'd been on his property— the sight of them chilled his blood.

He put a hand over hers without thinking. She didn't seem to notice.

"Those skid marks…" she said, pulling back inside. "Is that from the person who set off the alarm this morning?"

"Yep."

"They left in a hurry to skid out like that," she said.

"Whoever it was didn't know I knew they were on the property. I think they saw me leave the house and got out quick."

"Are we talking some random thieves like my grandparents experienced? Someone just looking to see what they can take, or—" She swallowed.

"I don't know," he said. "But I'll be prepared, whoever they are."

She nodded, her gaze moving back out the loft doors, and she shivered.

"Come on—we need hay."

Conrad picked up a bale by the twine and tossed it down the hole that led back down to the main floor. It landed with a thump, and a cloud of dust rose up from it. A second bale quickly followed.

"I said I'd pitch in with the work, didn't I?" she said. "I seem to be holding you up."

She bent down to grab a bale, and he watched as she lifted it no more than a foot off the dusty floor. It was too heavy for her, and Conrad reached over her arms and snagged the twine from her fingers. He couldn't help but notice the faint scent of flowers around her, and it mingled nicely with the sweet scent of hay.

"I got it," he said.

She stood back as he tossed the bale down. It landed with a wobble on top of the others.

"Let's head down," he said, and he grabbed the handle of the sliding barn door and hauled it shut. But just before the door slammed fully closed, his gaze landed on that spun-out scar in the dirt at the side of the road once more. Someone had come on his property, and while he wanted to believe that this was about cattle or horses, there was a footprint in his garden that suggested otherwise.

ANNABELLE CLIMBED DOWN to the main level and waited until Conrad's cowboy boots hit the concrete floor next to her. He hoisted a bale of hay and tossed it against the wall, then lifted a second bale on top of the first. Then he grabbed the third and jutted his chin in the direction of the cow and calf.

"At least we aren't bottle-feeding this one anymore," he said. "That gets tiring fast when you've got to time everything to feed a young calf on schedule."

He didn't wait for her to follow, but carried the bale over to the stall, pulled a knife out of his belt and popped the twine. He used a pitchfork to toss some hay between the rails. Then he leaned against the top one. His expression had softened. The calf was drinking from the cow, milk dripping from the corners of his mouth. As a kitten, her cat, Herman, had been a whole lot smaller than that calf, but he'd been the runt of a litter and she'd fed him with an eyedropper.

"There is nothing quite so satisfying as seeing a baby animal with milk on their chins, is there?" she said.

Conrad looked over his shoulder. "It means something is going right."

"You mentioned bringing them out to your field," she said.

"I don't know. I'm not sure it's the right thing to do yet. There's something about having a little haven in times of stress, you know?"

"Don't I."

He smiled faintly. "Maybe these two can just hunker down here in the barn for a few more days. It won't hurt anything."

And it wouldn't hurt her to stick around here for a few more days, either. But there was a timer ticking in the back of her head. She'd have to make a solid choice one way or another soon—was she testifying or not?

She cleared her throat. "Can I ask you something?"

"Sure."

"Are you getting paid overtime or anything for the bother of having me here?"

Conrad chuckled. "Nope."

"So they just volunteered your personal ranch, and you get nothing back?" Annabelle leaned against the rail next to him. "That hardly seems fair."

Conrad was silent for a moment, and his dark gaze caught hers. "I volunteered."

His voice was quiet, but something in his gaze was more intense than the words, and her breath caught in her throat.

"Why?"

He turned his attention back to the cow and calf, but his voice stayed soft. "I guess I understood how scared you were. Your face was white, and you had that emergency blanket around your shoulders, and you were still shaking. You saw something terrible, you saw who did it and you were scared out of your mind, but you still came to me and told me what you saw."

"Was that you I told?" she asked. It was all a blur now. She'd seen a uniform, and she'd headed straight for it. She had been terrified, and the cop had marched her straight to the sheriff and she'd been ushered into an interview room... But she hadn't realized that the first cop she'd told had been Conrad.

"Shock will do that," he said. "But yes, it was me."

Her mind swept back over that afternoon. She'd been terrified, and all she'd wanted was for someone to fix it—she hadn't even been thinking straight.

"So you thought you'd just take me home with you?" she asked with a low laugh.

"Not exactly." Conrad shot her a grin in response to her joke. "We were discussing where we should hide you until the trial, and this ranch ticked every box."

"So that was it?" she asked. "It was a good solution?"

If so, he was possibly the most professional man she'd ever met, willing to sacrifice his own privacy and downtime for a case.

"No." Conrad licked his lips. "I told you before that I see a lot on this job... I see bad things happen, and we have to pick up the pieces. The one thing that makes me feel better is knowing that people heal, and that they feel better afterward. And when I saw you so freaked out, shaking, your face as white as paper, I had a feeling that it would haunt me. Because some cases do."

Annabelle sucked in a breath. Conrad still didn't look at her, but he did flex his big hand into a fist, then slowly relaxed it.

"I'd haunt you?" she whispered.

"Yep." He turned to look down at her. "You already do."

She could see the fine lines around his eyes, the scruff on his chin, as he hadn't shaved that morning. He looked tired, worn, but something deep inside him glowed with life.

"I just needed to see you happy," he said. "I needed to know you were safe. It was the only way I was going to have any peace."

"Oh…" Annabelle breathed. "Do you feel like that with all the people you help?"

Or was she special? That was what she needed to know…

"There was a boy who was abducted by his father last year, and it did me good to see his mom walking him home from school after that. It makes it all worthwhile if you know that the things you've seen are fixable."

"And I'm fixable," she said with a faint smile.

"No, you're…unique." He shook his head. "I don't need to fix you. I need to protect you—stand between you and whatever might come at you." He cleared his throat. "Sorry, *need* is a strong word, isn't it? I don't mean to dump any of my emotional garbage on you. This is why I try to keep that professional line drawn."

"I wouldn't call it *garbage*," she said quietly.

"It's not the way I'm supposed to feel." He

looked down at her, and she could see the battle in those stormy eyes.

"You're a human being, you know," she whispered.

"So I've been told." His lips curved up into a smile.

"Maybe this isn't about what we're supposed to be feeling," she said. "You're caught up in this mess, just as much as I am. Your home is at risk because of me."

"My feelings aren't your problem, though," he said.

"But you said I'm different… Is it because you knew me from the soup kitchen?"

She half expected him to joke about her being too stubborn, or about having to share his personal space with her, but his dark gaze locked on to hers, and he wrapped his fingers around hers.

"I wish I knew why," he murmured.

He bent down and pressed a kiss against her forehead. For a moment, they were motionless, his breath warm against her skin, and then he pulled back. His dark gaze flickered down to hers once more. This was crossing lines—she wasn't a fool. And yet it felt strangely right. She wasn't the only one with feelings here, and knowing that there was a real, breathing, warm man underneath that professional exterior was a strange relief.

"I probably should have let them place you somewhere else," he said.

In a hotel somewhere, or a safe house where she'd be stuck inside with a TV and an impenetrable officer standing guard...

"I think I prefer being here," she said. "The great outdoors, horses, cattle, Amish neighbors. You couldn't have known that there'd be...attraction...between us."

"Well, let's just say I didn't know you'd feel it, too."

Her breath felt lodged in her chest, and she was halfway afraid to ask.

"Did you feel this way before?" she whispered.

Conrad was about to answer when the barn door opened, and Annabelle turned to see Wilder. He pulled off his hat, then slapped it against his leg.

"Oh, you got to the cow, I see," Wilder said.

Conrad straightened, and she could feel the moment slipping away. She wouldn't get her answer...and maybe it was for the best.

"Yep, just finished." Conrad's tone had changed, too. Gone was the soft, low voice he'd been using with her.

"The calf still feeding well?" Wilder asked.

"Yeah, yeah." Conrad glanced down at Annabelle, and she read some apology in his expression. Then he turned back to his brother. "I'm thinking we should give them a few more days in the barn—just to avoid getting the calf stolen, if nothing else."

"Yeah, that's a good idea," Wilder agreed. "I looked in on Wollie's cattle, and everything's in order there. I'm going to head out and check our western pasture."

"Sounds good. We should get back to the house."

Conrad headed for the door, and Annabelle followed. She gave Wilder a smile as they all emerged into the morning sunlight. They parted ways—Wilder swinging back up into the saddle, and Annabelle and Conrad turning toward the house.

"In answer to your question," Conrad said, his voice low. "Did I feel this way before? Yes, I did."

She hadn't realized he was still thinking about it. And his answer gave her a jolt of surprise. She'd never suspected.

"Why didn't you ask me out?" she asked.

"Because I'm a little more world-weary than

you are," he said. "I doubt I'd be any good for you."

"Isn't that up to me to decide?" she asked.

He slowed, stopped, then turned toward her.

"Yeah, probably," he said. "But here's the thing. I know what I want. I want a woman I feel passionately drawn toward...and someone I won't be too much for. And you're younger than me, a little less battered by life. I figured I was doing you a favor."

She wasn't sure how to answer that.

"We should get back," he said. "And you can feel free to forget I said anything. This is about you—your safety and your needs. I'm very clear on that."

So he'd felt something for her...something powerful that he was willing to set aside. She hadn't even considered the possibility, and her heart hammered hard in her chest.

"It looks like Linda left us some berries on the step," he said, and he started forward, forcing her to jog to catch up.

There were two plastic tubs overflowing with plump crimson strawberries sitting on the step next to the side door. There was a note tucked down between the two tubs, and he unfolded it.

"Linda said they have more than enough berries and thought we might enjoy some, seeing as we had company. They're also inviting us to dinner tonight." Conrad handed the note over. "They like you."

She looked down at the neat handwriting, then over toward the Schmidt house, where Jane was climbing up an apple tree. She waved from a low branch.

"Good morning!" Jane hollered. "Hello!"

Annabelle waved back, and Conrad did, too. Then he looked down at her, and he smiled sadly.

"I didn't know you felt anything for me," she said quietly.

"It's okay." He shrugged. "Annabelle, don't worry about it. Okay? It's fine."

Conrad picked up one tub of berries and opened the screen door. Annabelle gathered up the second tub and followed him inside.

"Do you think you could make some of that strawberry cake you mentioned?" he asked.

Back to normal. At least, that was what he was trying to do.

"Sure," she said.

Maybe it would be good for her to have something else to focus on than this big man standing guard over her. Because he wasn't just an attractive cop now—he was turning out to be a whole lot more human, and while he insisted that his feelings weren't her problem, she couldn't help but wonder what else lay under that tough exterior of his.

He felt something for her…something that had been brewing for some time…

She'd be wise to watch her own heart. Conrad would be a very easy man to fall for, but she still didn't know if she'd testify. While Conrad would do anything to protect her here, he wasn't the entire justice system, either. He wasn't the only one who could complicate her life, and his best intentions might not be enough to keep her out of Stephen Hope's clutches.

She couldn't let her heart start guiding her where her brain needed to lead.

CHAPTER NINE

CONRAD HAD SAID too much. He hadn't meant to say anything at all… His feelings weren't her problem, so they could have remained unsaid. What had he been thinking? He'd overstepped. Wildly. He was awash in regret. He should have known better than to suggest she come here, knowing how he felt about her. This might be the safest place for her to hole up before that trial, but he'd been too cocky about his own abilities to keep this professional.

He pulled down some metal mixing bowls and put them on the counter. Annabelle stood at the sink, rinsing strawberries in a plastic colander. Her blond hair swung down in front of her face so he couldn't see her expression.

"Do you have an electric mixer?" she asked.

"Yeah." He opened a drawer and took out a handheld mixer, then rooted around for a minute before he located the metal beaters that went with it. He put them on the countertop. "Just call me if you need anything else. I'm going to watch for Wollie and give him a heads-up about that trespasser."

She didn't answer, but she cast him a smile, then turned back to the strawberries. They were both trying to get back to some sort of normal balance.

I'm an idiot, he thought, and he headed out onto the side porch, letting the screen door bang shut behind him. He'd called the sheriff's department that morning to fill them in on the trespasser, and Conrad looked down at his phone now to see that he'd missed a text from Sheriff McCann.

I'm coming by this morning so you can fill me in on the details in person. I also have a package the female officers put together for Annabelle.

Apparently, there wasn't much faith that his home would have what a woman needed to be comfortable, and they weren't exactly wrong. He doubted that Annabelle would describe her experience as comfortable.

Conrad did as he'd intended and warned his neighbor about the trespasser. Then he set about double-checking all his perimeter alarms. Maybe it was just the stress of having someone lurking on his property that had made him confess his attraction to Annabelle.

Sheriff Eugene McCann arrived a half hour later in an unmarked SUV. He was a portly man with iron gray hair and a mustache to match. He got out of his vehicle carrying a cloth grocery bag.

"Good morning, boss," Conrad said.

"Good morning." The sheriff scanned the property. "We caught Stephen Hope at a traffic stop at around two this morning. He was with two other men who have no prior convictions, so we have no reason to hold anyone but Stephen Hope."

"But you've got him," Conrad said with a grim smile.

"We have him, all right."

"And the men he was with had no priors?" Conrad frowned. "Is it possible that they were unconnected?"

"I don't think so," the older man replied. "Unless Stephen Hope isn't our guy after all. These two knew him and claimed that they were with him the day of the robbery in a completely different town."

"What do you mean, if Stephen Hope isn't our guy?" Conrad asked.

"If our witness identified the wrong man."

"She was very certain."

The sheriff shrugged.

"Are we checking up on the two men with him?" Conrad asked.

"I have two deputies looking into it now," he replied. "But all three looked a little too cocky. They told us to check the security footage, and it's almost as if they knew that there were three men of similar height and build in nondescript clothing who won't look into cameras."

Conrad felt the breath seep out of him. "Any alibi they're trying to support?"

"They claim he played cards with them all day."

"Cards."

"Poker, specifically. Obviously, we don't believe it, but it'll be enough for the defense lawyers to work with."

"They're setting up an alibi for if Annabelle balks at testifying."

"Exactly."

And she very well might after this…

"I saw the skid marks you mentioned," the sheriff went on. "And I got the picture of the footprint. I'll take a cast of it. There seems to be a unique wear pattern at the heel that

we might be able to match up. Who knows if
we'll need it, but I'd rather have it than not."

"I did interrupt some rustlers the other
night," Conrad said. "So I don't know if this
is just angry cattle thieves who don't like
having their racket interrupted, or if it's connected to the Stephen Hope trial."

"The trespasser came to the house, not the
stable or the barn..." the sheriff said.

"Yes, sir. Not to the stable where I keep my
horses, and not to the neighbor's cattle, either.
My brother is checking cattle that are grazing
farther out, but I highly doubt we'll see any
problems. This seems...targeted."

"The chances are high this is connected to
the trial." The sheriff nodded.

For the next few minutes, Conrad and Sheriff McCann took a plaster cast of the footprint in the garden, and Conrad took him on
a quick tour of the outside of the house. The
sheriff had a grandfatherly look about him,
but anyone who knew him knew that no one
was tougher or more observant than Eugene
McCann.

When they came back around the side of
the house, the sheriff nodded toward the side
door. "Should we head inside?"

"That's a good idea." Conrad led the way

up the side steps and into the kitchen. Annabelle stood at the counter cutting strawberries into a bowl with a paring knife. She looked up when the sheriff walked inside, and her gaze flicked between them.

"Hello," she said, her voice tight.

"I come bearing gifts from the women at the department," Sheriff McCann said with an easy smile. He handed over the bag. "Some toiletries, a few magazines, a couple novels…"

"That's really kind," Annabelle said. "Thank them for me."

"Absolutely."

Annabelle put the bag on the counter next to her. "Have you caught him yet? The one who shot the guard?"

Her lips were pale, and she parted them as if she was going to say something else, but stayed silent.

"Yes," the sheriff said quietly. "He's in custody. We picked him up last night at a roadblock. I wanted to come tell you in person."

"Do we have any idea who was lurking around here last night?" Annabelle asked. "If you picked up Stephen, then…it wasn't him, right? So maybe it was nothing?"

Stephen. She'd called him by his first name. That was rather casual.

"Well, we have two other accomplices who are so far unidentified," the sheriff replied. "So no, I wouldn't call it nothing. But that's why I'm here—we'll piece it together. I'm sorry we don't have more nailed down for you, but we're working on it. And that should be more reassuring than it sounds."

Annabelle nodded.

"Maybe we can go talk in the other room," Sheriff McCann said, glancing back at Conrad.

"You bet. You okay here, Annabelle?"

"I'm fine." She gave him a forced smile. "One strawberry cake coming right up."

Conrad led the way into the sitting room, and he crossed his arms over his chest. The sheriff's expression turned grim once they were out of sight.

"So how is it going with Annabelle?" Sheriff McCann asked, his voice low. "She didn't give a lot of reaction there when I said we got Stephen Hope into custody."

"I don't know what reaction you're expecting," Conrad said.

"Just noticed. That's all."

Yeah, so had he. "This is all pretty intense for her. She's scared, and a little bit skittish."

"Skittish how?" the sheriff asked with a frown.

"She saw a man killed, and the man who did it knows she's the only witness who can identify his face. She's wondering what's safer for her—testifying, or saying she didn't see anything and skipping town."

"Was that because she isn't sure about who she saw, or she's scared of him?" the older man asked.

"She knows who she saw," Conrad said. "I'm sure of that. But she's scared."

"Should I sit down with her?" the sheriff asked.

"We've got Hope in custody now, and that should relieve some of her fears." At least, he hoped it would. It was a step forward, at least.

"Do you need more backup here?" the sheriff asked.

"We could use a bigger law enforcement presence. If they got to us once, I'm worried they'll come back better prepared."

The sheriff nodded. "We'll have the deputies ask around about cattle rustlers. That'll give us an excellent excuse to put more officers in the area without alerting Hope's accomplices. If it is them."

"I'd rather be safe than sorry," Conrad replied.

"Me, too."

There was a rustle by the door, and Conrad looked up to see Annabelle standing there. She was wearing an old barbecuing apron he hadn't seen in ages, and her worried expression flipped between them.

"What's going on?" she asked.

"Just discussing logistics," the sheriff replied. "We'll have more deputies patrolling out here to make sure you don't get a repeat of last night."

She nodded. "Did Stephen Hope say anything? Did he admit to doing it?"

"No, he hasn't confessed," Sheriff McCann said. "We don't really expect him to. We'll need your testimony to prove he was there."

"What about the other two?" she asked. "Did you get them?"

"I'm not at liberty to talk about that," the sheriff replied. "Do you know anything about them?"

"They didn't remove their masks," she replied.

"True. But if there is something you know…"

"There isn't." She took a step back. "I was just wondering how safe I am at this point."

"With Conrad here, you're incredibly safe." The sheriff gave her a gentle smile.

"Okay. Thanks."

Annabelle turned back toward the kitchen, and Conrad caught the thoughtful look on the sheriff's face as he watched her leave.

"Should we move her to another location?" Conrad asked.

"Do you think we need to?" The sheriff raised an eyebrow. "Because keeping her here, even if they've discovered where she is, gives us the upper hand. They'll come to us. Otherwise, I have a sneaking suspicion we won't get anything to stick on the other two."

"You want to use her as bait," Conrad said.

"I want to put some violent criminals behind bars and keep her safe at the same time," Sheriff McCann replied. "I believe she's safe with you. But if you disagree, you should say so now."

"She's safe with me, sir," he replied. "But maybe she should get the choice there."

"We'll ask her," he replied, but his expression remained clouded. "It looks to me like Stephen Hope works with people who have no criminal past. It's an interesting development."

Conrad wasn't sure he liked where this was leading.

"What are you getting at, sir?"

"See if there's any connection between her and Hope... It's unlikely, but I've seen entire cases come together on unlikelier links," the sheriff replied.

"You think Annabelle's connected?" Conrad said.

"I'm not saying she is or that it's even probable. I'm just saying it's a possibility," he replied. "And I don't like to discount anything."

"She had no reason to tell us anything if she was involved," Conrad said. "All she would have had to do is keep her mouth shut. I don't think she's involved."

"Unless murder wasn't part of the deal, and she panicked." The sheriff shrugged. "He had her keys, after all."

"She lost them."

"She also didn't tell us that until much later. That's important. I get that she might forget in the heat of the moment, but it took her several days to say anything? Eyes and ears open, Conrad. Keep me posted."

"Of course."

But Conrad didn't like the direction the sheriff's mind was moving. Annabelle wasn't

involved in this… There was no way. He'd
seen her tear-streaked face when she told him
she'd seen the shooter. She'd been shaking
so hard that her teeth just about chattered. It
was tough to fake that level of shock. He also
knew her a little bit better than the sheriff did.

Sheriff McCann headed through the kitchen.
Conrad followed him, as did Annabelle's veiled
gaze.

"Before I leave, Annabelle, we were discussing moving you to a different safe house location," the sheriff said. "I don't think it's strictly
necessary while you have Deputy Westhouse
with you, but we wanted to check in with you.
Do you want to be moved?"

Annabelle licked her lips. "I want to go
home, but if that's not possible yet…"

"Not yet." The sheriff gave her a sympathetic smile.

"I'm still safe here?"

Conrad nodded. "You're safe." He'd make
sure of it.

She inhaled a slow breath. "Then I think
I'd rather stay. At least there are things to do
here. I don't want to be cooped up in a hotel
or something. And I trust Conrad."

"Sounds good." Sheriff McCann shot her
a reassuring smile. "Try to relax, if you can,

and do whatever Conrad tells you. He's the best we've got. That's a guarantee."

"Thanks." She smiled faintly. "I appreciate it."

And then Sheriff McCann pulled open the door and stepped outside.

His boss's words were still rattling uncomfortably around in Conrad's mind. The sheriff had only hinted at it, but Annabelle was an unofficial suspect. And Conrad didn't like that one bit.

AN HOUR LATER, Annabelle pulled the fluffy strawberry cake from the oven. The kitchen was hot—she'd pushed open the window and propped open the door to get some cross breeze. She had an uneasy feeling in her stomach. The sheriff had been perfectly nice. He seemed like a kind older man, and he'd given her good news—Stephen Hope was in custody. But something felt off...

"It smells great."

She turned to see Conrad in the doorway.

"Once it cools it's really good with vanilla ice cream, or whipped cream on top," she said. "And the fresh strawberries, of course."

"Of course." He smiled.

"Conrad, are you allowed to lie to me?" she asked.

"What?" He came all the way into the kitchen. "What are you talking about?"

"I've been thinking about it," she said, turning toward him. "Are you allowed to tell me things that aren't true to further the case? I've heard about that—the police using lies to get someone to confess, that kind of thing."

"You aren't a suspect, Annabelle."

"Still. I just want to know… Can you lie to me, as a witness?"

"No," he replied. "We can't ask you to testify and lie to you about it. But we can…omit details that might need to stay on a need-to-know basis for your own protection, or for the furtherance of the case."

That was what she'd thought. "I have a feeling you're omitting a few."

Conrad was silent, and he pressed his lips together.

"I thought so," she said.

"Look, Annabelle, I can promise you that whatever I don't tell you is for your own good… if you're telling me everything."

And that was the problem, wasn't it? She wasn't telling him everything, either. She was holding back to protect herself.

"What's bothering you?" Conrad asked.

"Nothing."

"If you lay it out for me, maybe I can see what I *can* tell you to make you feel better," he said.

Annabelle took the apron off and hung it over a kitchen chair. "I'm scared I'll be implicated in this robbery."

"Because of your keys," he said.

"Yes."

"Okay…" He let out a slow breath. "I can assure you that lost keys aren't enough to implicate anyone."

But it wasn't just the keys. It was something about how the sheriff had talked to her. She couldn't put her finger on it, but she didn't feel like that man was fully behind her. They needed her testimony, but there had been no promises beyond that.

"Your priority is getting a bad man behind bars," she said. "And you need my testimony to do that. I get it. But it isn't always about who did it. Sometimes it's about who has a better lawyer. So trusting my future to the outcome of a criminal case—that scares me!"

"You're afraid he might not be found guilty," Conrad said.

"Yes." She let out a huff of breath. "And

I'm afraid he'll lie about me—get some revenge on me for having testified against him.
That's what I'm afraid of."

Conrad nodded.

"And you can't promise me he won't!" she
said. "You also can't promise me that you'll
side with me if he does."

"Me?" he asked. "Yes, I can. You're innocent, and I know it. I've seen people work up
some tears to lie before, and that wasn't you.
You were honestly freaked out, and I'm not a
guy who looks at evidence with blinders on.
I listen to my gut, so I can tell you straight—
I'll be on your side, Annabelle."

"Based on…" she said hesitantly.

"I know you," he said. "I know you better
than anyone else does on this case, and I've
seen you at the soup kitchen, and I've gotten to know you here. Look, I told you that
I needed to see you safe for my own peace
of mind, and I don't know if you realize just
how powerful that need is…

"I can understand how you might feel like
just a cog in a machine here—one small piece
of putting a very bad man behind bars. But
you're more than that…to me."

He was more than that to her, too, and lately
she'd started thinking about telling Conrad

about the text message she'd gotten from Stephen Hope. She'd been hiding it, because it would show that he knew her—there had been a personal connection. It would make her look guilty, and maybe Conrad would change his mind about how innocent she was. Did she want to risk that?

Conrad went to the freezer and grabbed a plastic bucket of ice cream, depositing it with a thunk on the counter. "What do you say we start on the cake?"

How could she refuse? There was something comforting about this big, rugged cop and his belief in her that he couldn't shake.

It was no guarantee, but it would be enough for today.

THAT EVENING, ANNABELLE went with Conrad and Wilder to the farmhouse next door. She wore a pair of jeans and a tee. It was all she'd brought. But she did use some tranquility spray she'd been gifted by the women at the sheriff's department that smelled of lavender and vanilla. It was nice to feel pretty for an evening, and she did notice that Conrad stepped a little closer to her as they headed toward the neighbors' house.

Wollie and Linda had set up a table and

the kitchen chairs underneath the shade of a spreading oak tree beside the garden. Jane was obviously freshly bathed, and she wore a little dress with a white apron tied in front in an exact replica of her grandmother's. Her hair was still wet from her bath, and tendrils were drying in the warm summer air around her face.

"How are you doing, Jane?" Annabelle asked.

"I'm good!" Jane said. "My *daet* says I can stay up late tonight because you're here to visit. Otherwise, I'd have to go to bed at seven thirty."

"That's a treat," Annabelle said with a smile.

"And my *daet* says I have to stay home and not go wandering around because sometimes *Englishers* are up to no good," she said.

"I, uh, I meant that there are some *Englishers* around these parts that are up to no good lately," Wollie interjected.

"It's okay," Conrad said with a chuckle. "We understand."

"My aunt is *English* now," Jane said. "She left before she got baptized, so she didn't get shunned. If she got baptized first, she'd be shunned. That's very bad. And very lonely. And you don't want to get shunned."

"No, that does sound bad," Annabelle said, and she glanced toward Linda, whose face was growing pink. She said something curt in Pennsylvania Dutch, and Jane clamped her mouth shut.

"Your sister jumped the fence?" Wilder said.

"That's what they call leaving the community," Conrad murmured in Annabelle's ear. "'Jumping the fence.'"

"My sister made bad choices for a long time," Wollie said. "She wouldn't live like a good Amish woman, and she left. She's missed out on...everything."

"Where did she go?" Annabelle asked.

Wollie shook his head. "I don't know."

"*Why* did she go?" Conrad asked quietly.

"Why does any young person jump the fence?" he asked. "She wanted freedom. She didn't want to be held to our rules."

"I hope she's okay," Annabelle said. Maybe she'd disappeared and was living a quiet, contented life somewhere. Maybe running away and starting over was an actual, realistic possibility...

"She's cut off from her family, her friends,

her roots—" Wollie shook his head again. "Our life here is about family. We don't forget our parents when they age. We get together often—cousins play together, and siblings stay connected and in each other's lives. My sister left all of that for a life away from us. Leaving doesn't change who she is or the family she came from. She's not okay, even if she thinks she is. She's making do."

"Can I get you some lemonade?" Linda asked with a little too much cheeriness in her tone.

Annabelle looked down to see Jane watching the adults intently, and Annabelle cast Linda an apologetic smile.

"Let me help you get that," Annabelle said.

"Oh, it's ready to go, but we can fill some cups," Linda said.

Annabelle followed Linda over to the table, and the older woman lowered her voice.

"Sue didn't just disappear…"

"No?" Annabelle asked.

"She's been in touch with me since she left, but I haven't told Wollie about it."

"Why not?" Annabelle whispered. "He seems really worried about her."

"He's also very traditional in his views," Linda replied. "He sees one path for Sue—

marriage and babies. And Sue...she never did like that sort of thing. She was very smart, and she loved math. She could have made a proper Amish life for herself, but it wouldn't have been anything Wollie approved of."

"Oh, I see," Annabelle said. "But you understood her."

"She's my daughter," Linda said. "I understand her better than anyone. But sometimes people need to have their freedom before they understand why the rules are there. Then they can appreciate a calm life. For young people, tranquility is boring. For those of us who have lived longer, it's a blessing."

"Do you think she'll come back?" Annabelle asked.

"I do hope so," Linda replied. "Because that little one—" she nodded in the direction of Jane, who was chewing some purloined bit of food very quickly "—is just like Sue was. She's just as smart, and energetic, and full of mischief. Just like her. And I'd rather we find a solution than have history repeat itself with Jane."

Was that a serious worry? Jane was a handful—that was clear—but she seemed to want to be good.

"She's a wonderful little girl," Annabelle said. "I think she's a lot of fun."

"The world can be a dangerous place for a lot of wonderful girls," Linda said softly. "I see that spark in you, too."

"Thank you?" Annabelle said hesitantly.

"It's a compliment," Linda said with a small smile. "But it's also a warning, my dear. Be careful."

"Of what?" Annabelle asked.

"I'm not even sure," Linda said thoughtfully. "I've just lived long enough to know that bright young women with ideas and energy can stumble into trouble if they aren't careful. And you seem…like someone who might have stumbled into trouble."

"I'm just visiting friends," Annabelle said feebly.

"Hmm." Linda nodded. "Two big, burly men, one of whom is a cop. Perhaps I'm wrong, but it feels like you might have come here for help."

Annabelle's breath caught, and for a couple of beats, Linda simply met her gaze. There was no demand, no judgment, just a friendly look.

"I can't really talk about that…"

"I suspected as much," Linda said and gave

her arm a squeeze. "You come by anytime you need it, okay? Sometimes we women need another kind of help—the kind that comes with friendship and a little understanding. I'm hoping my Sue realizes that sooner rather than later."

Annabelle felt tears mist her eyes, and she nodded quickly. "Thank you."

Was she really so obviously in trouble that the Amish neighbors could see it half an acre away?

"For the record," Linda said, casting her a smile, "if my Sue needed help, I hope she'd find someone as decent as your big deputy over there. The Westhouse men are good people."

And perhaps that was the vote of confidence that she needed. Because Annabelle was very much in trouble, and the only one who seemed to be in any position to help her was Conrad.

CHAPTER TEN

THE DINNER WAS DELICIOUS—fried chicken, corn on the cob, potato salad and a noodle casserole that Linda always made that Conrad couldn't get enough of. He enjoyed watching Annabelle chatting with Linda and playing with Jane, but as the sun sank lower, he knew the evening was drawing to a close. There were chores to do, and when Wollie cleared his throat and stood up, that was the sign that it was time to get back to work.

"Thank you for coming over," Linda said, folding her hands in front of her apron. "And take care of that young lady. None of us are quite so tough as we think."

Conrad smiled. "I intend to."

As they headed back toward the house, the evening brought a cool breeze.

"I'm so full," Wilder said. "I love Linda's cooking."

Conrad and Annabelle both murmured their agreement. There had been a lot of food, and

Linda had a way of sneaking a few scoops of noodle casserole or an extra piece of fried chicken onto a plate without a man noticing or feeling like he could decline. The only option was to eat it—which wasn't exactly a hardship.

"Do you ever have them over?" Annabelle asked.

"Sometimes," Conrad said. "They're more comfortable hosting, but we've had them over a few times."

"I think they don't like how Jane is drawn to the TV, or the microwave, or pretty much anything that plugs in," Wilder added. "We're a bad influence."

Conrad couldn't take her hand like he wanted to as they walked back toward their own land. Maybe it was good that his brother was here to put a stop to those impulses. Conrad had to cut this out...

"I'm going to go check the cow barn," Wilder said. "Are you able to do the horses tonight, or...?"

"Sure, I can do it," Conrad replied. "If you're not too tired to come along, Annabelle?"

He glanced over at her, and she met his gaze with a warm look.

"It's no problem for me," she said.

Wilder peeled off in the direction of the cow barn, and Conrad walked just a little closer to Annabelle now that his brother was gone.

"You're a good sport with all the work around here," he said.

"I actually like it," she said. "I could get used to this."

Could she? He pushed that back. There was no use thinking about what a future with her might look like. This wasn't personal—it couldn't be. This was a job, and even though his emotions were getting more and more tangled up with this woman, he knew that her safety depended on his clear thinking. He couldn't make the same mistake twice.

But he had to admit that he liked having a feminine touch around the place. A strawberry cake, the smell of feminine products steaming from the bathroom late in the evening when Annabelle went for her shower, and the extra person at the table who was a far sight easier on the eyes than Wilder was.

Annabelle made a good addition around here. He hadn't been expecting that. He'd assumed she'd be a fish out of water, and that they'd all be eager for her to get back to her regular life. He'd been hoping that seeing her safe would flush her out of his system.

So far, that wasn't working.

Sophie and her colt were out in the corral, and Conrad pulled open the stable door and held it for Annabelle to go inside with him. Sophie pranced uneasily at the center of the corral, and Conrad looked at her for a moment and then did a quick turn to scan the area.

"What's wrong?" Annabelle asked.

"The horse is skittish," he said.

It didn't necessarily mean anything more than there being a few coyotes around or a storm on the way, but all the same, he examined the property, looking for anything out of the ordinary. All was quiet—the sun sinking in the west, painting some far-off cumulus clouds in pink and orange. The birds were silent, though. And that was strange. He'd keep Annabelle close—he wasn't taking chances.

"The weather channel is calling for high winds tomorrow. She might just be sensing some changes in air pressure," Conrad said. "I'll get the stall ready first."

He grabbed a shovel from where it hung on the wall and sauntered toward the largest stall that housed the horse and her new foal at night. The other horses stayed in the field, but Conrad liked to give the new mother and her baby a little more time of being coddled. Besides, with these cattle rustlers about, a colt would be prize pickings, and he didn't want to risk it.

Annabelle followed him and leaned against a stall railing as he added some fresh hay and some grain as a treat to the feeder.

"Linda told me a little bit about her daughter, Sue," Annabelle said.

"What did she say?" Conrad asked. "Wollie's never said much—just that she'd left the community."

"She's a free spirit, apparently," Annabelle said. "But Linda has been in touch with her, so she isn't missing."

"Really?" Conrad shot her a surprised look.

"I guess Wollie is pretty conservative," she said.

Annabelle seemed to have gotten more information out of the neighbors in a few days than he and his brother managed in two years. Maybe it was just the female friendship that did that, but he suspected it was more. Annabelle was special, and it was a mild relief to know that he wasn't the only one to notice it.

"I don't think free spirits fit into the Amish

life too easily," Conrad said. "They've got a simple life, but there are a lot of rules to keep it that way."

"I thought you liked rules," she teased.

Conrad laughed out loud. "I do. I like them a lot. But I'd never be able to live an Amish life. I like my modern conveniences too much. But they make for some good neighbors."

"Hmm."

Conrad eyed her. "What about you? Could you live Amish?"

"It might be a good way to disappear," she said softly, but the joking was gone from her tone.

Conrad eyed her uncertainly. "Are you thinking about disappearing?"

"I mean, if I had to," she said, and she shook her head. "Sorry, maybe I shouldn't have said that out loud."

"You really are safe with me, Annabelle," he said. And he meant that in every way possible. "I'm not letting anyone at you—*anyone*."

That included the sheriff, he realized. He wasn't going to let her be a default suspect here. But he did believe in the system and he was convinced that there was a solution within those boundaries, even if it meant paying for a fancy lawyer. He wouldn't abandon her.

"You have a job to do," she said. "I get it."

"Hey." Conrad stepped closer to her, and he plucked a stray piece of straw from her hair. "You *are* my job, and my job has had my top priority for a decade. You being my job means you're safe." He swallowed. "But you're not *just* my job, okay? That's the way it's supposed to be, but I—" He shouldn't be saying this. "Never mind."

"Are we friends?" she asked, a hesitant look in her eyes.

Friend... It hardly encompassed the level of protective ferocity he felt toward her, but... "Yeah," he said. "We count as friends."

Annabelle smiled, but didn't say anything as he pulled open the stall door and headed over to the other side of the stable. He pulled the sliding door open for the horses.

"Come on, Sophie," he called.

The mare looked over at him, then put her ears back. What was with her?

"Come on, girl," he called. "It's just me." He shot Annabelle a warning look. "You might want to back up and get out of the way. She's out of sorts tonight."

Annabelle did as he asked and backed up to the other side of the stable. Conrad went and got some hay, holding it out invitingly.

"Come on, Sophie. Let's get you brushed down. You like that."

The horse came forward, took the hay from his hand and chewed in grinding circles as she clopped into the stable. Her colt stayed at her side. Conrad gave her a clear path to her stall, but when she started backing up again, he put a reassuring hand on her shoulder.

The horse startled and stepped sideways, a shoed hoof landing on his foot. The pain was instant and excruciating. He let out a huff of air and pushed Sophie hard to the side to get her off his foot.

"Inside," he said through gritted teeth, and Sophie finally did as she was told and went into the stall. Her foal followed her, and he limped over, pushing the gate shut. Then he closed his eyes against the pain.

"Conrad?" Annabelle seemed to materialize at his side, and he felt her hand slip under his arm.

"Ouch," he muttered. "That's going to leave a mark."

He tried to take a step, and he hissed in pain.

"Let's get you back to the house," Annabelle said. "Here, lean on me."

"No," he said.

She looked up at him. "I don't think you

have a choice, Conrad. I'm stronger than I look. Unless you can walk on it, I'm your option."

Conrad put his foot down, testing the pain. It hurt, and he wasn't going to be able to walk on it without icing it right away. He didn't need this. He was supposed to be her personal bodyguard, and he shouldn't be this easily incapacitated.

"All right," he said grudgingly. She was safer in the house anyway. He put an arm around her shoulders and did his best not to lean on her too much, but all the same, he felt her dipping under his weight.

He grabbed a stall rail to steady himself and hobbled toward the door with her help.

"Now, I'm going to get the house secured," he said through gritted teeth, "and I'm going to—"

"How, exactly?" she interrupted. "Conrad, *I'm* going to get you inside and get some ice on that foot. And then I'm calling your brother, and we just might be driving you to an emergency room if it looks broken."

"No," he said gruffly. "I'll have to call the sheriff and get you moved to a different safe house if I can't—"

"Oh, stop that." She staggered under his

weight as they made it to the house, and when he grabbed the porch rail, he let out a sigh of relief.

"Stop taking care of you?" he asked incredulously. "That's why I'm here!"

Heck, lately, it almost felt like this was why he'd been born. He wasn't going to stop now.

Annabelle shrugged. "Unless there is some evil genius out there who orchestrated a horse stepping on you in order to get at me, I think what we have here is a hurt foot, a bruised ego and an evening ahead of us where I'm the one giving the orders." She smiled sweetly. "Now, let's get you inside."

WITH HER ARM around his waist, Annabelle could feel the tightness of Conrad's muscle and the solidness of his build. He was a big man, and if he wasn't trying so hard not to lean on her, she'd easily collapse under the weight of him.

But she'd seen his face go white when the horse had connected with his foot, and her stomach was still roiling in sympathy with that pain. Every hobble would be incredibly painful, and she tried to support him as best she could. Right now, Conrad needed her, and while she knew he probably didn't like this turning of the tables, she was the one who could help him.

Once they got inside, Conrad used the walls and counters to steady himself until he sank into a kitchen chair. His face was white still, and he shut his eyes for a moment, then opened them.

"Let's see how bad it is," Annabelle said and knelt on the floor in front of him. She carefully rolled his sock off his foot. Even his feet were larger than the average man's, and she cradled his heel against her legs as she inspected the damage. There was a clear indentation where the horse's hoof had connected with the top of his foot, and a red bruise was already starting to spread. Conrad leaned in to get a better look. Then he lifted his foot off her lap.

"Yeah, I'll live," he muttered.

"You need ice," Annabelle said, and she pushed to her feet and headed to the freezer. She poked around until she came up with a bag of corn nibblets. It would have to do. She pulled another kitchen chair over, then lifted his leg up and put the plastic package directly onto his foot. He winced.

"Sorry," she murmured. "I hope it isn't broken."

"It isn't," he muttered.

"You sure?" She rose to her feet and leaned against the kitchen table.

"I know what broken feels like," he said. "This isn't it. It'll be a good bruise, though."

She'd take his word for it, but some ice and a couple of Advil would help.

"I hate this," Conrad said.

"Being at my mercy?" She shot him a teasing smile.

He managed a rueful smile in return. "I'm much more comfortable bossing everyone else around."

"Get used to being challenged, then." She laughed softly. "Under ordinary circumstances, I'm no pushover."

He took her hand, his warm fingers running over hers. "You're no pushover under these circumstances, either. Anyone else would have been a mess by now."

"I hide my mess well." She looked down at his fingers moving gently over hers. His hand was strong and rough, but his touch was gentle—his strength supporting her.

"You don't have to." His voice was deep, quiet.

Freaking out didn't change things, either. She needed to keep her head.

"Do you ever imagine what it would be like to slip into a different life?" she asked after a moment. "Like an Amish life, maybe... To just arrive in an Amish community suitably attired and introduce yourself as So-and-So Yoder, or something like that?"

"You don't speak the language," he said. "It would be tough to blend in with no Pennsylvania Dutch."

"There is that..."

He still held her hand, almost as if he'd forgotten what he was doing, except that his fingers hadn't stopped moving over hers. She liked the feeling. It was comforting and made her wish she could twine her fingers with his...

"I'd want to just move into a farmhouse," she said wistfully, "to live a simple life with a few dresses, some chores to do and simple, logical requirements... No internet, no news channels, no problems bigger than a farmyard. I'd raise chickens, and sell eggs...and knit socks."

"The Amish have problems, too," he said, humor touching his tone. "Think of Methuselah, the nasty rooster."

"I forgot about him." She smiled faintly. "I'd sell Methuselah and get a nicer rooster.

Problem solved…" She let her mind wander over that coveted, simple life. "I know they have problems, too, but they also have an old-fashioned way of doing things, and as a woman, I might be protected."

Her father would hate to hear her say that. He always had wanted her to be more competent than any guy she came across. It wasn't that she liked those gender roles, exactly, but at least they didn't have to shoulder all the burdens alone. There was a woman's domain, and a man's. And a woman didn't have to worry about anything beyond her own job to do. It was someone else's problem… She could let go. It was an inverted kind of freedom.

"You *are* protected." The movements of Conrad's fingers stopped, and she looked up to meet his gaze.

"My problems are a whole lot bigger than a farmyard, though," she whispered.

He didn't answer that, but his gaze did soften.

"What if you just melted into a simple ranching life, gave up police work," she pressed. "Focused on calving season and cattle drives, and put your feet up in the evening and listened to the wind? Don't you ever imagine it?"

"Yeah," he said. "I've imagined it."

"Let someone else catch the bad guys," she said, lifting her shoulders.

Let someone else testify against them and put them away in prison.

"Someone has to face it," Conrad said. "I'd rather it be me than someone who isn't prepared."

And that was where they were different. He was trained for this.

"So maybe I'm the only one who fantasizes about running away from it all and living on the money I can make from selling eggs and socks," she said with a sad smile.

"You aren't joking, are you?"

"Maybe about how I'd make my living," she replied. She didn't know how to knit or care for poultry.

Conrad eased his foot to the ground and pushed himself to stand. She put a hand against his broad, muscled chest to press him back down into the chair, but it didn't work. He was a powerful man, and she swallowed.

"You should really get your foot elevated—" she began.

"Come here." He hopped once to get his balance and wrapped his strong arms around her. She didn't expect the sudden tenderness, and she looked up at him.

"Come here…" he repeated, his voice low, deep and so tempting that her knees felt weak. She tentatively leaned her face against his shoulder, smelling the musky scent of him. He adjusted his arms around her, guiding her closer against him. She slipped her own arms around his waist and let out a shaky breath. It was nice…too nice. She could feel her heart melting in his embrace.

"You can knit socks and sell eggs," he said quietly. "I'll raise cattle and carve birdhouses. And we'll forget about electricity and the news and anything else, and we'll just watch the sun set and the garden grow."

"You'd have to start taking care of your garden first," she said softly.

He laughed, the sound reverberating through his chest. "Probably."

"Maybe I'd take over the garden," she said. "And I'd sell lettuce and cucumbers at a road-side stand."

"And your knitted socks?" he asked, a smile in his voice.

"And socks." She lifted her head, and Conrad looked down at her, their faces suddenly closer than she'd anticipated. He froze—

seeming to be equally surprised—but neither of them moved. She could feel the soft tickle of his breath against her lips.

"We should run away together," she whispered. "We'll learn Pennsylvania Dutch and get you some suspenders."

He chuckled. "Don't tempt me."

That deep voice sent a shiver up her spine. His lips hovered a breath away from hers, when she heard the sound of boots on the step.

She took a step back, and Conrad's hands dropped to his sides. Wilder had the most impeccable timing.

"You should elevate that foot," she said, then dropped her gaze.

The side door opened and Wilder came into the kitchen. He looked between them. Then his face colored.

"Sorry to interrupt," he murmured.

Annabelle ran her hands down her shirt, wondering just how obvious it was that she'd been in Conrad's arms. She felt her face heat.

"You aren't interrupting anything," Conrad said, sounding annoyed. "Sophie stepped on me. She was all skittish today. Annabelle's helping me ice my foot."

"Ah." Wilder's gaze moved to the corn

nibblets on the table, already growing warm from being outside the freezer. "The cows are skittish, too. They must feel that storm coming."

Annabelle let out a soft breath. Just a storm. And storms passed.

Wilder's boots clunked against the linoleum floor, and he hauled open the freezer. He rummaged around for a moment, then came out with an ice pack.

"Here." He handed it to Conrad with a smirk. "So you got stepped on by a horse, huh? Might want to leave the actual ranching to me."

"Shut up," Conrad said with a short laugh, accepting the ice pack and sitting back down on the kitchen chair. "I've never seen Sophie like that before."

"We might want to really batten things down for the storm, then," Wilder said.

The brothers met each other's gazes, and some wordless communication seemed to pass between them.

"Is anyone considering bringing Conrad to the hospital for an X-ray?" Annabelle asked.

Wilder bent down and looked at his brother's foot. "Nah."

"It might be broken," she said, voicing her earlier concern.

"It's not," both men said together, and Annabelle rolled her eyes.

"You two figure out your plans," Annabelle said. "I'm going to bed early. You might be used to all this outdoor work, but I'm not. I want sleep."

Conrad caught her eye, and his gaze was tender. "Thanks for the hand getting back inside."

There was something in his gaze that suggested he was thanking her for more than that. She didn't trust herself to answer, so she turned and left the room, the sound of Wilder's and Conrad's voices filtering down the hallway after her.

She wasn't really tired, but she needed some time to herself. Something was developing between her and Conrad that was yards past the bounds of friendship. As he'd pointed out, he was older than her, more jaded, and the man responsible for bringing her back to Wooster to testify. He was also the man she didn't trust enough to tell all her secrets to. He thought he could protect her, but he didn't know everything, did he? She needed to be careful.

But right now, all she could think about was

the way his gaze softened when he looked down into her eyes, and how much she'd wanted him to kiss her.

CHAPTER ELEVEN

CONRAD WINCED AS he put the ice pack back on his foot. He wiggled his toes just to make sure he could. No, his foot wasn't broken, but he could feel the swelling starting in earnest now, and he adjusted the ice pack.

"So what's going on there?" Wilder asked.

"What do you mean?" Conrad tried to tamp down the irritation.

Wilder didn't answer, but he did smile ruefully.

"She's younger than I am, under police protection and very likely being chased down by a killer's gang connections," Conrad said.

Wilder frowned. "She's a witness to that robbery in Wooster where the security guard was shot, isn't she?"

There weren't that many active cases in this area that would warrant the kind of protection he was providing for Annabelle. He'd said too much, but it was only a matter of time before his brother put together the pieces.

"She's a witness to something. I can't confirm what. But her life depends on no one knowing where she is."

"I know, I know," Wilder said, shaking his head. "You were very clear on that before. And I haven't said anything. The only ones who know about her are the Schmidts next door. Which brings us back to what's happening between you. I know you're protecting her, but there's a connection there."

"There shouldn't be," Conrad replied tersely.

"Should or shouldn't, there is," Wilder replied. "And I've been throwing available women at you for years, and I've never seen you really connect with any of them. Not since Terri."

"That was…a unique situation," Conrad said.

"That was deeply traumatizing," his brother replied. "And you've been scared to take a chance with a woman ever since."

"I've dated a few women," Conrad countered.

"Dated, but never really deeply connected with one."

His brother had a point. He hadn't dated a woman for longer than six months.

"It wasn't always so cut-and-dried," he replied. "For the most part, I wanted a more committed relationship than they did."

"Because you chose women who weren't ready to settle down yet," Wilder said. "I'm not exactly a relationship expert myself, but even I can see your pattern. You'd find a woman fresh out of a nasty divorce, or someone who just wasn't that into you. Every single time. And why? Because you're scared of the real thing."

Maybe he was. Conrad sighed. "My job comes with certain risks. If I have a family of my own, I have a weakness that criminals can target."

"So you're going to live alone?" Wilder asked. "Grow old with me? Because I'll get married again one of these days, and you'll be the third wheel. Guaranteed."

"Yeah, yeah," Conrad said.

"Other cops have families."

"I know." He nodded. "And I'll get there. But I need someone who gets it—understands me. You know how it is. Women at the gym, at the grocery store, even at work think I'm good-looking and like the muscle, but they don't even care to understand me on a deeper level. Terri was different that way. She did understand me—she was my partner!"

"But she wasn't meant to be," Wilder said. "Are you pining for her?"

"Far from it. I'm happy for her. She sent a Christmas card last year, and she and Will had another baby. A boy. She looks really happy, and Will is still absolutely smitten with her. She's got the life she deserves."

"Might be time for you to get the one you deserve, too," Wilder said.

"Not with a protected witness," Conrad said.

Wilder shrugged. "Whatever. I get how inappropriate it is, but she's not going to be a witness for much longer, is she?"

"No, she's not…" And it was only occurring to him now that Annabelle might not be so different from the other women after all. They were locked down together—forced proximity. She hadn't chosen this, and once she got back to her regular life, whatever connection was between them might just melt away.

"So what are you saying?" Conrad asked.

"I don't know." Wilder sighed. "Just don't discount something real if you can find it. You might be right, and Annabelle might be absolutely wrong for you, but I haven't seen you look at a woman like that in years. And I'm tired of being your old-age plan."

"You are *not* my old-age plan," Conrad chuckled.

Wilder grinned. "Good. Find a woman, get married and have some kids. Maybe you'll unwind a bit."

But he couldn't unwind now. Conrad pulled out his phone and pulled up the perimeter alarm app. He flicked through a few different screens. Everything looked fine, which was good considering the state his foot was in.

"I'll unwind once this case is over," Conrad said.

As much as he ever did. At least when Annabelle was safe, he'd be able to process this on horseback and go out in the fields, away from pressure and duty.

And yet even as he considered it, he was picturing the scene that Annabelle had painted for him—a little house with chickens outside, some cattle, and Annabelle at the heart of it all. For some reason, the only thing that soothed his jangling nerves was the thought of her there.

He would have kissed her if Wilder hadn't interrupted them. He knew it. Because Wilder was right—Annabelle was different for him.

He'd felt it when he saw her at the soup kitchen, and it was only magnified after the robbery. She was connected to his own peace of mind—and that was a very bad sign.

Annabelle was beautiful, sincere and deserved a life free from danger. And if that was going to happen, she might need to do exactly what Terri had, and get as far from him as she could once this was over. He might have to accept that the kind of woman who captured his heart deserved better than he could give. And the connection that he longed for—the kind he knew was possible, because he'd found it again in Annabelle—might not be in his future.

It was rare and precious...and right now, completely against the rules. Conrad was a cop to the bone.

"I'm going to watch some TV," Wilder said. "You coming?"

"In a bit."

Wilder grabbed an apple off the counter and headed out of the kitchen, leaving Conrad in solitude. He heard the sound of the shower starting in the bathroom where Annabelle would be getting ready for bed, and the TV turning on in the living room, where his brother was settling in.

He knew Annabelle was feeling something, too. That magnetic draw was mutual, but he needed to be the stronger of the two of them. She was caught up in something bigger than her, and he was the one assigned to guide her through it.

No matter how right his brother might be, Conrad's heart couldn't be part of the equation.

THE NEXT MORNING dawned overcast, and a warm, moist wind blew from the west, smelling of rain. Annabelle stood at the side door, watching as the wind whipped the treetops into a froth of leaves.

She'd had a fitful night's sleep. She dreamed of her parents in Wooster. In her dream, she was in her parents' living room, and she was asking for help. Her father's back was to her. He just kept shaking his head and saying, "I thought I warned you about this…" and he wouldn't turn around.

Dad? Dad! Look at me! I need help!

But he wouldn't turn.

She'd woken up with an unsettled, restless feeling not unlike that gusting wind outside. And despite the dream, she missed her parents with an ache deep inside her chest.

If she ran away from testifying, she certainly wouldn't ever sit in their kitchen again, or sit in a lawn chair in their backyard with one of her father's barbecued burgers on a paper plate in her lap. She wouldn't enjoy any more family gossip sessions with her mother curled up on the worn sofa in the living room... Wollie had said that his sister couldn't truly be happy disconnected from her family, and this morning she felt the truth in those words in a very personal way.

If she ran away from it all, she'd never erase her roots, but she would be destined to a life without the family, friends and hometown that she loved. Would it be a happy life? Or would it be, as Wollie put it, making do?

"Penny for your thoughts."

She turned to see Conrad at the kitchen doorway. He wore a pair of blue jeans and a blue plaid button-up shirt that was snug around his biceps. She had a feeling most store-bought shirts would be. He came into the kitchen limping.

"How is your foot feeling?" she asked.

"Better."

"Still looks sore to me," she said.

"Yeah, well, I can handle that," he replied.

"I iced it last night, and it made a big difference."

"I guess you were right—it's not broken," she said.

"What can I say?" He smiled faintly. "I know what broken feels like."

He knew what it felt like, but she didn't. She'd never experienced a broken bone. She was starting to think that a broken life felt like this—adrift, uncertain. Or did she have a broken spirit? That robbery had been the first thing to change her on a fundamental level, and she was still figuring out her new normal.

She felt her own smile slip. "My dad told me not to testify, you know."

"Did he?" He turned to face her.

"He and I don't really talk much anymore. It's tense between us, but he did tell me not to do this."

Conrad was silent.

"He made sure I knew how to take care of myself. That was his mantra—a woman needed to be able to take care of herself without leaning on a man."

"I think it's forgivable to lean on a cop." A smile turned up Conrad's lips.

"What are the chances I could call my parents?" she asked.

Conrad shook his head. "You can't."

"If anyone would keep my secrets, it's them."

"If you call your mom, she'll be scared, upset by what she can't control. She'll call someone close to her—an aunt, maybe?—and she'll swear that other person to secrecy. Then she'll do what every normal person does in times of stress—she'll share the burden."

Annabelle swallowed. Not everyone did that, did they? Would that apply to Theresa, too?

"I don't think she would," Annabelle said. "I'd tell her how important the secret is. But they'll be less worried if they hear from me."

"They can contact the sheriff's office at any point and check that you're still okay," he said. "I can even ask the sheriff to call them on your behalf, but, Annabelle, you can't put that burden of secrecy onto their shoulders."

Annabelle felt a wave of uncertainty. "Some people are able to keep secrets."

Conrad met her gaze, and he pressed his lips together in a thin line.

"I have people who truly care about me, Conrad. They wouldn't sacrifice my safety. They know exactly how much this matters."

Theresa had seen that guard shot, too. She knew. She just hadn't seen Stephen's face.

Conrad pushed a hand through his hair and shut his eyes for a moment. "Who did you tell?"

Annabelle swallowed.

Conrad opened his eyes and fixed her with a steely stare. "Annabelle, if you told someone where you are, I need to know who."

"Theresa Willard."

He nodded a couple of times. "Why?"

"Because I was letting people know I'd be away for a little while, and she was really worried! She thought I'd go into witness protection and completely disappear. She's my best friend, Conrad. I told her that I'd be tucked away on a ranch where no one would find me. That's it! That's all I said."

Conrad was silent, but she could see the snap of anger in those gray eyes.

"And I should add that since I'm still in one piece, and you haven't shot anyone yet, she obviously kept the secret, which proves that there are some people who can be trusted!" she continued.

"Obviously?" he demanded. "We had that trespasser the other day!"

"And no one else since!" she replied. "Who knows? Maybe it was connected to the cattle rustling!"

"If it was connected to that, they'd have gone to the stable and made off with the colt!" he shot back. "Or down to the barn, or better yet, to the herd in the fields. They would have been focused on stealing livestock and wouldn't have been anywhere near the house!"

Annabelle felt her chest constrict. "Who would Theresa tell?"

"Anyone!" he said. "Her boyfriend, her cousin, your coworkers who might be asking about you, the neighbor… When people are stressed, they *talk*, Annabelle. To anyone who will listen. It's why interrogations are so successful. There is something inside the human psyche that makes people want to unload their emotional burdens."

"I'd trust Theresa with my life," Annabelle said, her throat tight.

"Good, because you just might have!"

"You know what, Conrad?" A lump rose in her throat. "I'm a regular person! And we aren't just a bunch of sheep who wander around mildly confused and stupid! I have people in my life, and I trust them. What use is living without people? So yes, I chose to trust my best friend. And yes, I'd choose to trust my parents. They brought me into this world, and they'd literally lie down and die to protect me. So if you think I'm some sort of fool for trusting someone, you're wrong!"

"I didn't call you stupid," he said tersely.

"But you were thinking it," she shot back.

"I've seen more than you have," he countered. "I've seen people's own families betray them—not that I'm saying yours would do that. But bad things happen, and I'm here to stop them from happening to you."

"You've been to hell and back—I get it. And that brings some hard lessons. But I'm not so far behind you, Conrad. I'm going through more right now than most regular people can even imagine! And I'm on my feet still. I'm not cowering in a corner somewhere."

He put his mug down with a thunk.

"Have you changed your mind about having me around?" she demanded.

"No!" His voice reverberated through the kitchen, and he closed the distance between them in two limping strides where he towered above her. Her breath caught, looking up at him. "I haven't. You still make me feel things I don't want to feel! And I still care more than I should about what happens to you, which would make it a whole lot worse if those lowlifes out there got ahold of you!"

"They won't." She was well hidden, and Theresa wouldn't jeopardize her safety like that. If she couldn't trust her own best friend, who could she trust?

"You're right. No one is getting anywhere near you," he retorted. "But not because your friends are so trustworthy under high stress. It's because *I'm* still here." He headed toward the door and grabbed his hat off a peg on the wall. "Now, we've got a storm moving in. We've got to get the animals locked down. Wilder is heading out to the field to drive the cattle toward the shelter of the trees if they aren't already there. You and I have to make sure the cow barn and stable are locked up tight."

Annabelle blinked at him, and he winced as he plunged his hurt foot into a cowboy boot.

"Normally I'd give you a choice," he added, turning back toward her, his eyes ablaze with repressed anger. "But not this time. The livestock depend on us, and I need you with me or I can't guarantee your safety."

"I've cooperated with everything you've asked of me since I arrived," she said, her chest tight. She blinked back tears that threatened to rise, and she went over to where her borrowed boots stood next to his and stepped into them. "I've made one mistake. One."

"So you admit it was a mistake?" He looked down at her pointedly, and she wanted to fight, to argue, to turn this into a battle. But that would be stupid. No, she didn't think trusting her best friend was a mistake, but she wasn't going to say that now.

"Yes," she said. "It was a mistake."

Conrad nodded and adjusted his pistol holster on his belt. Without another word, he pushed open the screen door and stepped outside.

CHAPTER TWELVE

CONRAD'S FOOT WAS still plenty sore, but he could push through it. Of all the things that could injure him, to be stepped on by a horse had the least dignity. But right now, he was mulling over the fact that Annabelle had just lied to him. She'd just said that telling her best friend was a mistake, but he'd read the lie all over her face.

She'd lied…

The truth was, he couldn't fully blame Annabelle for having told her best friend where she'd be. Annabelle was a regular civilian. She faced life with little to no understanding of the dangers out there that people like him kept at bay. In fact, people like her were the very reason he worked so hard to maintain the peace— because she *deserved* a normal life. She'd now stepped outside of normal, and the learning curve was a steep one. But couldn't she see that she'd messed this up? It was pretty clear to him.

"Do you trust anyone?" Annabelle was at his elbow as he strode toward the barn.

"Of course," he retorted. "I trust my brother to keep his mouth shut about you being here. I trust my mother to keep the secret when I buy someone a birthday gift. I trust my colleagues with my life some days. We're human—we have to trust someone."

"I think I'll be okay," she said. "I do. I know it was a mistake, and I certainly won't repeat it, but I think I'll be fine."

Conrad turned, and a gust of wind blew Annabelle's hair in front of her face. She was so young, so unblemished. The sky had already darkened with gathering clouds, and he could see the smudge of rain in the distance. She pulled her hair away from her face, squinting at him.

"No, you don't think it was a mistake," he said.

"What are you talking about?"

"You don't think you messed up. You're just saying what will make me happy."

She was placating him like she had to protect herself, and he hated that.

She opened her mouth to answer but didn't say anything.

"And I don't like being lied to," he said.

"Disagree with me. Call me an idiot. Say what you mean, but don't lie to me."

"I was just…" She didn't finish, and she didn't have to.

"I'm not the threat here, Annabelle," he said. "I'm not going to hurt you. You don't have to lie and worry about my reaction." He felt the anger seep out of him, and he softened his tone. "This won't last forever. You'll come out the other end of this and go back to a regular life. But right now, you have to trust *me*. Okay? I have one job right now. That job is taking care of you."

Annabelle blinked, then nodded. "Okay."

He felt a bit better then, and he reached back, grabbing her hand. "We've got to get moving—that storm is coming fast."

He limped briskly across the scruffy grass, Annabelle jogging next to him. At least with her hand in his, he knew exactly where she was, and that was a powerful relief. His cell phone pinged, and he pulled it out to see that the perimeter alarm had been triggered. He turned, scanning the yard and the drive behind them.

"Someone there?" she asked.

He shook his head. "I don't see anything.

There's a lot of wind. It could be anything blowing past."

Still, her grip tightened on his. He looked down at her and saw that she was still scanning the yard behind. The alarm pinged again, but he couldn't see any movement—at least, nothing more than branches and blowing leaves.

"Come on," he said. "The alarm is an aid, not the whole solution. If you're with me, you're safe."

He led the way toward the barn, and Annabelle stayed close enough that he could feel the warmth of her side against his arm. The wind was gusting, and she ducked her head down, seeming to blindly follow him. He planted his free hand on top of his hat and plowed forward.

The barn door rattled in the wind, and when he pulled it open, it slammed against the side of the barn.

"Inside!" he said, and Annabelle plunged into the barn. He pulled the door shut after them and put the lock in place. They were both breathing hard, and he looked around the interior.

"I'm just going to make sure all the doors are secure," he said. "Just wait for me, okay?"

He paused and grimaced, letting his sore foot rest a moment.

"You're in pain," she said.

"I'll live. I just need a second."

She watched him, her wince mirroring his own.

"I'm fine," he said, smiling faintly. "It's a bruise."

This was a job he had to do himself. There were a few doors to the barn—a sliding door that opened out the back, the hay door six feet off the ground, and then the two sliding doors on either side of the loft above. Each needed to be properly secured or it might end up flying off and hurting someone. Or just being one more door to be replaced after the storm.

He worked quickly, locking doors down, dropping bars into place to keep them secure, and snapping down latches. The cow shuffled in the stall, and when Conrad stepped back down from the loft ladder, he saw Annabelle forking some hay into the cow's stall.

"That's perfect," he called. "A little extra food to get her through the storm is a good idea."

She had a knack for ranch work, he thought. It was empathy and work ethic that mattered most on a farm, and she had both in good supply.

"Come on," he called. "Let's go lock up the stable, and then we're done."

As Conrad pushed open the door, another gust of wind flattened her shirt against her, and he reached out and grabbed her hand.

"We want to beat the rain," he said, tugging her close against him.

Conrad dropped a two-by-four into the slots across the barn door, limiting the rattle that the wind could do. Then he ducked his head against the gusts before pushing back in the direction of the stable.

Conrad pointed to a gate that led to the nearby field where the horses grazed. They were all packed together, waiting to be let back into the corral, and ultimately the warmth and security of the stable beyond it.

"Hold this gate!" he called to Annabelle, and he swung it open. She hooked her arm around it and held on as the horses trotted through. Conrad moved ahead of the animals and heaved open the stable's sliding door. He beckoned Annabelle, and she pushed the gate shut and latched it, the wind tangling her hair. He waited for her to duck through the door before he went inside to get the other three horses into their stalls.

His phone pinged again—the perimeter alarm. He ignored it. There would be a whole lot of false alarms during a windstorm, and he didn't have time to bother with them.

"Thanks," he said. "I need to secure this door, and then we'll head out the front."

Annabelle didn't have much space to move, and he slid a hand along her waist as he hauled the door shut. He hadn't thought before he reached out and touched her—it had just felt natural between them now—but as the door slammed shut, cutting off that gusting wind, he found himself looking down into her up-turned face. Her hair was tangled, and she blinked up at him. For a moment, neither of them said anything.

"I'm sorry I told Theresa," Annabelle said. "I was lying. I didn't think it was a problem, but it probably is. You'd know more about this side of things than I do."

"It's okay." He swallowed. "At least I know."

Looking down into her face, he felt a surge of tenderness toward her. "I got mad because I got scared."

She didn't say anything, and when he leaned closer, she rose up onto her tiptoes and her lips pressed softly against his. It was all kinds of wrong, but all of his logical reasons to back off melted away in the pounding of his heart. He leaned over her, pulling her close as he took over the kiss. When he finally pulled back, her cheeks were flushed and her eyes glittered in the low light of the gathering storm.

"Just let me keep you in one piece," he said gruffly.

"Deal." She smiled, and he stepped back.

"I have to get these feeders filled," he said.

He shouldn't have kissed her, but technically, she'd kissed him. Not that that detail would matter to Sheriff McCann.

As Conrad filled the last of the feeders, Annabelle headed for the door and pushed it open.

"What's that sound?" she asked.

"What sound?" He didn't hear anything but the howling wind. The door flung against the side of the building with a bang.

"Conrad?" She sounded surprised.

"Yeah?"

He dropped the scoop back into the bag of grain. Annabelle disappeared outside. He limped across the stable to the door. He could see the flutter of her hair just around the side of the building, and he pulled the stable door

shut, pushing a dead bolt to keep it locked
from the outside.

"What is it?" he called, and Annabelle
emerged from around the side of the building, little Jane in her arms. The girl had a
smudge of dirt across one side of her face,
eyes red-rimmed from crying, and she clung
to Annabelle's neck with a fierce grip.

"Jane!" Conrad said. "What are you doing
out here?"

"Methuselah ran away!" Jane wailed. "I
came to find him!"

Jane trembled in Annabelle's arms, crying
with big hiccupy sobs. Annabelle had spotted
the girl crouched next to the stable, her eyes
squeezed shut. She wasn't very big, and the
strength of the wind seemed almost strong
enough to carry her away. She looked even
younger with her face all blotchy from crying, and her baby-soft hair tangled with some
twigs and leaves caught in the silky strands.

"He ran away!" Jane sobbed. "And I saw
him come this way, and he went right under
the fence, and I saw him!"

Annabelle turned in a full circle, scanning
for a runaway rooster, keeping Jane clasped in
her arms. She couldn't have put the girl down

if she tried, but all the same, she was keen to keep her close. The last thing they needed was a runaway child to join the rooster, and the strength of the wind was downright frightening.

Annabelle looked helplessly at Conrad, who stood there with one hand on top of his hat, his dark gaze drilling into them. Her own cheeks suddenly heated. She'd just kissed that man.

"Jane, we've got to get you home," Conrad said, the wind whipping his voice away as he spoke. "There's a storm coming. It isn't safe out here!"

"I have to find Methuselah!" the girl sobbed. "He's going to die in the storm if we don't find him, and then what will his hens do?"

"Let's get her home," Conrad said to Annabelle.

Without any warning, Jane suddenly loosened all of the muscles in her body and slipped out of Annabelle's grasp as easily as if she were Jell-O, then took off. Annabelle had to run to catch up with the girl and caught her by the arm.

"Jane, please!" she said.

"But Methuselah is here somewhere, Annie! Help me look for him!"

Conrad muttered something that was probably best not heard by little ears and looked at Annabelle.

"We have to get you home," Annabelle said firmly.

"But Methuselah!" the girl wailed.

She wasn't going to give in—that much was clear. But this child needed to be brought home...or brought inside somewhere. The clouds were boiling gray and almost greenish, and the daylight around them had sunk to almost twilight.

"Okay, okay!" Conrad said. "I'm going to look around the stable for him. He came this way?"

"Yes, he came over here! I saw him!"

"I'm going to look for him. Sometimes chickens will find a safe spot to wait out a storm. If I don't find him, we have to go home, though, okay?" Conrad said.

Jane nodded hurriedly. "Okay."

Conrad stomped off, ducking and peering this way and that as he went. Was it for show, or was he honestly going to search out that rooster? Annabelle wasn't sure, but Jane would need to be convinced they'd done all they could before they'd get her back home again. Annabelle scooped the girl up in her arms.

"He's a naughty rooster," Jane said into Annabelle's ear. "He's a terrible rooster. He's always bad. He should be punished for running away. No fresh grain for him. Not any!"

"You can't stop feeding him," Annabelle said with a low laugh. She started in the direction that Conrad had disappeared, and he suddenly emerged in front of her with a raggedy rooster held out in front of him. There were some bloody nicks on his wrists. The rooster's sharp clawed feet were bicycling in the air in front of them.

"You found him!" Jane exclaimed. "Oh, thank you!"

"Come on," Conrad said gruffly. "We're getting you home. Your family will be worried sick, Jane!"

As they headed across the field toward the Schmidt house, Annabelle heard Linda's voice faintly calling, "Jane! Jane!"

"Mammi!" Jane shouted back, and she wormed out of Annabelle's grasp again and dropped to the ground.

Wollie appeared around the side of the house, followed closely by Linda, who threw up her hands when she saw them. Wollie started toward them at a jog. The wind was stronger now, and Annabelle felt the first drops of rain hit her face.

When Wollie reached them, he gathered his daughter into his arms and smoothed a hand over her hair, pulling a twig out. He asked her something in Pennsylvania Dutch, and Jane answered him in a long stream of chatter that made Wollie shake his head.

"That stupid rooster!" he exclaimed. "He deserves a night out in the storm!"

"He might deserve it, but we found him now!" Jane said pleadingly.

Linda arrived then, and she looked at the rooster with a downturn of her lips.

"I am ready to put this rooster into the pot!" she declared. "He's more trouble than he's worth."

"No!" Jane said. "Not yet! He's got to take care of his hens. Cook a hen, *Mammi*."

Annabelle couldn't help but chuckle at the child's logic. Farm-raised children certainly did see the world in a different light. Conrad passed the rooster over to Linda, who grabbed him tightly in an expert grip that immobilized the bird.

"Thank you, Conrad," Linda said. "I have no idea what we'd do without you."

"Eat chicken soup, no doubt," Conrad said.

Linda rolled her eyes. "No doubt. But thank you for bringing our little girl back. Jane, that was very naughty of you to run away."

"I was chasing Methuselah. He's the naughty one!" Jane retorted.

Wollie gave Conrad and Annabelle a nod.

"Stay safe. You ready for the storm?" Wollie asked, raising his voice to be heard.

"We're ready," Conrad replied. "You?"

"We are now," Wollie replied, patting his daughter's leg. Annabelle noticed that he hadn't put his daughter down yet. Everyone would feel better once that child was safely indoors. "See you when the storm stops."

The rain was coming in bigger drops now, a proper downpour imminent. The Schmidt family started back in the direction of their house, and Conrad grabbed Annabelle's hand in his, tugging her comfortably in next to him. She didn't need any more encouragement to duck her head and jog along with him across the prickly grass. Would they have to talk about that kiss in the stable?

In the distance, thunder rumbled over the land, and she felt the tremble in her stomach. Annabelle shivered. The wind was no longer summer warm—it had a nip to it. Goose bumps rose on her arms.

"I'm glad you spotted her," Conrad said, leaning down to be heard. "I wouldn't have seen her. I can't imagine a little girl out in this storm."

"She's with her family now," Annabelle said. "But I know what you mean. That could have been bad."

Conrad tightened his grip on her hand, and she heard the faint beep from his phone. She recognized it now from the perimeter monitor.

"Is that thing going to beep all night?" she asked, leaning closer to be heard.

"Probably," he replied with a short laugh. "It's okay. Technology gets glitchy in thunderstorms. It's more of a fair-weather solution. I'll feel better once I've got you inside."

His arm felt warm against hers, and his body blocked some of the wind as they hurried toward the house. A flash of lightning lit the sky, followed three seconds later by a heart-stopping boom. The rain started in earnest then, a steady pelting drive of huge, warm drops.

Annabelle looked over her shoulder once, and she saw the soft golden glow of light coming from the Schmidt farmhouse. But then Conrad's hand tightened almost painfully on hers, and she whipped around to see a figure at their side door.

It wasn't Wilder—she knew that in a second. This was someone dressed in dark clothes, a hoodie pulled up over his head, and he seemed to be fiddling with the door.

Conrad released her hand and put his arm out to block her way. Then he pulled the gun from its holster and ran silently ahead of her toward the intruder.

The black-clad man turned and saw Conrad coming for him, then bolted toward the drive.

"Freeze!" Conrad barked, but the man only sprinted faster.

Conrad took off after him, and Annabelle shielded her eyes against the rain to see Conrad come to a stop at the edge of the drive. She heard the spin of tires as an unseen vehicle took off. Conrad stood in the rain for a few beats, then turned in a full circle. She crouched next to the steps, water dripping down her face and neck as Conrad moved around the property, his gun held in front of him. She saw something on the steps—a yellow manila envelope getting drenched in the rain. She crept forward and grabbed it.

"Okay—we're clear," Conrad said, coming up around the back of the house. "There are no broken windows, and he didn't get the door open. Let's get inside."

"Who was he?" she gasped. "Did you recognize him?"

"Don't know." Conrad put a protective hand on her back, and she could feel how she was shaking now as she hurried up the steps to get into the house. Conrad unlocked the door and followed her inside.

"Is it the same people from last time?" she asked as he slammed the door shut and flicked on some lights. She let the envelope drop onto the counter, and her teeth chattered.

"I'm thinking so—whoever they were, it was a pickup truck parked in the same spot as I saw the tire tracks last time." Conrad looked down at the sodden envelope. "What's this?"

"It was outside," she said.

Conrad opened the flap and pulled out some damp photos. There were five of them, all black-and-white, and printed on regular paper from someone's home printer. But the images were all familiar.

"That's my apartment building," she said. "And that's my neighbor Hilda. She takes care of Herman for me sometimes if I'm out of town." She flicked to the next picture. "That's the corner store by my place…"

Annabelle's fingers trembled as she pushed them aside. The last two photos made her blood run cold.

"That's my parents' house," she said, pushing a picture toward Conrad, and then she stopped at the last one. It was Herman, sitting on the windowsill in her apartment in his little faux-jewel-encrusted collar. The photo was taken from outside.

"Your cat?"

She nodded. "What is this…?"

"This is a threat," Conrad said. "I think we can now safely assume that the last trespasser was definitely after you, and not the cattle." He pulled out his cell phone and dialed.

For the next couple of minutes he talked with someone at the sheriff's department, giving a description of the vehicle, of the trespasser and of the pictures left in the envelope on the step. He went through the information with the cold detachment of a law officer, but instead of reassuring her, her stomach got heavier. When he hung up the phone, she rubbed her hands over her face.

"How did they know where to find me?" She could hear her voice shake, but she couldn't help it.

Conrad met her gaze easily enough when she looked up again, but he didn't answer her.

"Theresa wouldn't breathe a word!" she insisted.

"Did you tell anyone else where you were?" he asked.

She shook her head. "No one. I promise."

"Then we either have a leak in the force, my brother got chatty with someone or Theresa breathed a word." By the look on his face, she could see which one he suspected. Theresa would have had all sorts of people asking her questions, pestering her for details about the robbery and about where Annabelle disappeared to.

"It could have been the local rumor mill," Annabelle said. It was remotely possible.

Annabelle felt the tears rising inside her. It wasn't the Amish people, was it? She'd told Theresa, and in a moment of stress, Theresa had told someone else. Word was out. All it would have taken was one confidence shared...

"Oh, I'm so stupid," she said, trying to swallow back the tears.

Conrad put his arms around her and pulled her against him. His touch was confident, and comfortable, and he smoothed a hand down her wet hair, then leaned his cheek on the top of her head.

"Not stupid at all," he murmured. "You're normal. That's not a bad thing…"

But what was done was done. Word was out—and she wasn't safe here anymore.

CHAPTER THIRTEEN

THAT NIGHT, AS the trees thrashed and the wind howled around the house, Conrad sat on the couch and Annabelle curled up next to him with an afghan tossed over her legs. Wilder had gone to bed, but Conrad couldn't bring himself to put a hallway and two closed doors between himself and Annabelle. Not tonight. Not after someone had gotten in this close to them *again*.

The sheriff didn't want to move Annabelle right now. They were going to stick to the original plan with plainclothes officers around the area and see if they could catch the accomplices in another attempt. Except they hadn't caught him this time, and that was worrying...

And yet with all these very good things to occupy his mind, his thoughts kept slipping back to that kiss in the stable.

It had felt like a culmination of all the things he'd longed for in one soft kiss. He hadn't brought it up, because he didn't want to embarrass her. He also didn't have a right to ask for anything else. That kiss might be nothing more than a reaction to a strange and intense season of her life, and it might not mean anything at all, but he replayed it in his mind, all the same.

"At least they don't have my cat," Annabelle said. Conrad had called the sheriff and filled him in about the photos left on the doorstep. Sheriff McCann had contacted Annabelle's parents immediately and confirmed that they had the cat with them. So whatever that picture had meant, it wasn't to inform her about a kidnapped animal.

"They're trying to scare you," Conrad said.

"They're succeeding," she said. "They know where I live, where I buy milk at the corner store, the neighbor I talk to... Those are weird details to get right. And my parents—they know where they live."

"Your parents now have deputies stationed in front of their house," Conrad said. "They're safe."

"They're going to a lot of trouble to keep me quiet," she said.

"All the more reason to put him away for good," Conrad said.

"Unless he's got more up his sleeve," she

replied. "He's not working alone. Maybe he's got friends ready to exact revenge once he's behind bars."

"How do they know so much about you in this short amount of time?" Conrad asked.

"That's what I want to know..." She shivered. "You know, my dad wasn't wrong."

"Hmm?"

"I didn't speak to him for a full three years after he kicked me out at eighteen," she said softly. "I was furious with him. He said I was a legal adult and it was time to stand on my own two feet. And he wasn't wrong."

"I don't know about that," Conrad said. "If you weren't ready..."

"He wanted me to be self-sufficient," she said. "And while I might not have liked his methods, I did become self-sufficient."

Conrad looked down at her. "What are you getting at?"

"All this time, I've been looking to the police, to my friends, to my support network to help me during this whole episode. But there's a time to take things into your own hands, too. I have to take responsibility for how my life turns out," she said seriously. "And being the linchpin for this case is a big risk. If that man has ways to hurt people I love, or ways to ruin my life, I'm the one who suffers—not you. Not Sheriff McCann. Not the judge, or the jury, or my coworkers. Me. And if he implicates me, and I end up in trouble for something I never did…even if I didn't do jail time, I'd have a criminal record. I'd be an ex-con for life. Talk about ruining opportunities."

Conrad was silent.

"If it was you," she said, turning toward him, "would you do it? Would you take the chance and testify?"

"I'd have to think about it really carefully, I guess. But I'm a cop. So it would be different for me."

"Well, I'm thinking about this really carefully," she said quietly. "Because if I'm looking for the justice system, or even a particularly sweet cop, to make this go my way, then I'm just leaning on someone else, aren't I? And my dad did have a point about standing on my own two feet. They say if you want something done, you have to do it yourself."

"And sometimes, we have to work together to get a job done," he countered.

"But only one of us would pay with her freedom if this goes wrong," she said.

"A key isn't enough to incriminate you, Annabelle," he said.

She didn't answer. Was there more that she was holding back? The thing was, the whole department was banking on her being on the witness stand. She was their hope of getting a conviction, but this was more than a case. This was a woman's life… *Annabelle's* life.

"I might not testify," he said after a few beats of silence.

"What?" She looked up at him.

"If my own freedom were at stake, I might not testify," he said.

Lightning cracked across the sky, illuminating the room in a flash. There was a heart-stopping beat of silence and then the boom. Annabelle shifted closer to him, and he put a hand across her knees.

"If I decided not to, how would I go about it?" she asked.

"You're asking me to help you make an escape plan?" he asked.

"I am."

This was crossing a line. As a deputy, he was supposed to be protecting her for a reason— one that would put a criminal behind bars. He wasn't supposed to be helping her evade her duty.

"This could get me into trouble," he said.

"Who would I tell?" she asked softly. "All

you'd have to say was that I was lying. And they'd believe you over me."

"Yeah, but I wouldn't lie," he said.

"I'm not saying I'll use it," she said. "But if I needed to, what would be my best way to avoid testifying?"

"Well…" Conrad sucked in a breath. "You'd have to say you questioned your own memory and you couldn't swear to who you saw. That would make you an unreliable witness, but you'd still have Stephen Hope to worry about. And he'd be on the streets. Criminals who want to avoid incarceration don't tend to let witnesses off on a promise that they'll keep their mouths shut."

"So I'd have to run away," she said.

"Yes."

She leaned her head on his shoulder.

"And you'd need to pay with cash for a while. No credit or debit cards. Those are traceable. It's tough to live that way."

"Would I have to change my name?" she asked.

"You could," he said. "Annabelle, I hope you don't do it. It's a hard life, and if you just give us enough time, we'll get the evidence we need to put Stephen Hope and his accomplices away for good. But you have to trust us."

He adjusted his position so that he could put his arm around her. She felt good against him, warm and soft, and she smelled nice, too. He wanted to sit here and hold her, but every minute she was in his arms, his heart kept pulling toward her, and he knew this wasn't good for him. He shouldn't be letting himself long for her this way...

"Linda told me a story about a man named Dirk Willems that the Amish people idealize," she said quietly. "Do you know the story?"

He shook his head.

"He was in jail for his beliefs, and he managed to escape. A soldier followed him and fell into a frozen lake. Dirk Willems went back to fish him out and saved his life. He ended up being recaptured because of it and put to death."

Conrad frowned. "Dark."

"Yes. Very. The point is, he believed in something so strongly, he was willing to risk his life. That sacrifice has been remembered, and honored, for hundreds of years."

"But?" he asked softly.

"I think Stephen Hope deserves jail. I think he's a monster. I want to see him pay for what he did. But I'm not willing to risk my life or the people I love for that. It means I can't see myself as any kind of modern-day heroine, risking it all for truth and honor. But that's how I feel. I only have one life to live, and I won't waste it on him."

"I wouldn't ask you to," he said quietly.

"They've found me out here, and they're trying to shut me up. How far will they go? I don't want to find out."

"I won't let them touch you."

"I do believe that." She smiled faintly. "But my bigger worry is that they'll try to silence me by implicating me."

He saw her worries, and they were legitimate. "I'll make you a promise. If I see things turning in a direction that will implicate you in the case, I'll warn you."

"You'd get fired for that," she said.

"Yeah, I would."

"Are you willing to risk your career for me?" Annabelle looked up at him.

"I'm not willing to risk your life, either."

She put her head back on his shoulder, and for another couple of minutes, they sat in silence. The rain lashed the windows, and lightning flashed, illuminating the room.

"Do you want to turn in?" Conrad asked. "I'll stay out here and keep an eye on things."

He felt her shake her head. "Do you mind if we just sit a little longer?"

It was a strange kind of torture sitting with her in his arms this way—knowing that whatever he was feeling now would hurt just as much when it was all over. And when it was over...would *he* have sacrificed everything that gave his life meaning to protect her?

Though he was sure they would get the evidence they needed, he'd be watching closely to see that the case didn't take any unlikely turns.

He tightened his grip on her. Let her feel safe. He'd untangle his own emotional turmoil later, when he was alone once more.

BY MORNING, THE storm had passed. Conrad heard his brother get up—the creak of the floorboards, the bathroom door closing. Outside, the sky was lighter, but the sun still hadn't crested the horizon.

Throughout the night, they'd adjusted their position so that Annabelle was lying on the couch, her head resting on his leg, and he'd put his head back. It hadn't been a deep or restful sleep, but it had felt too nice to be this close to her, and he hadn't wanted to wake her up.

Let her rest...

He carefully moved, easing off the couch

and settling her so that she could continue sleeping. She nearly woke—inhaling deeply and then resettling as he lowered her head so that she could lie flat.

Conrad stretched his back, then walked over to the window and looked outside.

There were a few fallen branches from the trees, a scattering of debris from the wind and lashing rain the night before, and a glittering expanse of dew covering the grass in the soft light of dawn. The first couple of sunrays glittered through the trees, and he noticed a gray pickup truck driving slowly past on the road in front of the property. That was an unmarked sheriff's department vehicle, and he felt better seeing it.

He'd need to go out there and reset the proximity alarms after the windstorm. He glanced down at his phone. There was a new message from his boss.

Four units patrolling. Two more in position.

They'd increased police presence, and he felt his blood pressure lower. Annabelle would come out of this safely—and she'd have more than just him making sure of it.

But would she testify? That was the question. *Should* she testify?

Wilder's footsteps padded down the hallway, and Conrad headed toward the kitchen to intercept him.

"Morning," Wilder said.

Conrad put a finger to his lips. "She's sleeping on the couch."

"Oh…right," his brother whispered. "I didn't sleep well. Every sound woke me up."

"Me, too," Conrad replied. "I'm going to head out and reset those perimeter alarms. If I can even find them again after that storm. Would you mind just staying in the house with her for a few minutes?"

"Sure." Wilder headed for the coffee maker. "I'm not going anywhere before coffee anyway."

Conrad glanced over his shoulder into the living room, where he could see Annabelle's legs under the afghan. She was asleep, and he felt a tug of tenderness toward her that he tried to tamp down.

He had to focus on his job, because his emotions were only going to get him into trouble.

CONRAD RESET THE ALARMS—several of which had been dislodged during the storm. He spotted another unmarked vehicle far down the road, and he got a call from his boss.

"Just sit tight," the sheriff said. "If we can draw them out, we're in a better position to prosecute. They're serious about intimidating our witness. With you there, I'm not worried about her safety, but I'm betting they'll make another attempt at contact."

"If his accomplices don't have criminal records, they might not have a lot of experience in breaking and entering, either," Conrad said. "They've had some beginner's luck, but I'm counting on them messing up one of these days."

"Unless we can get Hope to give them up," the sheriff said.

"Yeah, I'm not holding my breath there," Conrad said with a short laugh.

"Okay, well, just hang tight. Watch for anything suspicious, and we'll keep an eye out here," his boss replied. "You need anything?"

"I'm good."

"Okay. Take care."

This sitting-duck routine was making Conrad jittery. He'd rather chase someone down and pummel them himself than sit here and wait, but this was the job, and it wasn't only about protecting their witness, but also making a watertight case that would put Stephen Hope and his accomplices behind bars for a good long time. Annabelle's safety relied upon that, too.

By the time he got back inside, Annabelle was awake, and the sounds of a shower came from down the hallway. Wilder headed out, and Conrad pulled some ingredients from the cupboard to start breakfast for when his brother returned from chores.

Conrad had some potatoes frying by the time Annabelle came into the kitchen, her hair wet. She was dressed in a pair of jeans and a fresh T-shirt, her feet bare.

"I saw you putting those motion sensors back up," she said.

"Yep, we're secure again," he replied. "And we've got a bunch of plainclothes officers in the area."

"Hmm." She nodded, her gaze moving toward the window.

"You need to eat," he said.

"You sound like a grandmother." She smiled and headed for the fridge.

"I sound like a reasonable person," he said with a laugh. "How do you like your eggs?"

"Over easy." She pulled some orange juice from the fridge.

"Coming right up."

He was getting used to her being here…
More than used to it—he was enjoying it.
Her presence around this house softened the
entire place. She made mornings just a bit
brighter, and she gave him something to look
forward to in his day…even when having her
here messed with his routine.

The side door opened just as he was cracking an egg into the pan.

"You're back," Conrad said without turning. "How do you want your eggs?"

"Scrambled," his brother replied. "I just
talked to Wollie."

"Yeah?" He glanced at his brother, who had
pulled his hat from his head and tossed it onto
a peg. "How'd they fare through the storm?"

"They had another calf stolen."

"What?" Conrad turned in surprise. "During that storm they came for cattle?"

"It's smart, you have to admit," Wilder said.
"No one was out there."

"How are our cattle?" Conrad asked.

"All accounted for."

So they were still targeting the Amish
herds.

"I thought Wollie had his cattle under a
shelter," Conrad said.

"There are wheel tracks across the field."

"They're getting bold." Conrad met his brother's steely gaze. "Obnoxiously so."

"Yep, that's what I said." Wilder sank down into a kitchen chair. "What do you want to do about it?"

He was feeling things slipping out of his control these days, and this was a chance to get his hands on some bad guys and resolve an issue.

"I want to lure those cretins onto our property," Conrad said. He nudged the spatula under the cooking egg, then flipped it. "And then I want to arrest them."

"Like, put a couple of calves near the fence and wait?" Wilder asked.

"Pretty much. I have a feeling they'd find some unattended calves close to the property line hard to drive past. What do you say?"

"Let's do it tomorrow night," Wilder said.

Annabelle stood by the table, silent. Her blue gaze moved between Conrad and Wilder, and she tucked her hands into her jeans pockets.

"What do you say?" Conrad asked her. "You up for a good old-fashioned stakeout?"

A smile touched her lips. "Sure."

"It'll be late and on horseback," Conrad

said. "You are allowed to say no. This can wait."

"No, it can't," she said. "I'll be fine. Let's do it."

She caught his gaze and a smile twitched at the corners of her lips. That little mischievous smile of hers had a way of turning his heart inside out. A midnight stakeout was one more thing that would be just a bit sweeter because Annabelle was a part of it.

THE NEXT DAY, Annabelle did a little weeding in the overgrown garden. It was something to keep her hands busy and mind distracted, because it was hard not to think about those photographs. They were an obvious threat, and the one who dropped them off had gone to some personal risk to do it.

She should take warning, shouldn't she? But something was holding her back from bolting. Conrad seemed so certain they could find the evidence they needed, and if they could, Annabelle would get her life back. She didn't want to be on the run. If she had a chance of going back to her regular existence, she wanted to do it. She was trusting Conrad more than she had planned on—both to keep her physically protected and to prove her innocence. Was that too much to put onto one man's shoulders?

The storm hadn't damaged any of the plants. In fact, the downpour had given the garden some new growth—mostly in weeds. Little Jane came over to help weed, and Linda waved, showing she'd given her permission. They pulled weeds and dropped them into old ice cream pails, clearing black, moist earth from around some sprawling pea plants and green beans that seemed to have been neglected for the summer but were still sprouting fruit. An extra couple of ice cream pails were used to collect the harvest of edible green beans and peas that hadn't gone to seed already. Jane seemed particularly good at separating them.

"That's too tough," she said, holding up a huge green bean. "You boil it, and you'll chew it for a week."

Annabelle chuckled. "You're probably right."

"Even *Mammi* wouldn't make me eat it," she went on. "But the cows will eat them."

"Will they?" Annabelle asked.

"Oh, *yah*. They like it. You could give them to the mama cow that lost her baby. *Daet* says that the orphaned calf is making her feel happy again."

The day slipped by with the chattering little girl at her side. They even visited the cow and calf in the barn, and the "baby horse" in the corral with Sophie. She brought some of those tough, overgrown green beans and pea pods for the cow, who gobbled them up like candy. The calf, who'd grown fond of human contact, came to Jane for head scratches.

Conrad seemed antsy, though, unable to settle down and just enjoy a lazy, hot afternoon. Although Jane's presence and the farmwork had helped settle her own mind, she understood. His mind was on other things, and when she'd catch his eyes questioningly, he'd smooth his feelings back behind a professional reserve again.

"You're thinking about cattle rustlers, aren't you?" she asked as they walked back toward the house after Jane had gone home.

"Hard not to," Conrad replied. "They're getting too bold. We have to get them now before they start robbing houses."

"So the sheepdog never does get a vacation?" she asked.

"Theoretically, I do. But you can't turn it off. Even if you go lie on a beach somewhere, you're noticing potential pickpockets and scams aimed at tourists." He shot her a wry smile. "I'm not much fun."

"I think I could loosen you up." She laughed softly. "You know, given time."

She hadn't meant it to sound quite so flirtatious... She felt her face heat.

"You like a challenge, do you?" He nudged her arm and then caught her fingers in his. She leaned into his arm, and he slowed his pace. It was wildly inappropriate—she wasn't deluding herself here—but it felt wonderful to hold his hand and feel his strength. Walking together in the afternoon sun, she wished that they could slow time down and never think about court cases or the future.

"Are you getting hungry?" he asked.

"A little bit."

"I'll start cooking," he said.

And for a little while, she'd pretend that the outside world didn't exist, and that the biggest problems they had were some cattle rustlers and some green beans gone to seed.

THAT EVENING, AFTER they'd all had a meal of fried chicken, biscuits and gravy, Conrad and Wilder saddled the horses. Silvery moonlight washed over the rolling fields, and a cool breeze brought up goose bumps on Annabelle's arms. She could feel fall in the air—a chilly hint of colder days to come.

"Here." Conrad handed her a jacket—too big, but it would do the job. "You'll need that later."

"Thanks." She laid it over the pommel in front of her.

"Now, we're going to ride out to the west pasture," Conrad said. "There are some good blind spots where we can hide and let the horses graze while we keep an eye on the road."

"And what do we do if the rustlers take the bait?" she asked.

"*We* don't do anything," he replied with a small smile. "You sit tight, and I'll take care of the rest."

"Right." She rolled her eyes, but she wouldn't argue. He was the professional here, and she was only along for the ride...and possibly for the coffee in Conrad's thermos.

The Schmidt house across the way glowed with kerosene light. Annabelle could see Wollie Schmidt walk in front of the window, his little girl in his arms. He was bouncing her, and while Annabelle couldn't hear, she could feel the laughter from that house. Wollie was a good father, and there was something so simple and appealing about a dad playing with his little girl. Unlike Annabelle, Jane wouldn't be expected to do it all herself. Jane was being raised to do the exact opposite—to get married and have kids, and to let her husband take care of the man's work. It was a different way of life...one that had its appeal considering the stress could be cut in half. But it also included trusting a man to keep doing his job, and to never let her down. Therein lay the problem.

"Let's head out," Conrad said, and he and Wilder heeled their horses into motion. Mona followed without any prodding necessary from Annabelle.

The horses' hooves plodded in a comfortable rhythm through the grass, and Annabelle let her back relax into the rolling motion. Conrad rode ahead of her, and he glanced over his shoulder, catching her eye and then turning forward again.

They followed the fence line, before heading west, away from the Schmidt cattle. Her horse followed Conrad and Wilder ahead of them, keeping a perfect pace, allowing Annabelle to look around. The trill of frogs suggested that some ground farther down the hill was marshy, but she couldn't see a difference from here.

She half listened to the brothers' conversation as they rode ahead of her. There was talk about the next calving season, some stud bulls that Wilder seemed to think were overpriced for their services, about a new tick medication and the fact that they were running low on baling twine. She let her attention roam, looking over the ribbon of road ahead that was illuminated by moonlight, an Amish buggy moving slowly along it. She could tell because of the bouncing, battery-operated headlights on the buggy. Farther beyond the road, she saw the flutter of laundry on a clothesline, glowing in the moonlight. Had something happened in that home to disrupt the routines, causing someone to leave the laundry out? Missing cattle, perhaps?

Conrad slowed his horse and eased in next to Annabelle.

"My brother is going on ahead to drive some cows with calves down closer to the fence. He's the natural cowboy around here."

"What if they actually get a calf?" she asked.

"They won't." Conrad cast her a half smile.

"You're pretty confident," she said.

"I am, and for good reason. We're prepared, and there's no way anyone is running off with a calf faster than I can respond. Besides, the sheriff's department knows what we're doing tonight, and they're patrolling other roads to give us our space and push the rustlers onto this stretch. We're corralling them to where we want them to go, and giving them some nice tempting, easily snatchable calves. When I call, we'll have backup."

"Very organized."

"That's the way I like it."

Wilder turned in his saddle. "He was the kid who had his baseball cards alphabetized."

"Seriously?" Annabelle chuckled.

"Hey, I could pull out any card I owned in a split second. My brother had a lake of them spread across his bed and was continually losing them. You tell me who had a better system."

"You had an adult system," Wilder retorted. "And you were ten."

Conrad shrugged. "I was an early bloomer."

"Imagine him now," Wilder said with a laugh.

Conrad chuckled and shook his head. "I'm organized where it counts."

"Like his sock drawer," Wilder joked, and

he ducked his head as Conrad threw something at him. "Okay, I'm going ahead. You two come up behind to block off easy exits."

Wilder heeled his horse into motion and trotted off. Annabelle stood in her stirrups to get a better look at the cattle over the crest of the next hill, dotting the landscape.

Still, her mind came back to Conrad's attention to detail. The longer she stayed on the ranch, the easier she could be caught if this case changed course... And the very characteristics that made Conrad a reliable sheepdog would also make him a reliable bloodhound if she ran.

"Are you really that organized?" Annabelle asked, trying to sound casual.

"Not really," Conrad replied. "I am when it comes to work. But work takes up about ninety-five percent of my life, so it's an easy mistake to make."

Conrad led the way to a copse of trees. There was a picket line already set up there— a stretch of rope for the horses to be tethered to while they grazed. Conrad swung to the ground and tethered his horse. Annabelle's legs were a little stiff from the long ride, and she was grateful when she felt Conrad's warm hands against her hips, catching her on her way down.

"Thanks…" she breathed.

They were alone, behind the horses, and while she could hear Wilder a couple of yards away, there was a feeling of privacy here. Conrad's gaze caught hers, and for a moment, they just looked at each other.

"You brought coffee, right?" Wilder said quietly.

Conrad touched her chin with the pad of his thumb, then stepped away from her, out of the horse's shadow.

"Yeah, I've got it in my saddlebag."

"Those shrubs over there are probably our best spot," Wilder said, his voice still low.

"I agree. It's a good line of sight…"

Annabelle looked around at the rolling hills, the scattered cattle lying down or standing with drooping heads as they slept. Conrad and Wilder were turned away from her, and she realized that if she wanted to get away from here, escape her duty to testify and simply disappear for a year or two, then this would be exactly the way to do it.

Amish country was a wild place—populated by simple people. If there was anywhere she could get a new name, work for cash and disappear into the countryside, Amish country was the place to do it. It didn't have to be here in Ohio. She could head out to Pennsylvania or Indiana. An Amish dress and *kapp* might be just what she needed to blend in on a country road, and her gaze moved down to the fluttering clothesline again.

But then she looked back at Conrad and felt a heartrending tug toward him. He was trusting her. He hadn't kept her locked up inside. And there was an undeniable connection between them that would make disappearing hurt that much more—for both her and Conrad.

She wouldn't run tonight. Her heart wouldn't let her. That was all she could decide upon right now.

CHAPTER FOURTEEN

CONRAD TOSSED SOME hunting cushions by the wild raspberry brambles, and they settled onto the ground. On one side of him, Wilder opened up the thermos of coffee, and on the other, Annabelle was looking thoughtfully down the incline toward the road and the Amish house beyond where some laundry was fluttering on a clothesline.

If his brother weren't here, he'd ask her what she was thinking about so hard. Instead of saying anything, he touched her knee. Annabelle's gaze flickered toward him.

"Coffee?" Wilder said, passing a tin cup over. Annabelle accepted it and took a sip.

Wilder poured the next cup for Conrad and then filled the thermos lid for himself. For a moment, they all sat in silence in the coffee-scented air. Conrad drained his cup, set it aside and leaned forward to get a better view of the land.

One of the cows had lain down beside the

fence, her calf almost disappearing into the grass next to her. The other calf had taken the opportunity to drink milk in the silvery moonlight. The house across the road extinguished the light in an upstairs window, just as Conrad's phone blipped with an income text. He pulled it out of his pocket.

Black Ford F-250 pickup truck with cattle trailer coming southbound down RR365.

"We've got a possible suspect coming this way," Conrad said.

He could hear the country music playing before he saw the vehicle. It came slowly down the road, headlights slicing into the darkness. It didn't slow down, but the cattle trailer was very much like the one Conrad recognized from the other night. Still, his pulse sped up in anticipation. But it didn't stop, disappearing into the night.

"I thought that was it," Wilder said quietly.

"I guess not," Conrad murmured.

Conrad settled into surveillance. He was used to this—the long hours, the boredom. As the next hour passed, Annabelle put her head down and closed her eyes. Wilder, on the other hand, picked up a piece of wood and pulled out his knife to whittle.

Conrad's phone blipped again.

Same vehicle. Second pass.

And sure enough, that same black pickup truck came into view coming back from the other direction, carrying the same trailer behind it. If it was just a local farmer, why pass this way twice at this time of night?

This time, the music was turned off, and the truck pulled to a stop at the side of the road and the headlights blinked out, leaving them in darkness.

He put his hand over Annabelle's and she startled awake. He pointed to the truck. "No one moves but me," Conrad whispered. "You two stay here. If they're armed, I don't want either of you getting shot."

"Solid point," Wilder muttered.

Suspect stopped. Going closer for better surveillance, he typed.

He eased away from the shrubs and slipped back to the tree line to make his way down toward the road. The cab light came on in the truck, and he saw a woman in the passenger side. The man hopped out and circled around the front of the vehicle. The woman got out and went to the back, opened the door and pulled out the ramp.

"Bingo…" he murmured to himself. But he had no proof until they touched a calf.

The man hopped over the ditch and headed for the barbed-wire fence. He pulled out wire cutters and went to work, the wires curling back in a coil as he snipped them. Conrad felt a rise of anger.

It was so casual—just cutting a fence and walking in.

The woman carried a plank of wood and dropped it over the ditch with a thud. The last wire snapped and coiled back with a springing sound that carried all the way over to Conrad. Then he stepped through the gap and headed for the closest calf.

The cow roused then and gave a moo. The man stopped, put a hand out. She mooed again and stepped forward. The man pulled out a cattle prod and jabbed it at her. She stumbled back, stunned, and the man bent down to pick up the calf, still warily watching the cow.

Send backup was all Conrad needed to text.

"Get in here!" the man barked. "I need help. This is a big one."

The woman came into the field behind him, and she squatted, trying to help him gather up the calf. Conrad took two quick pictures, pocketed his phone and then pulled out his gun.

The man and woman were both quite focused on the calf and the cow, who was coming back to protect her baby, and they didn't see Conrad running silently toward them through the shadows—still favoring that one sore foot—until the woman looked up, dropped the calf and started stumbling backward.

"Freeze!" Conrad barked. "Wayne County Sheriff's Department."

The command had the opposite effect, and they both sprang apart and started to run. Conrad had no intention of shooting his suspects. All he needed was to take out a couple of tires on that truck. He aimed, let all the tension seep out of him and then squeezed the trigger. There was the bang of the gun and then a hiss as the front tire flattened. He aimed again just as the woman jumped into the passenger seat of the truck, and took out the back tire. The entire vehicle lurched to the side, and Conrad hurtled forward. The man started to drive, but the truck kept pulling dangerously to the side, and he finally hit the brakes and put his hands in the air.

"Get out of the vehicle!" Conrad ordered, jogging up to the driver's side. He was glad to be able to stop running, as his foot was still sore. "You're under arrest."

The man didn't move, so Conrad opened the driver's door and grabbed one of his raised hands by the wrist. He twisted hard and pulled the man out.

The woman sat frozen in her seat, staring at him. Conrad could almost see the wheels turning in her head. What was *her* game plan here?

Conrad grabbed the keys out of the ignition, and when the man took a step forward as if to try to escape, Conrad caught his boot behind the man's ankle and tripped him flat on his face.

"I meant it," Conrad growled. "You're under arrest. You have the right to remain silent. Anything you say and do can be used against you in a court of law. You have the right to an attorney…"

When the man was cuffed, Conrad stood up, hoisting him to his feet at the same time. The sirens of approaching squad cars were already whooping in their direction.

"Ma'am, I need you to step out of the vehicle," Conrad said.

The woman sucked in a breath. "I don't know what's happening. I just came out for a ride with my boyfriend."

Right. And that was why she was preparing the back of the trailer for the calf. But she'd obviously decided on her next step here, and she wasn't going down with her man.

"Step out of the vehicle," he repeated.

"I'm not a part of this," she told him. "I haven't done anything. Tell him, Rueben. Tell him I don't know what's going on."

"That true?" Conrad was honestly curious about what the man would say. Would he protect his woman?

"No, it's not true!" Rueben snapped. "Out for a drive? This was her idea!"

There it was... The honorable gentleman was throwing her right under the bus, as Conrad had expected. When he looked over his shoulder at the Amish house across the road, he saw an entire family of husband, wife and six children all standing on the porch in their nightclothes watching them.

At least with Amish families, you wouldn't find YouTube videos of yourself arresting someone later on.

The squad cars arrived then, and two uni-
formed deputies got out. One took the man
into custody. Conrad circled the vehicle and
opened the passenger door.

"Let's go," he said, and she sighed and got
out. She turned teary eyes up at him.

"This isn't fair. I'm not involved," she
pleaded.

"You opened the trailer. You brought a
board to cross the ditch. You helped your accomplice to pick up the calf." He raised his
eyebrows. "Any of that familiar?"

The teary look evaporated and she pressed
her lips together. "I want an attorney."

"Great," Conrad said. "There's plenty of
time for that, too."

He passed the woman into the other deputy's
hands, and he watched as they were loaded up
into two separate squad cars. He accepted a
clipboard with some forms to fill out from his
colleague, and checked his watch for the time
before he started to fill out the arresting information and the details of what he saw while
they were fresh.

For a few minutes, Conrad took care of the
arrests, gave the other officers an update, and
when all the patrol vehicles but one pulled
away, leaving them in silence again, Conrad

nodded to Annabelle and Wilder that they could come down.

"So this is it?" Annabelle asked quietly. "These are our cattle rustlers?"

"Seems like it," Conrad said. "Two of them, at least. We'll question them and see if we can get them to rat each other out. The woman will probably give us more names, if there are any. She's doing her best to get herself out of this."

Wilder raised his eyebrows. "Do you want me to take the horses back to the stable? Or are you riding?"

Conrad looked over his shoulder toward the last deputy, who was waiting on him.

"Sure," he said. "Why don't you take the horses back, and Annabelle and I will catch a ride. That'll give me time to get some forms filled out to start the process of pressing charges."

"Sure," Wilder said. "No problem. I'm glad you got 'em, Conrad."

He shot his brother a grin. "Me, too. Thanks for your help."

Annabelle's face looked rather pale.

"You okay?" he asked.

She licked her lips. "Is it common for couples to commit crimes together?"

"More than you think," he said. "It's not just a thing in the movies, although it's a whole lot less appealing in real life." Then he slid a hand behind Annabelle's back. "I'm going to get you into a squad car before anyone sees you, okay? Then we're heading back."

ANNABELLE SAT IN the back of the squad car, although the window between the front seat and back was left open so that she could hear everything said between Conrad and the deputy. She was in the back because that was where there was room for her since another deputy was driving them home, but it felt like a cage.

Would she find herself in the back of a squad car again one of these days, this time with criminal charges against her? Conrad and the other deputy both seemed pleased with having arrested the two cattle rustlers, and while there might be more criminals in the ring, this was a strong start.

"They seem local," Conrad said. "I don't know... Just a farm truck and a trailer. I'm willing to bet there's a ranch with a whole lot of fudged cattle brands. Hard to sell at auction, but there's a market for anything. It's hard to believe the Amish would accept stolen cattle, though."

"There's a first time for everything," the other deputy said.

"True enough. The fact remains, if there are rustlers, there's a market for the stolen cattle. They wouldn't go to the trouble otherwise. We just have to find it."

They sounded excited—all the possibilities, all the crooks they could take down. And it sent a shiver through her. Not that she wasn't grateful for bad guys being dealt with, but it was so impersonal.

What if that woman *was* innocent? What if she really didn't know anything about it? Annabelle had seen that much—the pleading. She'd even felt a snap of jealousy when the woman had looked up at Conrad like that, but Conrad hadn't been moved by her tears. At first, she'd felt a wave of relief. It meant that Conrad's reaction to her situation wasn't just a man who responded to women who needed a champion...but he hadn't even taken a moment to consider the possibility of her telling the truth.

What if she'd done something stupid, not realizing what she was getting involved in? It didn't seem very likely from where Annabelle sat, but Annabelle's own innocence might not seem likely if Stephen started making claims about her, especially if he told the cops about their previous romantic involvement. Conrad knew nothing about that.

But what if she was the one on the other end of those cuffs?

The deputy dropped them off at the house, and Annabelle waited while Conrad opened the back door to let her out. Her legs felt shaky, and she stood back as Conrad said a cordial goodbye to the officer. The squad car pulled out, and they were left in the velvety darkness.

Conrad's phone blipped.

"Perimeter alarm," he said with a small smile.

She tried to smile in return, but wasn't sure she managed it.

"Annabelle, are you okay?" he asked. "You seem…shaken." He shook his head. "Maybe that was stupid of me to go after rustlers right now. I'm sorry. You're under enough stress as it is, and I forget that seeing someone arrested might be really scary and—"

"I'm fine with your job," she said, letting out a shaky breath.

"I have to act the tough part when I'm dealing with someone breaking the law," he said. "Just so you know."

"I know." She nodded. "Conrad, you don't scare me. Okay? That's not what this is. I know you're a good guy."

"Then what's wrong?"

How to explain! She pulled her hands through her hair. "What if she's innocent?"

"Oh..." He nodded. "Look, I've seen this a lot. They all claim innocence at first. 'Officer, I don't know what happened. He was alive five minutes ago.' 'Officer, I don't know how this block of cocaine ended up in my backpack.' 'Officer, it was all his fault, and I had no idea what was going on.' My job ends at pressing charges. The rest is up to lawyers."

"What if she was telling the truth, though?" she pressed. "What then?"

"It's not a perfect system, but I have to trust it. Her lawyer will dig up evidence that proves she's innocent—ideally. But, Annabelle, she was opening up the trailer, putting down a board for him to use to cross the ditch... This wasn't her first time doing this. And then she was helping him to lift the calf. I mean, she knew what she was doing. She just knows how to work up tears, too. That's it."

"Do you think that about me?" she asked.

"What?" He shook his head. "No. Wow. Where is this coming from?"

"If things looked bad for me, would you change your mind about me?" she asked. "Would all of this time together, getting to know each other, would it mean nothing if evidence pointed at me?"

"Are you talking about the lost keys still?" he asked.

"No, I'm not talking about the keys!" Her eyes misted, and she turned away. She wasn't going to cry. He'd only think she was trying to manipulate him. He caught her shoulder, and when she pushed against him, he released her.

"What is this, then?" he asked. "Annabelle, seeing someone arrested is tough. This is on me. This is entirely my fault—"

"Stephen Hope is going to say I'm his girlfriend," she said, and the words came out in a rush.

"Why?" His tone changed then to something more cautious, and she turned to face him.

"Because two years ago, I dated him for a few weeks," she said. He'd find out anyway. All anyone had to do was check far enough back in her cell phone history.

"Wait—" He frowned. "You *know* him?"

"I *knew* him. Past tense. I met him at a restaurant. We talked for a few hours. We met up again. We did a lot of talking, honestly. And then we got romantic. But he had a real temper, and he could get in these really morose moods. I couldn't handle him. I broke it off."

"How did he take it?"

"Pretty well, actually. He agreed that we probably wanted different things, and we went our separate ways."

"Were you working at the bank then?"

"Yes."

"Did he know that?"

"Yes, of course. It's one of those first date things you find out—where the other person works. He was working for a catering company, doing the driving."

"So when you saw him during the robbery—"

"I knew him immediately." Her voice shook. "That's how I was so sure who he was. And I'd just seen him shoot a man dead. He looked me in the face, and he knew me, too."

"Did he look surprised?"

She shook her head. "No. Not at all. He… winked."

Conrad winced. "Why didn't you tell me this before?"

"Because he had my keys! And—" She swallowed. "And he sent me a text. He made it sound like I was involved in the robbery. He said I was getting a cut—a lie, obviously—but it was going to look really bad. And he said that if I said anything, he'd bring me down with him."

"Did you have any contact with him after your brief relationship?" he asked.

She shook her head. "Not purposefully."

"What does that mean?"

"It means that I remember a couple of times I saw him around town. In a place the size of Wooster, that happens. Once he was behind me in line at the movie theater, and I dropped my coat. He picked it up for me. Another time, we ended up in the same checkout line at the grocery store. Things like that."

"How close together at the grocery store? Was he right behind you again?"

"Um—" She nodded. "Yes, he happened to be. He looked as surprised as I was. We had a stilted conversation, and he…walked me to my car. Helped me load my groceries. He was being sweet."

"Did he try to reconnect with you romantically?" he asked with a frown.

"No. He was just being nice. Or so I thought.

I thought he was someone who wasn't for me, but who wasn't a bad person."

"Did you see him at the bank ever?"

"He was parked in front of the bank a few times," she said. "But there are a lot of stores on that street. People park along there all the time, and I never saw him come inside."

"Any other times you can think of?" he asked.

She shook her head. "No. That's it. I didn't run into him any more often than I ran into anyone else in Wooster! I mean, I know just about everyone. If you aren't coming across acquaintances in Walmart, it's the grocery store, or at the gas station, or just walking down the street. I didn't think anything of it until he said he'd bring me down with him."

"If he made a big friendly show in front of security cameras, he might be able to make a case. When did you see him at the movie theater?"

"A couple of months ago?"

"The last time you saw him at the grocery store?"

"A few weeks ago, I think."

"The last time he parked in front of the bank?"

Panic started to rise inside her. "A month

ago? I don't really remember. I didn't know I'd have to! Why?"

"Because if he can remember the dates, then he can 'prove' you were in a relationship with him." Conrad swallowed. "Annabelle... This looks really bad."

"I know." She nodded, tears welling. "I know." She wiped her eyes. "And I know I look like I'm trying to manipulate you, but these tears are *not* for you! They're because I know exactly how bad it looks. This is *my life* we're talking about."

Conrad crossed the few feet between them and gathered her into his arms. She leaned her face against his chest and let out a shaky sigh. His embrace was strong, and she could feel the powerful beat of his heart beneath her cheek. He wasn't panicking. He wasn't blaming her. She wanted to stay here in his arms, shut her eyes and let the rest of the world roll on by without her, but he was only a man, after all. What was he thinking, though?

"I believe you," he said quietly.

Her heart skipped a beat and then hammered hard to catch up. "What?"

"I believe you," he repeated.

Annabelle pulled back and looked up at him. Her head swam a little, and she searched his face for some sign of a lie. But he looked down at her, meeting her gaze evenly.

"Why?" she asked feebly.

"For the same reason I told you that I believed you last night," he said. "That hasn't changed."

"Oh..." She felt like the vise around her chest suddenly released. "You do believe me."

"A hundred percent." He swallowed. "But it's going to look bad. You were right about that."

She nodded. "I know. And until I saw Bonnie and Clyde down there, I still thought this might go away. But that's why I can't testify. My only chance is if I keep my mouth shut. He'll leave me alone then."

"Will he?" Conrad asked.

"Yes! I'll run away. I'll leave Ohio completely, find somewhere else to live—another state. I'll stay as far from him as I can, and he'll have no reason to involve me or anyone I care about."

"Because he'll be free." Conrad's tone held volumes. He didn't seem as convinced as she was.

"If I testify, he'll implicate me," Annabelle said. "And I'll end up in prison for something I never did. You know how it'll look..."

"I won't let it happen," he said, his voice a

growl. And he looked like a giant just then, his eyes blazing and his muscles taut. If it came down to one man battling another, or even battling a small army, she'd bet on him. But still…

"You're one man, Conrad! Granted, you're an impressive one, but you're still only human!"

"I'm not letting someone I love go to prison!" he said, and the steel in his eyes suddenly melted to molten softness. "Annabelle, I won't let it happen…"

Had she heard that right? It was like the whole ranch spun around them as his words sank into her heart.

"You love me?" she breathed.

CHAPTER FIFTEEN

CONRAD HADN'T MEANT to say that part aloud, and of course, it was what she'd stick on. His brain was still running ahead, trying to find a solution. He'd definitely said that out loud… But it did explain what had been going on inside him all this time. He was protective of her, more than he was of any other civilian he was honor bound to defend. And he thought about her constantly. Even before the robbery, she'd been on his mind. He just hadn't thought that a relationship between them would make sense! But lock them together for a few days with nothing else to do but get to know her better, and all of a sudden, he'd discovered a name for this roiling emotion…an inconvenient but honest name for it. He loved her.

"Yeah…" It was better to just admit the truth. "I do love you. And I shouldn't—I know that. This isn't appropriate. I'm not asking anything of you—"

But her deep blue eyes seemed to draw him in like a sailor drowning in the deep. His explanations and disclaimers... They all just seemed to drift away in the current. He slid his hands around her waist and lowered his lips over hers.

He loved her. It couldn't be helped, and the thought of anything happening to her simmered up a wave of fierce protectiveness. If he could stand between her and danger, he would.

When he pulled back, he cradled her face in his palms.

"Do you feel it, too?" he asked helplessly. "Because if this is just me, I've really overstepped and I'd have to immediately get the sheriff to find you a new place of shelter."

"Oh, Conrad..." She smiled. "I know it's fast, and crazy, but yes, I love you, too."

Those words were a tremendous relief.

"Good..." he breathed. "That's good."

"But I can't stay here."

Conrad froze. Had he overstepped after all? Was he pushing himself onto her? He let his hands drop to his sides. He couldn't force this.

"I think I understand," he said with a quick nod. "It's okay. Look, I've said it all along, but whatever I'm feeling isn't your problem, and I will absolutely get it under control. I'll call my boss, and—"

"Conrad!" Annabelle punched him softly in the chest. "You doofus! I said I loved you and I meant it! I'm not leaving because of you." Her chin trembled. "But there is no way I can testify at that trial."

"I'd be there with you," he said. "Every step of the way."

"I believe that," she said softly. "But things would not look good for me if Stephen Hope decided to drag me down. He had my keys. And even you've been saying someone must have been helping him from inside the bank, and I'll look like that someone."

"We'll find evidence of your innocence," he said. "Otherwise, you'll be running from him the rest of your life. We won't get the conviction without you, so he'll be free, and he'll be after you…"

The thought of that man chasing Annabelle down was enough to chill his blood.

"I can't do it…" She shook her head. "And, Conrad, you have this place locked down. It's to keep bad people out, but it also keeps me in. I need a head start—"

"You want me to look the other way," he said woodenly.

"Please." She searched his face, but he wasn't ready for this yet.

"Wait, Annabelle…" Conrad swallowed. "Don't run yet. Give me a chance to find more evidence, at least. We know he did it. There is no doubt in my mind, and I know you had nothing to do with that robbery. That means someone else helped him, and if I can track down who that was, then you're home free."

"And if you can't?" she asked.

If he couldn't, then all the blame would land squarely on Annabelle, and Conrad would be the only one willing to fight for her innocence. If he were to sit down with his boss and lay out his reasons for believing Annabelle was innocent, he could hear what his boss would say now. *Conrad, you're too close to this. Someone can be attractive and appealing, and also guilty as hell. You need to step back. Let us take it from here…*

"I won't have a choice there, will I?" Conrad said miserably. "I'll find the evidence. It has to be there… Someone gave him the information about that cash delivery, and they wouldn't have done it without a cut. It's a matter of following the money. We didn't see it on the first look through everyone's accounts, but there is obviously an account somewhere that just got flush."

His mind was spinning ahead. There was a case to win, and they weren't as close to closing it as the sheriff might like, but getting the right ones involved was important. Sheriff McCann couldn't disagree with that. If Annabelle looked guilty, then he'd just have to put in the hours to prove otherwise.

"The sheriff isn't on my side," she said, pulling him out of his train of thought. "He isn't on anyone's side. He's a very nice human being, I'm sure, but he's not seeing me as someone who obviously wasn't involved. I saw it in his face when he came here."

Conrad had seen the same thing.

"If I testify, this all lands on me," she said. "If I leave now and don't testify, then Stephen has no reason to even mention my name."

"And if he walks free after killing that man?" Conrad asked.

"He sent those photos. He's tracking me— and he has been for a while, because he took that picture of Herman through the window of my apartment. Herman is at my parents' place now, so that wasn't a new picture! The way I see it, I have to choose between my own freedom and his incarceration. I want both of those things, but I don't think I'll get them."

And that was the choice for Conrad, too, unless he could dig up more evidence.

"What if I could get you both?" he asked earnestly. "What if I could get you your own freedom, your life back and that monster behind bars?"

Because that was exactly what she needed—nothing less.

Annabelle swallowed. "Conrad... You can't promise that."

"Give me a chance!" he pleaded. "The evidence is there. I just have to find it."

In the very core of his being, he knew that she was both innocent and needed him now more than ever. Someone had to believe in her, or she'd end up slipping through the cracks. Stephen Hope couldn't get his pound of flesh from the woman who saw his face. This time around, Conrad was determined to protect her.

"Will you just give me some time?" Conrad asked. "I know you don't trust the justice system a whole lot right now, but you can trust me."

"Am I more than a job to you now?" she asked.

He looked down into her face, and he wondered how he could have ever told her that was all she was. It had been a lie from the start.

"You always were," he whispered.

She smiled faintly at that. "Then we don't have much time."

CONRAD SPENT THE rest of the day on the phone attempting to get those warrants for the bank employees' banking activity. He doubted that they'd simply deposit stolen money into an account, but they might pay off some debt here or there without any explanation as to how.

He called colleagues to get the latest information from the investigation—fingerprints, security camera footage, even the eyewitness testimony from customers who had been in the bank at the same time as the robbery. No one else had seen a face, or anything else that could identify Stephen Hope as the man who'd shot the security guard.

One person had gotten a look at the keys, though, and described them as "a ring of keys with a Snoopy key chain—like a little rubber cast Snoopy. I'd know them if I saw them again. It was unique."

And then there was the security code that

was used to get out the back of the bank. Every employee had one, and it was a unique identifier to let the security company know who came and left.

"Funny thing," Deputy Denise Churchill said. "The security code used to leave the bank after the robbery belonged to our witness."

"Our witness?" Conrad felt the air seep out of his lungs.

"Yes. I mean, they had to use someone's, but I don't recall any mention of the robber taking our witness to the door to let him out. Did she mention that to you?"

"No," he said, his mind spinning. "She didn't."

"Maybe ask her about it. That will come up in court, no doubt. We need a clear, concise answer."

So Stephen Hope had been thinking ahead about who he was going to pin this on…and if he went down, he was going to make sure that Annabelle did, too.

Was this more personal than she thought? Had he really taken the breakup as well as he appeared to?

Conrad found Annabelle in the kitchen, a

cup of cold tea in front of her, and her gaze trained out the window.

"Can I ask you something about the robbery?" Conrad asked.

"Sure." Her eyes looked tired, but she smoothed her expression and waited.

"How did Stephen Hope get out of the bank?"

"Through the back door," she said.

"Did he have anyone with him to let him out?" Conrad asked. "That door requires a code to be entered to let anyone out."

Her eyes widened. "I hadn't thought of that."

"So who was with him?" he pressed.

"No one. Just him and the two other robbers. The three of them left together. I remember hearing the door bang shut. How did they get past that door?"

"They, uh, had a code," Conrad said quietly.

Her face paled. "Whose?"

"Yours."

Annabelle visibly deflated. "Seriously?"

He nodded. "I just found out. Where were those codes kept?"

"Management had access to them," she said. "Whenever someone quit, a code would have to be deleted. But I think it was a process that included the security company."

"I'll look into the company and see if anyone accessed those codes in the last few months," Conrad said.

"But they used my code?" Annabelle's breath came quicker. "Mine?"

"Annabelle, someone got it. I'll find out who. How long have you had that code?"

"It was updated a couple of years ago."

"So at least two years."

"Yes."

"Could anyone have seen you use it?" he asked. "How protective of your exit codes were you at your branch?"

"We…" Her gaze moved around the kitchen. Then she shook her head. "It didn't seem that important to hide them like a banking PIN or something. We'd stand back when someone was using theirs out of courtesy."

"But someone—anyone—could have gotten a look at your code at some point over the last two years," he said.

"Yes. I suppose so."

Conrad sighed. "Okay, that's good to know. We'll look into the security company, and a lawyer could get the exit code thrown out of court based on the fact that they weren't that secret."

"A lawyer?" Her voice shook. "Whose lawyer? Mine?"

Conrad slid into the chair next to her and put his hand over hers. Her fingers were cold, despite the heat of the day. "I'm sorry that I'm being really businesslike here. I don't have a lot of time, and this is how I work to pick apart a case."

She nodded but didn't answer.

"We're gathering evidence, and I'm sifting through it on our end. Okay? We'll sort this out."

Annabelle didn't eat much at dinner that night, barely nibbling a slice of pizza Wilder brought home. She was scared, and that was normal. He wanted to fix this for her so badly that it hurt. If only they could rewind back to his earlier mission—protect her from someone who'd rather silence her. That was simpler—her physical safety was easier to defend. But this?

Someone wanted to ruin her life, not end it. That was harder to fight.

Wilder went back out to do evening chores, and Conrad and Annabelle stayed in.

"I'll do the dishes," Annabelle said. "There aren't many."

That was an understatement. A few plates and cups—the cardboard pizza box was already out in the recycling bin.

"Don't worry about it," he said.

"It'll give me something to do," she replied. "I don't mind."

Conrad's cell phone rang, and he saw the sheriff's number.

"That's the sheriff," he said. "Let me take this. It looks like a mess of a case right now, but it always looks this way before we sort it out."

She nodded, and he picked up the call, heading down the hallway to talk privately.

"How's it going, boss?" Conrad said, picking up.

"We have a bit more evidence that came to light. Are you alone?" Sheriff McCann asked.

"Yeah, I'm alone."

"We've looked into the cell phone messages of the bank employees, and there's a single text to Annabelle that is worrisome."

"Can you read it to me?" Conrad asked. Would it say the same thing Annabelle had said?

"Sure. It says 'You were part of it. You

helped us plan it. You had a cut of the cash. If you say a word, you go down with me. That's a promise, Princess.'"

Conrad let out a slow breath, the same kind of calming technique he used before he pulled a trigger. "She told me about that a few hours ago."

"And you didn't call me immediately?"

"I'm sorry, sir. I was going to talk to you this evening after I'd gathered a bit more evidence, if I could. I know how it makes her look."

"It makes her look like the bank contact he used to plan the robbery," the sheriff said. "We've done a little more digging, and this particular branch has a significantly higher rate of clients who've had their identities stolen than any other bank in the county."

"Really?" Conrad frowned.

"It's not too far a stretch to assume that someone has been selling customer information," the sheriff said. "It might be connected, or it might be a separate investigation. But it's important to note."

The more they dug, the more they found. Eventually, they'd get to the evidence that exonerated Annabelle, wouldn't they?

"There's more, sir," Conrad said, his voice

tight. "And I want to make sure we aren't jumping to conclusions when you hear it."

"Out with it."

"Annabelle and Stephen Hope dated two years ago for a very brief amount of time."

"Really."

"Sir, I believe that Stephen Hope targeted Annabelle, perhaps hoping to use her for an intelligence-gathering mission before a robbery. I suggest it didn't work—she broke up with him, and he took it more personally than she ever knew. He's been framing her to take the fall for this if she testifies against him, and it's pretty genius, if you ask me. If she says anything, then he makes her look just as guilty as he is. But without her testimony, he'll never see the inside of a jail cell."

"That is possible, Conrad," Sheriff McCann said, his voice low. "But it's also possible that he and Annabelle were still involved in a relationship, and things went sour when she identified him in that picture."

"I don't think so."

"Hear me out," the sheriff said. "Maybe he convinced her that it was a victimless crime— insurance would cover the lost cash, and no one would get hurt. Then he shot someone— and she hadn't anticipated that. She wouldn't be a part of killing the guard, and she turned on him. We're looking at accessory to a robbery, not murder."

"Sir, I don't think that's the case," Conrad said. "She's not like that."

"Do you know that for a fact?" the sheriff asked.

There was nothing Conrad could say that would convince his boss. What? He was in love with her, and therefore Annabelle was innocent?

"Let's just keep digging," Conrad said. "Because you have to admit, this is a bit easy. He could very well have another contact in the bank that helped him with details, and they're pinning it on Annabelle. He might even be connected to the identity thefts. They were threatening her with those photos that guy dropped off at the house. And someone was lurking that night—that had to be connected. They're trying to intimidate her into silence. If she were part of it, they wouldn't have needed to send her photos to show her that they knew where she lived, or anything else. There's more to this case. I'm sure of it."

"We'll keep looking, of course," the sheriff replied. "But, Conrad, I think you're too close to this."

He'd known that was coming. "I'm fine, sir. But I know her. She's not a criminal. She's caught in this, and she needs our protection, not our skepticism."

"I've seen cases like this before. So have you, for that matter."

"This is different. I can feel it. Sir, you've seemed suspicious of her for a while now."

"And you haven't been, despite the evidence," the sheriff replied. "You have better instincts than that. This is about closing a case."

"This is about a woman, not a case! She needs me to get her through this!"

"She needs *you*?"

Conrad winced at his slip.

"You *are* too close to this," the sheriff said more firmly. "If you're crossing lines, that could cost us a case. The defense would have a field day with that. You know the rules here, Conrad."

"She's being framed, sir. We just need to find more evidence."

"Then we'll look, and you'll have the time to focus on doing just that. You know I'm fair. And I want to protect the innocent as much as you do, but we need evidence. We're moving Annabelle to a different location. Have her be ready to go tonight. We'll get her into a safe house. You need some time to clear your head. It's been an eventful few days."

"That isn't necessary, sir," Conrad said.

"Do you want to be part of digging up that evidence or not?" There was a pause. "Conrad, be assured that I've heard everything you said and I'm taking it seriously. We'll look deeper. We're working on the warrant to look into all the employees' banking activity, and we'll get every scrap of evidence we can find."

"Thank you, sir."

"I have no interest in seeing an innocent woman incarcerated, either. Trust me on that."

"Of course. Understood."

When he hung up, Conrad felt a sinking feeling in his gut. But if he couldn't personally protect her, at least he could search for evidence while she was in the safe house.

And the cattle-rustling couple was still tickling the back of his brain. A couple locked in criminal activity together...a woman who might wish she wasn't involved and a man willing to throw her under the bus without any hesitation.

His phone blipped. The perimeter alarm...

He headed to the window to look outside. It was probably a bird or something, because there was nothing there.

ANNABELLE SLIPPED AROUND the side of the Schmidts' house, her breath coming fast. She'd thrown a stick past the motion detector leading out the main drive and then run east, past the stable, through the Schmidts' side garden and then around the house where she wouldn't be visible.

She couldn't stay—Conrad could see that, couldn't he?

And yet his words were still echoing inside her with every thud of her heartbeat: *I'm not letting someone I love go to prison!*

She knew that he'd defend her if it were up to him alone. But it wasn't. If she looked guilty, what was Conrad supposed to do—refuse to arrest her? Or was he supposed to leave his career on her behalf? Were they supposed to run away together until things blew over? With a cop on the run with her, it *wouldn't* blow over. Ever.

There would be no future with him raising cattle and her knitting socks. There was no pastoral life like the Amish lived for her and Conrad.

The only way either of them could continue was separately, with her as far from here as possible. Maybe Stephen Hope would forget about her. Maybe he'd do something else, something nonviolent, that he'd be arrested for.

Annabelle looked back toward the Westhouse farm, and her heart felt like it was cracking inside her. She'd never see him again, would she?

Her throat felt swollen with unshed tears. She turned toward the clothesline of dresses hanging in the last of the evening sun. She plucked at the hem of one of them. This was stealing, and somehow taking a dress made by Linda's own hands seemed even worse.

The screen door opened, and Annabelle turned to see the older woman looking at her curiously.

"It's laundry," Linda said with a teasing smile.

"I know." Annabelle couldn't even force a smile in return. "Linda, I'm going to need a big favor."

"What's going on?" Linda asked. "Come inside."

"I don't have time!" Annabelle looked in the direction of the Westhouse property. How long until Conrad noticed she was gone? "I need a dress, Linda. I have to blend in around here. I have to look Amish."

"You're running away?" Linda frowned.

"Yes." Annabelle licked her lips. "And I can't explain. But I can't stay, and if I go wearing Amish clothing, I'll be harder to spot."

Linda pressed her lips together. "I imagine if I turned my back, you'd just take a dress."

"I'd feel terrible about it," Annabelle said. "But I'm quite desperate. Would you…just turn your back?"

"You won't look Amish without a *kapp* on your head and an apron."

"Oh…" She hadn't thought of the finishing details.

"So you'd better come inside so I can dress you up properly," Linda said. "Grab a dress— any one will do. Come on. Hurry up."

Annabelle plucked the first dress on the line free of the clothespins and hurried up the steps.

"Our dresses are fitted with straight pins," Linda said briskly, and she took the pink dress and shook it out. "It's a good thing I didn't take the laundry in yet. I was feeling bad about being so lazy. Clothes off."

Annabelle did as she was ordered and stripped off her jeans and T-shirt. Then Linda dropped the dress over her head.

"Jane!" Linda called, and she rattled something off in Pennsylvania Dutch. There was a rustle overhead.

"Yah, Mammi!" The girl appeared a moment later with a pin box in hand, and her face brightened when she saw Annabelle.

"You came to visit!" Jane said. "And you're wearing a pretty dress!"

"Come here. Quick, quick," Linda said, holding out her hand.

Jane brought the pins, and Linda accepted them. "Now, upstairs and get one of my aprons from my drawer and a fresh *kapp.*"

Jane shot toward the stairs.

"And some hairpins!" Linda added.

"My hair isn't very long," Annabelle said.

"It just has to disappear under the *kapp,* that's all," Linda replied. "Are you going to tell me why you're running?"

"I look guilty for something I didn't do," Annabelle said.

"And Conrad doesn't believe you?"

"Oh, he does," she said, tears brimming in her eyes. "But he can't stop it. He'll try, but it's better if I go before he sacrifices anything."

"Hands up, please," Linda said, as she adjusted the skirt and started to secure it with straight pins. It appeared that it didn't much matter if a woman's size went up or down, since the waistline was secured with pins. It was incredibly clever.

Jane came back down the stairs with a white apron clutched in one hand and a *kapp* and a fistful of hairpins in the other. She slammed them down on the tabletop.

"Are you playing dress-up?" Jane asked.

"Sort of," Annabelle said.

"Are you going to be Amish now?"

"For a little while," Annabelle said, forcing a smile. "But not forever."

"That's too bad," Jane said. "I like being Amish. I think you'd like it, too."

And Annabelle very well might enjoy being Amish—but perhaps running suited her better.

Linda shook out the apron and put it over the front of Annabelle's dress. She circled around and tied it from behind.

"Now for your hair…" Linda eyed her uncertainly.

Annabelle looked out the window and saw

the mare and the colt grazing together in the field, and Wilder sauntering across the yard toward the house. No hurry… Maybe no one missed her yet.

Annabelle picked up her jeans from the chair where she'd left them, reached into her pocket and pulled out a hair elastic. She pulled her hair into a short nub of a ponytail.

"Will this do?" she asked.

"It'll have to," Linda said. She put the white *kapp* over the back of Annabelle's head and secured it with two hairpins.

Jane stared at her, perplexed.

"Jane," Annabelle said, leaning down, "I like you very much, and I'm going to tell you something very important. Sometimes life can get complicated, and if you want to end up better than me, you'll always listen to your father and grandmother and do exactly as they say, okay?"

Jane nodded mutely.

"Good." Annabelle pressed a kiss against the girl's forehead and then looked back at Linda.

"Am I okay with these running shoes?"

"We wear runners with dresses all the time," Linda said. "You look the part…just with hair a bit too short."

"It'll have to do," Annabelle said. "Thank you."

Linda stepped forward and gave her a quick squeeze. "I don't know what trouble you're in, but if you ever come this way again, you're welcome here."

Annabelle didn't trust herself to say another word. Through the window, she saw Wilder go into the house. It was only a matter of time now before they realized she was gone.

"I have to go!" she said, and she hurried to the side door and slipped back outside, leaving her regular clothes behind. She'd buy more when she got far enough away…or when she got a job that would pay her cash, because the cops would be following her bank account and credit card as soon as they knew she was missing.

She started across the field at a brisk pace. She kept her head down, not wanting anyone to look too closely at her, and she held her purse across her stomach. At least from a distance, she'd pass as an Amish woman. She looked over her shoulder once and saw Jane standing on the step watching her. Annabelle permitted herself one wave and then kept going.

That little girl might have her own heart-breaks in the future, but she had something so precious right now that she'd only take for granted. Because children and young people always took their security and happiness for granted. She'd done the same, hadn't she? Until it was gone.

The tall grass scratched her legs, and Annabelle picked up her pace.

This was the only way… But her heart kept stretching back to that ranch behind her where a muscular cop was doing his best to prove her innocence.

Because he loved her.

An Amish man stood at the fence in the distance, watching her approach. She broke into a jog, and when she arrived at the fence, panting with exertion, he took off his straw hat and scratched at his head. He was an older man with a full gray beard.

"Do you need help, young lady?" he asked in English. Apparently, she didn't look Amish to the Amish.

"Please…" She gasped for breath. "I need a ride into town. I just need to get to the bus station."

"Sure."

"I could pay you…"

"No need," he replied. "I was going to go later anyway to pick my daughter up from work, but I can go now."

"Really?" She squinted at him.

"Word around here is that some *Englisher* woman and the *Englisher* cop rounded up those cattle rustlers. A blonde woman with short hair, like yours. You're heroes around here."

"It was all Conrad," she said. "He's incredible. You're lucky to have him in your community. I was just along for the ride."

"All the same, I'm happy to return a favor," the man replied. "We've all been losing more cattle than we can afford, and two less rustlers is good for us."

"I'm really glad," she said earnestly.

"Come on, then," he said. "Just slide through the rungs there. I'll go hitch up."

Annabelle felt a surge of relief. She was one step closer to freedom.

Was there any way she'd see her parents again or her friends? Conrad? Or was she going to have to just let her heart heal and start over with strangers?

CHAPTER SIXTEEN

CONRAD WALKED BRISKLY through the house. He poked his head into Annabelle's bedroom— her clothes and toiletries were still there. He headed back into the kitchen and then out the side door. He took a quick tour around the outside of the house, and when he returned, he found Wilder standing with his thumbs in his belt loops, watching him.

"She's gone?" Conrad said.

"I don't see her," Wilder replied. "What about your fancy motion detectors?"

"There was one alarm," Conrad said, "but I looked into it, and there was nothing there. But there are a few blind spots."

Conrad muttered an oath and kicked the gravel. Annabelle must have figured them out.

"Why would she run?" Wilder asked.

"Because all signs are pointing to her being involved in a crime."

"Is she guilty?" Wilder asked.

"Nope." Conrad pressed his lips together. "She's innocent, but there are people who'd like to make her look otherwise."

"What are you going to do?" Wilder asked. "Is she in danger?"

"If she's staying with an Amish family, she's perfectly safe," Conrad said. "She can't have gone far. I mean, she might be able to hitch a ride, but where would she head? In fact, if she's run off without my knowledge, she might even be a bit safer."

"You mean, you're the *only* one who believes she's innocent?" Wilder said.

"I might be." Conrad sucked in a breath, and he looked across the fields in one direction and then the other. "The sheriff wants to put her in a different safe house, and I don't know if that's a good thing or not."

"She'd be out of your protection," Wilder said.

"But it would also free me up to find proof," Conrad said. "I think for the time being, she's better off without me, and I hate that a lot."

"She's smart," Wilder said. "And she's nice. That's a combination that will do her well out here."

Conrad was forced to agree. Amish country really was the safest place for her...even on the run. She'd be met with generosity and compassion, and for that, Conrad was deeply grateful.

He headed back inside, and he spotted a folded piece of paper on the floor. A note—brief and to the point. It must have blown off the table.

They think I'm guilty, and I can't let you sacrifice everything for me. You're a good cop, Conrad. You're an even better man, and I'll miss you with everything I've got... I'll try to contact you once I'm safe somewhere, but I can't promise. I'm sorry. I love you.

Her name was scrawled beneath the words, and Conrad folded the letter and put it into his pocket.

"Can I see it?" Wilder asked.

Conrad shook his head. "It's private."

But those cattle rustlers—the romantic couple working together—were still nagging at the back of his mind. It was just so common... and someone had given Stephen Hope that information from the bank.

Would another man have been in cahoots with him? Somehow, Conrad couldn't see it. But a woman—one who loved him, who believed that they'd have a future together, and who might have been shaken to the core when she saw him commit murder—might be willing to risk everything. Love did strange things to people. Look at him! He was willing to go against the entire sheriff's department in order to protect he woman he'd fallen in love with!

He pulled out his phone and dialed his boss's number.

"Hi, Conrad," Sheriff McCann said.

"She's gone," Conrad said. "She snuck off a few minutes ago. Her clothes and personal items are all inside the house still."

"And you're sure she left of her own free will?" the sheriff asked.

"No sign of a struggle. I was here the whole time. I would have heard it. No vehicles on the property. Only one perimeter alarm, and I investigated it. It was nothing."

"So she ran off," the sheriff concluded.

"Yes, sir."

"Okay… I'll put out an alert for our deputies to be on the lookout for her. She's on foot?"

"Yes, sir. All vehicles accounted for."

"That'll make it easier."

That also meant that they had very little time before someone picked her up, unless she went into hiding in an Amish home.

"Sir, I have an idea," Conrad said. "We have Stephen Hope in custody. Has he given us any more information about who helped him?"

"None."

"I think you should tell him that his girlfriend ratted him out," Conrad said.

"Annabelle told you something?" the sheriff asked.

Conrad clenched his teeth. "No, sir. I still think she's innocent. But I do think that a woman helped him with that robbery. It's just a hunch, but if you tell him his girlfriend has turned him over, he might say something interesting. You're assuming he'll finger Annabelle. I think she's telling the truth that she hasn't been involved with him in two years. Maybe he'll implicate someone else."

"Hmm." There was a couple of beats of silence. "Okay, I like it. I want you to join the search for our witness, though. You know her best. The sooner we can get her back into custody, the better it will be for her."

"Yes, sir."

"I'll give you a call after I've had a chat

with Stephen Hope. I'll let you know what he said."

"Thank you, sir. I appreciate it."

"If he identifies our witness, though, we'll proceed accordingly."

"Yes, sir."

The sheriff's department would, at least. He couldn't guarantee what he would do. Annabelle didn't want him sacrificing everything for her, but that wasn't her call to make. He'd grudgingly agree that her getting off this property was probably for the best, at least for the short term, but she couldn't live her life out of two-bit motels and money made under the table. What kind of existence would that be?

Conrad hung up the phone, and Wilder looked at him questioningly.

"I'm going to look for her," Conrad said.

"Do you know where to start?" Wilder asked.

"I think I'll start next door," Conrad said. "Do you think the Schmidts would lie to me if they saw her?"

"I don't know," Wilder replied. "I don't think they'd lie so much as clam up and not say anything. That's more to the Amish style."

"True." Sometimes silence spoke volumes.

In fact, Conrad wanted to give Annabelle a little more time to get away in case his ploy with the Hope interrogation failed.

And that realization felt like a rock in his stomach. What did that say about him as a man if she was safer without him?

"If she's not at the neighbors', I have a feeling she'll end up at the bus station eventually," Conrad said. "And if I find her out there, I don't know when I'm coming back."

"What do you mean?" Wilder asked.

"I mean I have to protect her, and I'll be figuring that out as I go. Just know that if I'm gone for a while, I'm okay."

"I don't like the sound of this," Wilder said.

"Me neither," Conrad said. "I just hope none of it is necessary."

"Is she worth all this?" Wilder asked. "I mean, slow down for a minute here and really think. I like her, too, but is this woman worth sacrificing your career for? You're a shameless workaholic, you know. Your job is everything to you."

He'd also end up a wreck if he saw Annabelle's life in ruins. He'd never felt like this for any woman before, and he was old enough to know that this wasn't going to come along in his life again. Annabelle was it—the woman who filled his heart. And he wouldn't leave her to struggle on her own.

"Yeah, she's worth it," Conrad said.

His brother nodded slowly. "Good luck, I guess."

"I'll need it."

Conrad would need more than luck, though. He needed an admissible confession from Stephen Hope, too. Because a life on the run with the woman he loved was still not the life he envisioned for them.

A year from now, he wanted a life right here on this ranch with Annabelle in his arms—no running, no deception, and a lifetime ahead of them.

That would take a whole lot more than luck.

THE BUGGY RATTLED over a hole in the road, thumping down with a jolt, and Annabelle put her hands onto the hard side of the buggy to brace herself. The Amish man next to her, Simon, winced.

"Sorry," Simon said. "I forgot about that one."

"It's okay." Annabelle slowly took her hands down.

The horse pulling them trotted at an even pace, but it was almost painfully slow. A car pulled around them, then sped ahead, and Annabelle wondered if she would have been smarter to get a cab.

But where? And with what phone? Conrad still had hers. This was her best bet if she was going to get to town.

Simon stood up to look ahead and steered his horse left a couple of feet to let another pothole pass beneath the buggy without another rattling jolt.

"This road needs repair," she said.

"Yah, yah..." He sat back down again. "We normally go out and fill the potholes in front of our own property with gravel to make it easier for everyone, but that can be hard to keep up with."

The community taking care of public roads... It was a different way of life. Did the young people here understand just how much they had in this simple existence? She hoped so, because life got a whole lot more complicated past the Amish boundary lines.

"Do you know if the police found our cattle?" Simon asked.

"No, sorry," she replied. "I didn't get an update on that."

"Hmm." He nodded slowly. "It would be nice if they find them. A lot of us have lost a good amount of money off stolen calves this season. I lost all but one."

"How many new calves did you have?" she asked.

"Six."

"Wow." She cast him a sympathetic look. "I'm really sorry. You'll be glad to have those two rustlers behind bars."

"No..." He let out a slow breath. "It isn't about punishment. I don't want to see them suffer. I'd rather see them reformed."

"That's very generous of you," she said. "But I doubt they'll reform. They've made a life out of taking what isn't theirs."

A sheriff's department cruiser pulled past them, and she let out a shaky breath.

"You never know, though," Simon said. "Life is long. It has twists and turns. And people grow."

"Do you really think so?" she asked.

"Once upon a time, I was a rash young man," he said. "You'd never know it to look at me now."

"How rash?" she asked with a smile, and she looked out the small opening in the back of the buggy. There was a pickup truck coming up behind them, but it didn't look like the sheriff's department. Did she blend in well enough to be ignored?

"I spent three whole years living *English*," Simon said. "We have what's called a Rumspringa. It's a year when young people can live free from our rules and explore the world a little bit. It's only supposed to last a year, though, and then they are supposed to see the wisdom of our way of life."

"I didn't know that," Annabelle said, turning forward again. "I thought they wouldn't have a choice."

"Oh, everyone has a choice," he replied.

"You obviously decided to return," she said.

"*Yah.* Well, I saw what I was missing out on. I was stubborn, and it took me a little longer. Most times you don't need to go all that far away to find yourself. That's why we travel by horse and buggy. This way, we're never too far from home."

Annabelle felt an unexpected mist of tears rise in her eyes. She was planning on running as far from here as she could…and *home* was starting to mean something more than just a connection to Wooster and her friends and family. Conrad was in her heart now, too, and the memory of that old ranch house, the barn, the overgrown garden… It all had gathered up inside her like a wildflower bouquet. It was fragile, but oh, so beautiful.

The pickup truck passed them—a middle-aged woman was in the driver's seat, and she gave the buggy a safe distance before pulling in front of them again.

Annabelle heard a siren from somewhere distant, the whoop of a patrol car. Had word just got out that she'd disappeared? She wondered what Conrad had thought when he read the note she'd left behind. Did he understand? Would he forgive her for this?

The siren was coming from ahead of them, and Simon reined the horse in at the side of the road.

"It's safer so the horse doesn't spook," Simon said.

"Understandable," she said, but her voice felt tight.

The siren turned off as the patrol car whipped past them, going well over the speed limit. The horse stepped sideways and nickered uncomfortably. The officers were looking for her—she could feel it. But they weren't expecting a woman in a buggy, dressed in Amish clothes.

Simon murmured something soothing in

Pennsylvania Dutch, then flicked the reins again and the horse started forward.

"So what are you running from?" Simon asked.

"Uh—" She swallowed.

"I imagine those patrol cars are looking for you?" He cast her a mildly curious look.

"Yes, they are. But I didn't do anything."

"Why do they want to find you, then?" Simon asked.

"They want me to testify against someone in court," she said.

"Ah. And you don't want to see the person punished?"

"No, I do," she said. "I'm not quite so good as you in that respect. But it comes with some risk to me and the people I care about, and I'm afraid."

He nodded slowly. "And your *daet*… What did he tell you to do?"

"My father?" She eyed him in surprise. "He wanted me to stay safe."

"I have a daughter your age," Simon said. "She's the one I'm picking up from work. You're, what, twenty-three? Twenty-four?"

"Twenty-five," she said.

"She's twenty-three," Simon said. "She's not married yet, so she's still living at home with us. She's a good girl, but she takes after me, I'm afraid. She's got the rebellious streak. She wants to open her own business and offer gardening services to *Englisher* people."

"And you disapprove?" she asked.

"*Yah*, I disapprove!" he replied. "She should get married already. Have some babies."

Annabelle smiled wanly. Such rebellion, when a woman wanted to work hard and build a reputable business. There seemed to be a price for the peaceful life the Amish lived. Sharing the workload between men and women was appealing, but it did close off any other options in a woman's life.

"But I think me disapproving makes it more fun for her," Simon said with a wink. "So I heartily and noisily disapprove. You have to give your *kinner* something to kick against sometimes. With no boundaries, they can't feel like rebels without going way over the edge. With a fence, they get the satisfaction of going beyond without tumbling over the edge of a cliff in the process."

Annabelle leaned back in the seat and smiled. There was wisdom in Amish country that she'd never guessed at.

"But if it were my daughter having to risk herself to do the right thing," Simon said, frowning slightly, "I'd tell her to do the right thing."

The exact opposite of her own father's advice.

"Why?" she asked.

"Because you can run away, but you'll never get far enough to sleep well at night. Dreams close the distance." He was silent for a moment. "But then, if it were my daughter, I'd also tell her to marry a nice man and let him take care of her."

Annabelle sighed. "There are some things a man can't protect you from, Simon."

"Hmm." He angled his head to the side in agreement. "There are. But the protecting, it's not just his job. You protect each other. You work for each other. You pull together, and two are stronger than one. A man likes to feel like he can hold up a whole house on his shoulders, but the truth is, he can't. He's just a man. He needs a place to rest his head, too. And if you take care of each other, you'll be okay…" He cast her a rueful look. "And your father will worry less."

"You don't know my father, then," she said. "He's a different sort of man."

He shrugged. "*Yah, yah.* And this little talk was meant for my own daughter. So don't take it too personally. I just want to see her happy like I'm happy. Happiness grows when it's shared."

Annabelle thought about Conrad, who seemed so strong, so tough, so able to handle anything at all that life threw at him, having needs, too. And who would shelter him when he was worn down by the pressures of his work? Who would be the one he could lean on, too?

The thought of another woman taking on that role boiled up some instant jealousy inside her, followed quickly by a sadness so deep that it nearly rocked her. She wanted to be the one at his side.

Maybe Conrad couldn't take on the whole justice system, but she also knew that that fact would stab deep for him. Because he was the kind of man who wanted to fix everything, save everyone, and be that sheepdog who kept his neighbors safe…who kept *her* safe. He *was* just a man, and that only made her love him more.

But life was so much more complicated than old Simon realized. It wasn't just about settling down, or about being Conrad's comfort. If Conrad ran away from danger with

her, it wouldn't change who he was at heart—
a protector.

Annabelle saw the buildings of the town approaching, and she wished most desperately that she could simply turn back.

"Sometimes the right thing to do is the most painful," Annabelle said softly.

"*Yah*, most times, actually," Simon replied. "And if you know that, you'll do okay."

She had two painful options in front of her—testifying against a man who would very likely bring her down with him, or leaving the man she loved behind.

What happened when all of a woman's options tore out her heart?

CHAPTER SEVENTEEN

CONRAD LEANED HIS elbows on his knees, feeling squished in the plastic bucket seat in the bus depot waiting area. Annabelle wasn't here, but he wasn't giving up yet. If she got a bus, she'd be gone for good.

He let out a pent-up breath. If Stephen Hope's people could get at her at his ranch, then they could find her here, too.

Conrad had spent a good many years growing his career in law enforcement. His brother was right—he was a workaholic who got a lot of his confidence and sense of self from the job. He felt good about protecting his community and rooting out the criminals who'd disrupt the happy lives of rural Ohio families.

So who would he be without that? What kind of man was he without the *Deputy* in front of his name? It was a scary prospect, but if he knew Annabelle was safe, that would have to be enough. Maybe he wouldn't be the cop who

protected all of Wayne County. He'd just be
Conrad, the guy protecting *her*.

A buggy rattled up next to the main window, and an Amish woman in a pink dress
hopped down. The light was getting lower
outside, and he couldn't make out much detail
past the reflection of the inside light against
the glass, but then she turned, and he startled.
That was Annabelle—and he hadn't given
her half enough credit! Had Linda dressed
her up in Amish garb? The older woman had
given him some cryptic answer about emotional journeys and spiritual journeys, and
some tangled story about two farmers who
had been fighting for years...and something
about how life was long and filled with twists
and turns. That was something he'd heard
Wollie say a number of times. None of it really
made any sense when it came to Annabelle,
though, and he got the feeling Linda was
evading the question, especially when she
kept sending Jane out on errands to keep her
away from the house while he was there.

Annabelle came into the bus depot, a purse
clutched in front of her, and he rose to his
feet. She froze when she spotted him, and her
gaze flickered around the depot nervously.

"It's just me," he said. "I'm alone."

Annabelle crossed the room, and she didn't pause for a moment—she just marched straight into his embrace, wrapping her arms around his waist. He held her close, his cheek against the top of her head, and for a few beats they stood like that, their hearts beating in unison.

"Are you okay?" he asked her.

She looked up at him, and without waiting for her answer, he kissed her. It was a wild relief to hold her in his arms again, and he didn't want to let her go. When he pulled back, he looked down into her face, and he felt that same swell of protective love that he'd never been able to curb with her.

"I'm fine," she said, pulling back. "Obviously, I don't hide as well as I thought if you beat me here."

He let her go, but his arms felt empty without her in them.

"Where else could you be headed?" he asked.

Annabelle sighed. "You have a good point."

"No one but Wilder knows I'm here," he said. "And I told him that if I don't come back, he isn't to worry about me."

"You mean…" She licked her lips. "Conrad, you know how this will end. If I go back and testify, Stephen Hope says I'm the one who helped him. If I don't testify, he goes free. And you can't be the cop who ends up with the witness everyone thinks is lying. You'd be giving up everything. Besides, you're right that he'd come after me. I saw him. I'm still a threat to his freedom. That doesn't change unless I'm—"

Dead. That was what she meant, and even the unspoken word felt like a rock in his chest.

"He'd have to get through me," he said.

She smiled tearily. "You can't give everything up for me."

"Sure I can," he said. "If you don't want to testify, we can start over somewhere else. We'll change our names. I'll learn to weld or something, and you can get started on that sock knitting."

"That's not the life you want," she said. "What about the ranch and Wilder?"

"I don't want a life without you," he said. "Besides, we still have one last shred of hope here."

"Which is?"

"I'm trying something—I'm pushing Hope's hand."

Her face paled. "No…"

"It's one last chance, Annabelle," he said.

"If he claims you're his contact, you and I disappear. Today. Right now."

Tears welled in her eyes. "That's not a life."

"And it's better if you do it alone?" he asked. "One thing the Amish say a lot is that life is long and it has twists and turns. Well, I want my life with you."

"The Amish man who drove me—he said that, too," she said.

"See? Amish are wise people. We have a whole lifetime ahead of us. Let's see where it leads." He sobered. "If you want that, I mean. You can turn me down, Annabelle. It'll hurt, but I don't want to pressure you into anything. If you want to leave without me, I'll never breathe a word of having seen you."

"Oh, Conrad..." Annabelle slipped back into his arms again. "I love you. And if you'd be willing to come with me, I'd never turn you down."

That was what he needed to hear, and it felt as if his heart came down around her like a shield. This was it—he was committed. Whatever life held, he was staying by her side. She might not be able to count on much else, but she'd always be able to count on him.

His cell phone rang, and Conrad had to let

go of Annabelle to take the call. It was from Sheriff McCann.

"Any news, sir?" Conrad asked.

"In fact, there is." The sheriff sounded downright cheery. "I did what you suggested and told Hope that his girlfriend turned on him and was offering her testimony in exchange for leniency in her own sentence. At first he didn't believe me, but then I said that I'd give her the deal and she wouldn't do any jail time, and it was like turning on a faucet. He was furious. He ranted and raved, called her names and swore..."

"Who?" Conrad asked, his heart stuck in his throat. "Who did he name?"

"Alana Fenwick, the head bank teller." The sheriff was almost crowing. "We've picked her up and put them in a room together. They're fighting like an old married couple. We have him, Conrad. And I've gotten a peek into Ms. Fenwick's finances. Hers are fine, but her mother is drowning in credit card debt, and she's been making lump sum payments against some of them—money we can't trace. We've got her, too."

Conrad couldn't help the grin that split across his face. Annabelle stared up at him, her face pale and her lips parted.

"Sir, I'm absolutely thrilled to hear it. Do I have confirmation that Annabelle would no longer be considered a suspect, even if Stephen Hope tries to pin this on her?"

"All the evidence is easily explained with Alana Fenwick," the sheriff replied. "Annabelle is completely off the hook. But her testimony will be much appreciated in this case."

"I've tracked her down, so I'll let her know," Conrad said. "And then I'll get back to you."

Conrad ended the call and filled Annabelle in on the details. She sank into one of the bucket seats.

"So what do you want to do?" he asked.

"Alana?" she breathed. "She was dating Stephen this whole time? She never told me anything! Theresa, Alana and I went out together all the time, and she never said a thing about even having a boyfriend."

"Well, she was also benefiting from his criminal activity, so…" Conrad shrugged.

"We were friends," she said.

"I'm sorry," he said. "I know it's a shock, but she wasn't a friend. I can promise you that. At least we know who was feeding him all that information about you now. And it clears you."

"You know who else it clears?" she asked with a small smile. "Theresa."

He smiled. "She probably told Alana where you were, believing that it would be safe. That one breathed word... But it wasn't Theresa aiding the criminals."

"There are good people out there, Conrad," she said. "And you're one of them. Thank you...for all of this. I'll testify, but only if you're my bodyguard until it's over. Tied at the hip, remember?"

"And we'd either drive each other crazy... or fall in love."

Her cheeks turned pink. "Look at you, Conrad. Was there ever any doubt which way that would go?"

"I'm glad you're insisting on me." He slipped an arm around her. "I wouldn't trust your safety to anyone else anyway."

THE NEXT FEW days were a flurry of activity. Annabelle was still under protective custody at a new safe house, as Stephen Hope's accomplices hadn't been apprehended yet. But that didn't last too long. The boot print from the garden was an exact match for one of Hope's poker buddies' boots, and the other accomplice folded the minute he was offered a deal. Conrad had been incredibly pleased with himself when he told her about it.

With further digging into Alana's work history, they were also working up a case against her for selling bank client information to Stephen Hope's criminal ring. Conrad seemed pretty certain she'd see jail time.

And then...it was over. All but the trial, but Annabelle was now allowed to go see her parents again. So on a Wednesday morning, Conrad drove her over, and she asked for a few minutes alone with her mom and dad before she introduced him.

Standing in the front yard, Annabelle gave her mother a hug. Conrad's cruiser was parked behind her. Estelle Richards squeezed her daughter close.

"I was worried sick about you!" Estelle said. "I called the sheriff's department every single day asking for updates, and all they'd tell me was that you were fine. Not where you were, not who you were with—nothing!"

"I know, Mom," Annabelle said. "It had to be that way. But it's fine now—they have everyone in custody. But Conrad is still keeping an eye on me."

Estelle looked over Annabelle's shoulder

toward Conrad's cruiser. "At least you were well taken care of."

"How is Herman?" Annabelle asked. "I've missed him, too."

"Herman is just fine," Estelle said, and then she shook her head.

"I was worried about him with Dad," she said. "You know how much he hates cats."

"Let me show you something," Estelle replied. "Come here."

She led the way across the lawn and stopped in front of the living room window. Annabelle shaded her eyes and looked inside. Her father was asleep on the recliner, Herman curled up in his lap.

"He's taken such meticulous care of Herman," Estelle said. "You wouldn't believe it."

"Are you serious?" Annabelle shook her head.

"He was worried sick, too, sweetheart," Estelle said. "I know he doesn't say it, but he loves you. And all he was able to do for you was take care of your cat, so he did it with all his might."

"So he has a soft spot after all," Annabelle murmured.

"I know he's a stubborn old fool, but you always were his soft spot," Estelle replied quietly. "He just wanted you to be strong and self-reliant so that you'd be safe. He thought he was right."

"He was wrong," Annabelle said.

Estelle smiled faintly. "I know. And now so does he."

"Does he really?" Annabelle asked.

"He said if he had it to do all over again, he would have raised you to come home when you needed help, instead of dealing with it on your own. He wanted to protect you himself."

"There were some very nasty people after me," she said.

"And he would have faced them for you." Estelle gave her arm a squeeze. "Annabelle, the older you get, the more you realize that your way isn't the only way. And you see your mistakes and your weaknesses... You'll need to be a bit easier on him, too."

Annabelle was silent.

"You haven't had a proper conversation with your father in years," Estelle said.

Her father always thought he was right, but as she looked at him in that recliner, he looked old. Did he really regret pushing her away the way he had?

"You and I talk, and you pass along the

message," Annabelle said. "Isn't that how our family works?"

"Maybe, but it's dysfunctional."

"Dad wanted me to be tough."

"He wanted you to be *happy*, and he thought he knew the path to get you there. You'll have to forgive him for getting it wrong, Annabelle. You forgave me for not standing up to him."

Her father roused then, and when he blinked his eyes open, Annabelle raised her hand in a wave. He reached down to move the cat to the side and pushed himself out of the chair. Annabelle followed her mother through the front door, and she paused in the foyer. Everything smelled so familiar—the perfume of an aging house, and the faint whiff of bleach from her mother scrubbing something down.

"You're back," her father said. "Good. It was stupid of them to lock you away like that, as if you were some kind of criminal."

"It was protective custody," Annabelle said. "And they have the real criminals in custody now."

"I told you not to get involved in this!" her father said, but he wrapped his arms around her, holding her close. He released her and stood back. "I'm glad you're okay."

"I'm fine, Dad."

"Herman, here—" He looked around himself. "Herman? Where did that cat go?"

Annabelle couldn't help the smile that tickled her lips. "Mom told me that you and Herman bonded."

"Yeah, well…" he said gruffly. "Herman missed you, I think, but I kept him distracted with tuna and a penlight. By the way, he needs tuna before he goes to bed."

"Does he?" Annabelle chuckled. The cat came out of the living room, and Annabelle bent down to gather him up in her arms. "Hey there, Herman. I missed you."

She kissed the top of his soft head, and Herman rubbed his head against her chin, purring loudly.

"I guess I should find his crate," her father said, looking around himself as if slightly lost.

"It's up in Annabelle's old bedroom," Estelle said.

"Oh, right. And you're staying for supper, at least, aren't you?" Her father cast her a questioning look.

"Yes, I'll definitely stay, so don't go getting the crate yet, Dad. Actually…" Annabelle looked out the long, narrow window by the front door. She could see Conrad's cruiser through the pane of glass. He was still her bodyguard until the trial was over, but even if he weren't assigned to her, she had a feeling that Conrad would be around. "I have someone you need to meet..."

"Who?" her father asked.

"The deputy who's been guarding me," she said. "His name is Conrad Westhouse."

"Right. Right. Yes, of course," her father replied. "He's welcome to come in for dinner. It's just bratwursts tonight. I should ask him what on earth he thought he was doing, cutting you off from your family like that. I don't know who they thought they were. Your mother called and asked about you daily, and I called and gave that sheriff a piece of my mind, too."

Her father opened the front door and beckoned toward Conrad.

"You've become...friends?" Estelle asked delicately.

"We're more than friends." She shot her mother a smile. "Make sure Dad is nice. I really like this guy."

It was time that Conrad met her parents anyway. If there was any future between them, it would include her family. Her dad might have raised her to be independent, but everyone came with people attached to them. Those were the relationships that made life sweet.

What had Wollie said…without those connections, it was just making do? That was wisdom right there. If anyone knew about families, it was the Amish.

Conrad came up the walk, and he met Annabelle's gaze with a warm smile. Her stomach gave a little flip of happiness.

"Conrad, meet my mom and dad," Annabelle said. "Estelle and Ray."

If they were going to have the future she was hoping for, this was the first step.

CHAPTER EIGHTEEN

NINE WEEKS LATER, Annabelle sat in the back of the courtroom, Conrad wedged in next to her in full uniform. He felt larger than life in that uniform—broader, tougher. But she knew him better now. Underneath that steely exterior was the softest heart she'd ever known. He reached over and took her hand in his strong grip.

"Ouch," she whispered.

"Sorry." He loosened his grip. Conrad was nervous, too. Stephen Hope's lawyer had been a good one, and he'd argued valiantly for all the doubts and inconsistencies that should let his client walk free, and they were down to the end of the line now.

The trial had lasted three weeks—testimony was given, the defense questioned and requestioned her about what she'd seen and how she knew Stephen Hope, but telling the truth was pretty simple. The hardest part had been having Stephen's icy gaze on her the entire time, but Conrad sat directly behind Stephen, and there was just no comparing the men. Conrad was twice as big, and twice as stony, his strength on display for her support. Stephen might be a strong man, too, but he couldn't intimidate her with Conrad looming behind him like an annoyed giant.

Now, after weeks of meticulous testimony, it was time for the jury to make its decision, and Annabelle leaned into Conrad's bulky shoulder.

"Stephen Hope, please rise," the judge said.

Stephen rose to his feet, dressed in prison greens. The judge turned to the jury and the forewoman cleared her throat.

"In the first charge of murder in the second degree, we, the jury, find Stephen Hope guilty…"

The courtroom erupted into clapping and the judge banged his gavel. "Quiet in the courtroom!"

"…and in the second charge of aggravated robbery in the first degree, we find Stephen Hope guilty."

Annabelle leaned back, realizing that she'd been clenching every muscle in her back. Guilty. He was going to be in prison for a good long time. She looked up at Conrad and he shot her a grin.

"You did great!" he whispered. "I'm proud of you!"

Stephen Hope's defense lawyer leaned over and whispered with him, and the judge made an announcement about when the sentencing trial would be held. It would be in another three weeks, and Annabelle intended to be back in this courtroom to see it. Stephen Hope belonged in prison, and she was determined to see the back of him. The courtroom was filled with excited whispers that grew into chatter and exclamations. The judge rose to his feet. Everyone rose, too, and then he left the courtroom.

Annabelle looked up at Conrad.

"It's over," she said.

"It's over," he replied. "I told your dad I'd text him when we got the verdict."

Annabelle smiled. "Go ahead."

Conrad had managed to bond with both of her parents over the last few weeks, and her father had taken a particular liking to him.

Three large officers came forward and put cuffs on Stephen's wrists before leading him toward a side door. Stephen paused, scanning the audience until his gaze landed on her. She felt Conrad lean forward, and she saw Stephen's face pale. He wasn't so sure of himself when faced with Conrad, and she felt a surge of pride.

"Down, boy," she said jokingly, putting a hand on his shoulder.

Conrad chuckled. "He needs to remember exactly who he's dealing with if he ever thinks of crossing you again."

They stayed seated as people filed out of the room. The hallway echoed with chatter and the call of reporters' voices. Slowly, the courtroom emptied, until Annabelle and Conrad were alone, all except for a bailiff standing at one door, and one journalist questioning a lawyer, a recorder held between them.

"So what now?" Conrad asked, turning back toward her.

"I guess we…get to go back to a normal life now. Isn't it weird to think that?"

"A little," he agreed. "But what do you want that to look like? Do you want to go back to work at the bank, or…?"

It was all over—the trial, of course, the danger and also that imposed time tied at the hip to this gentle, honest mountain of a man.

"I'm not sure if I want to keep working at the bank after this. Knitting socks has its appeal." She smiled jokingly. "I guess to start with I have to move back to my own apartment." It was the next step, and it would feel good to have her own things around her again.

Conrad reached out and touched her cheek. "Do you still love me?"

"You know I do. I'm harder to shake than that."

He didn't smile in return, but he did lick his lips. "Well, I love you, too, and my feelings haven't changed a bit. I didn't want to pressure you during the trial, but I don't think I can wait any longer to get an answer to this…"

Annabelle frowned. "What?"

"I want a life with you, Annabelle. I was willing to run away with you if I had to, and I'll keep on loving you that much—more, even. I don't want you to move back to your apartment—unless you really want to for a little while. But I'm hoping that you'll… I mean, if you feel the same way, I was hoping you'd want—" He let out a frustrated breath.

"You want to…"

"I want to marry you!" He cast her a hopeful smile. "I want to make you happy. I want to come home to you, and take care of you, and make dinner with you, and go to bed with you. I want to be your husband. More than anything."

Annabelle leaned forward, catching his lips with hers, and she let her eyes fall shut as she kissed him. When she pulled back, he searched her face.

"What do *you* want?" he asked softly.

"That. I want all of it!" she said. "I want to marry you, too."

"Really?" He caught her fingers in his strong grip. "You mean it?"

She nodded. "More than anything."

"Because I, uh, I bought a ring." His face flushed, and he reached into his front pocket, pulling out a velvet ring box. He opened it, and she saw a diamond solitaire twinkling from its depths.

"It's not a huge diamond," he said. "I'm a public servant, after all. But it comes with my heart, for the rest of my life."

"It's perfect," she whispered. He pulled the ring out and slid it onto her finger. She looked down at it in wonder for a moment and then kissed him again.

"Okay, so… officially," he said. "Will you marry me?"

"Yes!"

He exhaled a pent-up breath, then pulled her close and kissed her once more.

"I love you," he said.

"I love you, too!"

The journalist who'd been interviewing the lawyer was now looking at them in undisguised curiosity.

"I think that's our cue to run for it," Conrad said, and Annabelle laughed.

He grabbed her hand and slipped toward the back door.

"Excuse me?" the journalist called. "Can I just have a word? Did I just see a proposal?"

Annabelle couldn't help the laughter bubbling out of her as they jogged down the hallway hand in hand.

"Excuse me?" the journalist called after them, and Annabelle and Conrad erupted into the cold October sunshine.

With golden leaves fluttering in the sunlight, groups of people talking on the front lawn of the courthouse and news crews doing live updates, it all felt so impossibly free and beautiful that Annabelle could almost cry.

"What do we do first?" Conrad asked.

She looked down at the ring on her finger. There would be family to tell, a wedding to plan, friends to celebrate with, and all the excitement of planning a life together. But right now, Annabelle could think of only one place she wanted to be.

"Let's go back to Amish country," she said.

She wanted to look at it with new eyes, because alongside Conrad, it would very soon be home.

EPILOGUE

By spring, when Conrad and Annabelle were set to get married, Amish country was calm once more and the cattle grazed safely in new, lush grass. With the arrest of four more cattle rustlers, the ring had been broken up and most of the calves returned.

The wedding was held in a little church in downtown Wooster where Annabelle's parents had gotten married some thirty-odd years before. Their Amish friends hired vans to come to the ceremony—a little loophole they used when they needed to travel farther than a buggy could take them comfortably. The Schmidt family was there, as well as Simon Lapp and his wife and daughter. Conrad had been surprised by the strength of this new friendship, but Simon was deeply grateful for what Conrad had done in breaking up the rustling ring, and the Lapps were determined to be good friends in return.

Wilder was Conrad's best man, and Theresa

was Annabelle's maid of honor. That was the extent of the wedding party. They had wanted to keep things as simple as possible. Conrad's mother bonded immediately with Annabelle's, and it seemed like everything was falling into place very easily. For that, Conrad was grateful. They'd had enough drama to last them a lifetime.

Conrad stood in his tux, and he'd teared up when Annabelle came down the aisle in a flowing white dress and long lace veil. She was beautiful, and he couldn't wait to make his commitment official.

He didn't remember much of the ceremony. He remembered saying "I do," and the flood of relief he felt when she said it, too. They'd headed back down the aisle together and had pictures at the park. Then they'd gone to the best hotel in town for their reception, where friends and family, colleagues and cops, all danced into the night.

But Conrad and Annabelle ducked out early while the music was still going, and Conrad drove her back to the ranch.

He had a surprise for her. The Amish had their own way of saying thank you, and in preparation for Conrad and Annabelle's wedding, they'd spent the winter and the better part of the spring adding a *dawdie hus* onto the house. It was a little addition that was normally used as an in-law suite, but in their case, it would be where they lived, giving them some privacy since they'd be living on the ranch.

When they got inside, Conrad led Annabelle to the new door, and he swung it open. There was a kerosene lantern waiting for them to light, and moonlight spilled through a generous window.

"Wait," Conrad said, and he lifted her up into his arms. "Let's do this right."

Annabelle laughed, and her veil got caught in the door, so they had to stop and untangle it before he carried her through into the bedroom portion of the suite, with a large bed covered in a handmade Amish quilt.

"This is amazing," Annabelle said as he put her down on the edge of the bed.

Conrad lit the kerosene lamp, illuminating freshly painted walls and a polished hardwood floor. "No electricity in here, I'm afraid. It's a truly Amish refuge for you. But we've got a fireplace to cuddle up by during cold nights, and you won't find a more solidly built addition."

"I still can't believe they did this for us," she said.

"I think they've accepted us," Conrad said.

Annabelle reached up to unfasten her veil. Her hair had grown over the last few months, and blond tendrils spilled down her neck. Conrad took the veil from her and hung it up on a hook on the back of the bedroom door. Then he turned back toward her.

"Our first night as Mr. and Mrs. West-house," he said, and he felt a tremor of nerves.

"I like that," she said, and a smile turned up her lips. "Now come kiss me properly."

"I don't need to be asked twice."

He sank onto the side of the bed next to her and pulled his wife into his arms. He loved her. She had sunk into his very soul, and claiming her as his own felt right on a bone-deep level.

They had a honeymoon planned in Hawaii, but tonight would be spent in their very own home. Wollie had told him an Amish proverb that explained how he felt just perfectly. *A happy home is not just a roof over your head, but a foundation under your feet.*

And Annabelle was his foundation. He'd found his rock center. He was home.

* * * * *

*Don't miss the next book in
Patricia Johns's
Amish Country Haven miniseries,
coming August 2022 from
Harlequin Heartwarming.*

HARLEQUIN SELECTS COLLECTION

19 FREE BOOKS IN ALL!

From Robyn Carr to RaeAnne Thayne to Linda Lael Miller and Sherryl Woods we promise (actually, GUARANTEE!) each author in the Harlequin Selects collection has seen their name on the *New York Times* or *USA TODAY* bestseller lists!

#415 THE COWBOY'S UNLIKELY MATCH
Bachelor Cowboys • by Lisa Childs

Having grown up in foster care, schoolteacher Emily Trent readily moves to Ranch Haven to help three local orphans—just not their playboy uncle, Ben Haven. The charming cowboy mayor didn't get her vote and won't get her heart!

#416 THE PARAMEDIC'S FOREVER FAMILY
Smoky Mountain First Responders • by Tanya Agler

Horticulturist and single mom Lindsay Hudson looks forward to neighborly chats with paramedic Mason Ruddick. He was her late husband's best friend, but he can't be anything more. Unless love can bloom in her own backyard?

#417 THE RANCHER'S WYOMING TWINS
Back to Adelaide Creek • by Virginia McCullough

Heather Stanhope wants to hate the rancher who bought her family's land. Instead, she's falling for sweet Matt Burton and his adorable twin nieces. Could the place she longs to call home be big enough for all of them?

#418 THEIR TOGETHER PROMISE
The Montgomerys of Spirit Lake
by M. K. Stelmack

Mara Montgomery is determined to face her vision loss without any help—particularly from the stubbornly optimistic Connor Flanagan. Can Connor open Mara's eyes to a lifetime of love from one of his service dogs...and him?

HWCNM0222